对我们来说狗只是生命的过客,而对它们来说,我们是全部。

在我的有生之年里，我会竭尽所能在它们悲伤时，给它们慰藉，在它们开心时为它们增添几分欢愉。

美丽英文

第三辑

狗狗们的心事
The Soul of the Dogs

杨柳青　编译

天津教育出版社

TIANJIN EDUCATION PRESS

图书在版编目(CIP)数据

狗狗们的心事 / 杨柳青编译. —天津：天津教育出版社，2008. 10

ISBN 978-7-5309-5433-1

I. 狗… II. 杨… III. ①散文—作品集—外国② 随笔—作品集—外国 IV.116

中国版本图书馆 CIP 数据核字(2008)第 156924 号

狗狗们的心事		
出版人	肖占鹏	
责任编辑	匡威	
装帧设计	晨旭光华	
作　者	杨柳青　编译	
出版发行	天津教育出版社	
	天津市和平区西康路 35 号	
	邮政编码　　300051	
经　销	新华书店	
印　刷	北京中印联印务有限公司	
版　次	2008 年 10 月第 1 版	
印　次	2008 年 10 月第 1 次	
规　格	16 开（720×1000 毫米）	
字　数	300 千字	
印　张	14	
书　号	ISBN 978-7-5309-5433-1	
定　价	21.80 元	

读懂狗心

很久以前,读屠格涅夫的小说《木木》,小说中一个哑奴和一只狗的生死相依,无言而又至深的交流,使我在那一刻确信,狗不再是一个低等的动物,它也不仅是看家护院的恶犬或是贵妇膝上的宠物,它同样可以是穷人和奴隶的朋友,毫不势利的义士,甚至是上帝的信徒。它们忠诚、勤劳,但求付出不求回报。在某些世俗的人身上,这些品德已经逐渐消失殆尽了。狗性中深具超凡的神性,而人性中却潜藏着可耻的兽性。

在这个越来越世俗、越来越淡漠的现代社会里,似乎所有的人都在讲究效率,追求功利。为了追求所谓的物质文明,人们再没有耐性坐下来互诉衷肠,人与人之间的心灵隔阂越来越大,此时,还有谁在保持着不变的忠诚呢?还有谁不嫌你贫穷、不嫌你丑陋、不嫌你疾病、不嫌你衰老呢?还有什么值得你去倾注关怀,甚至喜欢你唠叨,让你呼之则来,挥之则去,不计较你的粗鲁和无礼,并无休止地迁就你呢?是啊,除了狗儿还有谁呢?

狗儿的要求最简单不过了——只求温饱而已。它虽然无法与人交谈,却懂得察颜观色,欢喜时它能与你一起欢呼雀跃,伤心失意时它会舔舐你的涕泣,愤怒时它可以当你的出气筒。

其实,狗从远古开始就伴随着人类成长,并在危机四伏的世界里守护着人的孤独。在所有的动物中,狗也许是与人类关系最密切的一种,同时它又是最具灵性的尤物。它带着晶亮忧郁的眼睛来到人间,感受人间的苦难和罪恶,也遭遇人的迫害

与放逐，但它始终是人类忠诚的朋友，义无反顾地追随着人类的脚步，似乎永远不会背叛人的情感……

狗和我们人类一样，都是地球生命的一部分，我们虽然没有相同的血缘，却有着相似的生活习性和丰富的情感。对狗类的了解通常也可视为对人类本身的反观，解析狗的意识、心理和情感，同时也可以说是人类对这个世界的进一步解读和沟通。因此，在《狗狗们的心事》中，蕴藏了无尽的知识和哲思。通过这本书，我仿佛看见另一个沉默的族类，如影随形地追随着人类的脚步，用它们特有的、原始而丰富的肢体语言，书写着对人类深刻而真切的情感，而这一切却全是我们所无暇顾及，或根本无视的狗的心理。

狗儿是我们最忠诚的仆人，最可信的朋友，为了巩固我们之间的情感，它们委曲求全，忍受了太多太多的痛苦和哀伤，临死还在感激着我们的收养（虽然很多时候，我们在收养它们的日子里并没有真心善待它们）。它们难道不正是一些宽容和无私的道士吗？

甚至为了取悦人类，狗还要竭尽所能地模仿人类的笑容。它们笑的时候，脸部表情愉悦而放松，两耳下垂、眼睛半眯、嘴唇柔软微启、双颊高耸。

在人类的面前，它们很不自然地缩紧双唇，露出牙齿，装出人类笑的表情。当它们"笑"的时候，还会四脚朝天，温顺服从地袒露腹部，这表示狗儿不但在笑，而且还在充分表达自己"笑"所代表的含义。我们可以设身处地来想它们的良苦用心，因为这是小狗对大狗表示顺从的动作，它们以此来显示自己的渺小和软弱，希望借此能够得到人类的关爱。

这样的动作不是也存在于我们人类吗？

我们把上帝称为天父，自己则是上帝的臣民，像小孩子一样在上帝面前弯腰屈膝进行礼拜。祈祷时双膝并拢，好像是想把上帝紧紧拥入怀中；双眼抬高仰望，好像

是为了迎接上帝垂视我们的慈爱目光。另外，我们也习惯在早晨或者晚上固定的时间向上帝祈祷，而很多狗也会在每天早上主人起床后对主人行礼如仪，露出腹部来道早安，没有人真正知道它为何会这样做。我想，狗只是把我们当成神而已。

我们认为上帝具有神秘而强大的力量，而狗却把人类看成是具有同样威力的自己的上帝，似乎人类所做的一切都有正当的理由，即使人们不停地辜负它们、背叛它们、伤害它们，但它们却永远是人类最忠诚的仆人，毫无怨言地陪伴着我们的孤独。正如英国诗人亚历山大·波普(Alexander Pope)的名言："凡人多犯错误，唯犬能见谅。"

这所有的一切都是狗儿对人类宽容的心态，读懂了狗心，便洞悉了这个世界上被我们忘却了的忠诚和仁爱，便也学会了接受别人或被别人接受。

那么，做一个快乐的爱狗人不好吗？

我认为，一本关于狗的书必须以人类的观点出发，并以此来解释狗的行为。《狗狗们的心事》虽只有几万字，却感人至深，把人与狗之间这种感情的默契阐释得淋漓尽致，难道不正是最完美的答案吗？

翻看本书中各种美丽的狗照，不禁一番爱怜。同时，行走在大街上，时常可见一些富贵气十足的玲珑小狗，在主人的脚边憨态可掬地闲逛，但想到还有多少失去宠爱的狗儿野居于荒郊野外，忍受着寒冷和饥饿的折磨，心中不禁又是一番感叹。不同的狗有不同的狗命，其间的天壤之别又何异于人类！读一篇优雅的关于狗的文字，反省一回百面人生，相信每个读者都会各有一番见仁见智。

曾经有过狗儿走进你的生命吗？你给了它一个什么样的命运？面对那一双双渴盼的眼神，你我可以只供温饱，可以置之不理，也可以忍心抛弃，当然你也可以选择自己成为爱狗族——只要你愿意。

——编者

目 录

第一卷 我们发现了彼此
We Found Each Other

第二卷 一起走过的日子

Friends Like Us

Contents

第三卷 我的快乐中有你
You Are in My Happiness

Contents

目 录

第四卷　你是我的命定天使
You Are My Fated Angel

目 录

我们发现了彼此
We Found Each Other

　　当我还是一只小狗的时候，我的顽皮总会给你带来快乐，让你开怀大笑。你称我为孩子，虽然家里的许多鞋子和靠枕被我啃咬得破旧不堪，你依然把我看做你最好的朋友。

第一卷

给生命带来奇迹的狗

佚名

谁能不嫌你贫穷,不嫌你丑陋,不嫌你疾病,不嫌你衰老呢?谁能让你呼之则来,挥之则去,不计较你的粗鲁和无礼,并无休止地迁就你呢?除了狗还有谁呢?

——尤金·奥尼尔

医生让母亲在家中度过生命的最后几天。母亲患乳腺癌已有15年了,并且在发现晚期肺癌期间,她还并发过两次心脏病。

母亲做着一份全职工作,含辛茹苦地养大了3个女儿,她还尽力为家人创造一个温馨的家庭。从小到大,我只知道有关母亲的两个特点:她的意志像铁一样坚强,并且,她非常热爱大自然。患病期间,她又告诉了我第三点:"我的一生很悲惨。"

父亲是一个难以相处的人,但母亲从来没有抱怨过,也许是因为她无法用语言完全表达出来吧。但当母亲的病情恶化时,在父亲眼里,她显然是个累赘。于是我和母亲都决定,母亲搬来和我一起住。

我利用3个星期的时间来安排一切。我更改了工作表,联系运输公司、肿瘤专家、心脏病专家、晚期病人护理机构,联系购买医疗器械,寻找能帮助她洗澡的护理人员。对于母亲最后的日子,我的安排很简单:让她生活在爱中,优雅地离开人世。

坐了5个小时的车,疲惫不堪的母亲到家了。她立刻接受了家庭护士的检查。护士把我叫到一边,问:"你觉得你的母亲还能坚持多久呢?"

我说:"2个月,也可能是3个月。"

护士悲伤地看着我,"你要有思想准备,"他说,"她只有几天的生命了,最多一个星期。她的心脏很衰弱，而且不稳定。"

我这个小而舒服的家，是4只猫和1只狗的天下。

我们安装好医用电动病床和氧气装置之后，那些猫吓得都不敢进卧室了。他们很不高兴，因为我还挪动了他们的用具。对于家里的一系列变化，那只还未成熟并有着坏习惯的狗显得很兴奋，他跳着，叫着，毛也掉得比平时多。

他叫奥托，只有他对医用病床、氧气设备和医药气味无所畏惧。他也不害怕病床上那个虚弱的女人，尽管她曾经喝斥过他。奥托会跳上母亲的床尾，并待在那里。

他也不害怕护士。当护士给母亲喂饭，或母亲去洗手间时，他很安静，也不捣乱。不管是给母亲换床还是洗澡出现混乱时，他都只是等着回到自己的岗位。除了吃食和大小便，奥托决不离开母亲的房间。

日子一天天过去了，母亲的病情开始有些好转。但别人告诉我："这很正常，这种好转一般是死亡前的回光返照。"

我很伤心。但奥托没有轻易地放弃母亲。借着母亲病情好转的机会，他从床尾挪到了母亲的身边。母亲用消瘦的手指抚摸着他柔软的皮毛。他斜靠在母亲的身上，似乎要抓住她的求生欲望。尽管母亲很虚弱，但仍然爱抚着他，不让我抱走。

几个星期过去了，母亲仍在和病魔作斗争。有一次，当护士们完成一天的工作离开时，我听到母亲的房间里有声音。我发现她的床头升了起来。奥托依偎在她的臂弯里，敬慕地听她读报纸。奥托用爪子抚摸着母亲的脸，这一幕令我永生难忘。

最终，母亲可以借助助行器在屋子里来回走动了，她的身后跟着奥托，还拖着氧气管。她停下休息，奥托也在那里休息。不管她走到哪里，奥托都寸步不离。我似乎忘记了她也是一位母亲。但奥托却明白，因此，这些日子以来他一直作为母亲的狗宝宝，并让她有了生活的目标。

转眼间，3年过去了，医用病床和氧气装置都已经撤了，所有的药物也都停了，护士也离开了。但母亲和奥托还在，重病期间他们建立起来的那份情感依然存在。

不久前，我们去看了肿瘤医生，他非常满意地说："卢拉，简直难以置信，你的癌细胞一点也找不到了，而且你的心脏也变得强壮了。当年你的女儿带你来看病时，我还认为你已经走到生命的尽头了。"随便医生怎么去想，但母亲认为这全是奥托的功劳。

非常幸运的是，母亲最终摆脱了死亡的阴影，奥托也仍然继续陪伴着母亲。他给予母亲的爱，是比医生的处方更有效的灵丹妙药。

Medical Dog

Anonymous

The doctors sent my mother home to die. A fifteen-year survivor of breast can-cer, she had suffered two heart attacks when advanced cancer was found in her lung.

Mom had struggled to raise three daughters while holding a full-time job, yet worked hard to maintain a cozy home for her family. Growing up, I knew only two things about my mother: She had an iron will, and she loved nature. During her days of illness, she told me a third: "I've had a miserable life."

My dad was a difficult man to live with, but my mom did not complain, proba-bly because she could not put words to her own need. But when it came clear that because of her progressive deterioration, my dad regarded her as a burden, she and I decided that she would move to my home.

I had three weeks to make a myriad of arrangements. I changed my work sched-ule, found transportation, an oncologist, cardiologist, hospice care, medical equipment, a caregiver and bather. My plan for Mom's final days was simple: she would live with love, and die with grace.

Upon her arrival, after an exhausting five-hour trip, Mom was examined by the home health-care nurse. The nurse took me aside and asked, "How long do you think your mother has?"

"Two, maybe three months," I said.

The nurse looked at me sadly. "Adjust your thinking," he said. "She has a few days, maybe a week. Her heart is weak and unstable."

My home, small and comfortable, was a heaven to four cats and a retriever. The animals had the run of my house.

We installed the electric hospital bed and oxygen machine, which frightened the cats from the bedroom. I'd moved their furniture, and they were peeved. The retriev-er, on the other hand, an immature dog with bad habits, was excited by all the changes in the house. He jumped up, barked and shed more profusely than usual.

He is Otto who was not afraid of the hospital bed, the oxygen machines or the medical smells. Nor was he afraid of the frail woman who had scolded him. Otto jumped onto the foot of Mom's hospital bed, and stayed.

He was not startled by the nurses. He did not interfere when Mom was fed, nor when she was transferred from bed to commode and back. Whether the disturbance was from changing her bed or because of bathing, he simply waited to resume his post. With the exception of eating and using the litter box, Otto never left Mom's room.

Days passed, and Mom started to rally. "Not unusual," I was told, "a rally is often a sign of imminent death."

I grieved. But Otto would not give her up so easily. He used her improved condition to reposition himself from the foot of her bed to her side. Her thin fingers found his soft coat. He leaned into her body, as if clinging to the threads of her will to live. Though weak, she caressed the dog and would not allow me to take him.

Days turned into weeks and Mom continued to fight. Once, after the nurses had gone for the day, I heard the sound of Mom's voice coming from her room. I found her with the head of the bed raised. Otto was tucked into the crook of her elbow, listening adoringly as she read from the newspaper. I will forever cherish the memory of Mom's face with Otto's paw, claws retracted, caressing the side of her chin.

Eventually, using a walker, Mom began to take walks through the house. She was trailed by oxygen tubing and Otto. Where she rested, Otto rested. Where she moved, Otto shadowed. It seems I had forgotten my Mom was a mother. Somehow, Otto knew, and during those days he became her dog child, giving her life purpose.

Exactly three years have passed since then. The hospital bed and oxygen machine are long gone. The medicines and nurses are gone, too. But Mom's still here. And so is Otto. And so is the bond that united them in days of sickness.

When we saw the oncologist a while ago, he patted himself on the back. "I can't believe it, Lula," he said. "I can't find your cancer and your heart is strong. When your daughter brought you to me, I thought you were a ship that had sailed." We let the doctor think what he likes, but Mom gives the credit to Otto.

Thankfully, my mother has put off dying, and Otto continues to share his gift of love—a medicine more potent than any drug a doctor could prescribe.

最佳女演员

· 林恩·阿尔科克

不曾养过狗的人，很难想象与狗一起生活是什么样子，养过狗的人，则无法想象没有狗的日子该怎么过。

——卡洛琳

萨曼塔是我丈夫杰克的狗，或者更确切地说，他是她的主人。而我则是喂养她、领着她散步，并照顾她的人，但对萨曼塔而言，连太阳都是围绕杰克转的。她爱慕着他，这种感觉是相互的。当她送给他一个猎犬温柔的"妩媚眼神"时，他整个人都融化了。

我们居住在西北地区一个名叫耶洛奈夫的地方，距北极圈有300英里远。杰克在部队，很少回家。我独自一人生活，非常感谢我的那些好朋友、一个非常愉快的工作环境，尤其是萨曼塔，她会在夜晚为我取暖。她在毯子下面慢慢地蠕动，并蜷缩在我的脚边——真是幸福极了。

北极的冬天极其漫长，萨曼塔耐心地等待着阳光与温暖的天气到来，很少出去。她是一种独特的猎犬，喜欢奔跑、追赶兔子和松鼠以及在湖里游泳。当那年春天终于来临的第一个温暖的日子里，我们外出散步。萨曼塔凭借着健康的体魄，总是很夸张地做出一些事情——以极快的速度跑过那些岩石，而这正是耶洛奈夫的美景。到了该回家的时候了，她走起路来却是一瘸一拐的，好像还忍受着巨大的疼痛。医生诊断出她是韧带拉伤，命令她静静地休养，几个星期之内不允许跑动。对于萨曼塔来说，这可不是一个好消息。现在，当我去工作的时候，她就被限制只能在门廊下面活动，我在家的时候就会带着她慢慢地走一小段路。几个星期过去了，她虽然走起路来还不稳当，但已经好多了，看着她逐渐康复，我也感到很高兴。

在这期间，杰克从周一到周五都没在家。周五晚上，他回来了，我们相互拥抱、亲吻着，萨曼塔紧紧地贴在他的腿边。整个周末，她都形影不离地跟着杰克，并因自己的伤痛而心安理得地接受着他的关怀。而我很清楚地明白,她跛行的原因很显然是因为杰克在家里。

夏末的时候,她的腿伤已经痊愈,她完全康复了。一个星期里,她奔跑、玩耍,追赶着她的球,一玩就是几个小时。当杰克回到家里,她的伤痛又神奇般地出现了,整个周末都卧在沙发上,得到了大量的拥抱、一条毛毯以及悉心的照顾。

我告诉杰克她的这些行为只是想要吸引他的注意。"这当然不可能了,"他说,"你没有看到她的腿伤仍然困扰着她吗?为什么不像兽医说的那样会复原呢?"我叹了口气,不再追究这件事了。

像大多数人一样,我和杰克都喜欢在星期日的早晨相互依偎着睡个懒觉。我们聊着过去一周发生的事情,再盛满咖啡,聊聊更多的事情,打个小盹,懒散地度过一天。萨曼塔躺在床下,也同样享受着这个特别的时刻。最后,我们起床、沐浴,并一起到厨房做早餐。我们也总是会给萨曼塔煎一个鸡蛋。她通常会在床上等着我们做好叫她吃饭。那天早晨,早餐已经摆好了,因为萨曼塔受了伤,所以杰克打算抱她下床吃饭。

"不,"我对他说道,"站在她看不到你的地方,看她接下来会做什么。"

我喊着萨曼塔,我们听到她跳下床,跑到餐厅。她的速度之快就像再也看不到明天似的,很奇怪,她的腿也不痛了,直到看到杰克。她停顿了一会儿,又立刻瘸了。我们看着她走了几步,你可以想象在这只猎犬的脑海中反复思考着:是这条腿还是那条腿呢?然后,她的另一条腿瘸了起来,接着,她被绊倒了!

我和杰克笑了起来,笑萨曼塔,也笑我们自己,萨曼塔本应该被授予"最佳女演员"的称号。相反,我们为她写了一张"西北地区最受欢迎的猎犬"的奖状,并颁发给她。看起来她为自己的表演以及获得的奖励感到很骄傲。事实上,我们都知道她是西北地区唯一的猎犬,但是我们不会告诉她——我们不想打破她的梦境。

Best Actress

Lynn Alcock

Samantha was really my husband Jack's dog, or more accurately, he was her human. I was the one who fed her, walked her and took care of her, but as far as Samantha was concerned, the sun rose and set on Jack. She adored him. The feeling was mutual; when she gave him that soft beagle "googly-eyed Look," he melted.

We lived in a place called Yellowknife in the Northwest Territories, three hundred miles from the Arctic Circle. Jack was in the army and away a lot. I managed on my own and was thankful for good friends, an enjoyable working environment and, especially, Samantha to keep me warm at night. She would crawl under the blankets and curl around my feet—what bliss.

It had been a long arctic winter and Samantha had waited patiently for the sunshine and warm weather to come and was raring to get out and about. A typical hound, she loved running, chasing rabbits and squirrels, and swimming in the lake. When the first warm day of spring finally arrived that year and we went out for a walk, in her exuberance, Samantha overdid it—running at top speed over the rocks that are the landscape in Yellowknife. By the time we reached the house, she was limping quite pronouncedly and appeared to be in significant pain. Her injury was diagnosed as sprained ligaments, and she was ordered to keep still: no running for several weeks. It was not welcome news for this beagle. Now she was confined to the porch while I was away at work, and then took short, quiet walks on a leash when I was home. As the weeks passed, her limp slowly but surely diminished; I was pleased with her progress.

During that period, Jack was away from Monday to Friday. On his return Friday evenings, there were hugs and kisses all around, and Samantha would be plastered to his lap. She followed him everywhere all weekend, lapping up the attention she received because of her "hurtie." It was clear to me that her limp became even more pronounced when Jack was home

By the end of the summer her leg was all healed and she was back to normal. She ran and played and chased her ball for hours on end—during the week. When Jack came home, her hurtie mysteriously came back, and she was placed on the sob for the weekend with lots of hugs, a blanket and treats.

I told that this was just an act for his attention. "Of course it isn't," he said. "Can't you see her leg is still bothering her? How come it's not healing like the vet said it would?" I sighed but let it drop.

Like most people, Jack and I love to sleep in and snuggle on Sunday morning. We chat about the events of the past week, reload our coffee cups, chat some more, nap and generally laze around. Samantha lies at the bottom of the bed enjoying this special time as well.Eventually,we get up, shower and head to the kitchen to start making breakfast. It was our routine to cook an egg for Samantha, too. She usually waited on the bed until it was ready and we called her to come and eat. That morning when breakfast was ready started down the hall, intending to lift Samantha off the bed and carry her into the kitchen because of her hurtie.

"No," I told him."Stand where she can't see you and watch what happens next." I called Samantha. We heard her jump off the bed and run down the hall. She was running like there was no tomorrow, and surprise, no hurtie—until she saw Jack. She stopped on a dime and immediately began limping. We watched as she took a few steps. You could see the wheels turning in her beagle brain: Was it this leg or the other? Then she started limping on the other leg. Caught in the act!

Jack and I laughed, both at Samantha and at each other, Samantha would have been given an award for "Best Actress in a Leading Role." Instead, we wrote, "The Best Beagle in the Northwest Territories Award" on a piece of paper and gave it to her. She seemed so proud of her performance and the award. Actually ,we knew that she was the only beagle in the Northwest Territories, but we didn't tell her—we didn't want to spoil the magic.

金色的眼睛

戴安娜·尼科尔斯

狗是我们与天堂的联结。它们不懂何为邪恶、嫉妒和不满。在美丽的黄昏，和狗儿并肩坐在河边，有如重回伊甸园。即使什么事也不做也不觉得无聊——只有幸福、平和。

——米兰·昆德拉

我6岁的女儿玛丽，拉着我的手走进了一家动物避难所。我们想挑选一只合适的小狗作为她的姐姐凯蒂12岁的生日礼物。我仔细地看着每一个笼子，看到那一双双渴求的棕色眼睛盯着我们。那是对爱和快乐家园的期盼，自从我和她们的父亲离婚之后，这些同样也是女儿们和我渴求的东西。

"这些都是新进的。"志愿者说着，便将我们带到一个笼子前面，那里有3只正在睡觉的小狗，漂亮的皮毛就像小熊一样。

"她们都是什么品种？"我边问边弯下身子近距离地看着她们。

"她们是中国混血狗，"那个志愿者说，"我从来没有见过这样看上去令人敬畏的狗。"

中间的那只小狗突然打着哈欠看着我们，我的心跳加速了。她令人感到惊奇，大大的爪子，脸上长着银黑色的狼斑。最主要的是她的眼睛，真是令我震惊，那么温和、可爱，就像她的皮毛一样，是金黄色的。冥冥之中好像有什么在告诉我，就是她了。

我永远无法忘记——当我们将凯蒂的新伙伴带到她面前时她惊讶的表情。"我要叫她夏安。"凯蒂愉快地说道。

在接下来的日子里，夏安完成了我所期望的一切。孩子们不再对我们失去的生活感到苦恼，相反，她们开始与她们的新狗狗做游戏。她们不再因失去父亲而感到沮丧，反而总是蹦蹦跳跳，开心地笑着。这所发生的一切给了我希望，她们会将这个艰难的过渡期过得更好，但愿有什么能够帮助我做同样的事情。

这是四月末的一个下午，事情发生了可怕的转变。女孩们和夏安在后院玩耍时，我去了商店。当我回到家，走上车道时，一辆皮卡车快速驶入我们这条街道。我下了车，手里拿着钥匙，看到夏安的绳索松了，她就像一阵烟似的从我的身旁跑过。

"夏安！"我喊道，"不！回来！"但是已经太迟了。她追赶着皮卡车，并撞在了车子的前轮上，身体被抛向了空中，"砰"地一声摔在了路边。

幸运的是，兽医院还开着门，他们收治了夏安。我一直守在夏安的身边关心着她，希望她在医生将她放到检查台上之前还活着。

"前肢看起来是受伤最严重的地方，"医生说着便用一个银色的夹子在她的脚趾间捏着，"神经已经受损，她没有任何知觉，我担心我们必须要把它切除。"

夏安手术的那一天，我度过了生命中最漫长的一天。当我们初次见到她，把她带到我们的身边是那么毫无准备。夏安躺在笼子里喘息着，眨着睡意朦胧的眼睛，从颈部到腹部都被剃得干干净净的。一条白色的绷带缠绕在她的肩部，那里原来是她的一条腿。一只塑料管也插在那里以帮助手术定位。她看起来是那么痛苦。当我看到夏安的尾巴虚弱地摇晃时，眼泪顿时流了下来。

那天晚上，我们都睡在地板上，陪着夏安。当她痛苦地呻吟，躺在一侧不能移动的时候，我在脑海中试图将她以前的样子描绘出来：跑、玩耍、跳到床上依偎在我的身边。我感到恐惧不安，怎样做才能让她恢复到原来那只无忧无虑的小狗。在某种意义上，我了解她身上所遭受的那种病痛。以前你过得开心，突然生活变得支离破碎了，你身处一个痛苦的世界中。

我和凯蒂在最开始的那几个夜晚轮流照顾她。我们注视着她，试着安慰她，给她止痛片，用勺子喂她香草冰淇淋。她打着盹，但是又经常因为疼痛而无法入睡。每过几个小时，我们都会将她抱到外面，帮助她站立，这样她就可以去洗手间了。我们都已经精疲力竭，但是没有什么事情能够比夏安回到我们的身边更重要了——即使她再也不是以前的那个样子。

周一，凯蒂去学校了，我不得不独自照顾她。玛丽忙着看她的卡通书，而我则不停地围着夏安转。我为她换了新的绷带，并确信她不会试着去咬它们。我拍着她的脑袋，不停地给她讲她是多么强壮。看着她痛苦的表情，看着血从排泄管渗出，我的心碎了一次又一次。我回忆着她用那充满爱意而又甜美的眼睛望着我，而不是如此痛苦。

"你是生还者，"我在她的耳旁低声说着，"我们需要你，所以你必须好起来。孩子们依赖你，所以请你……不要放弃，站起来度过这个难关。"

当我向她说这些话的时候，某些事物触动了我的内心。这些话语也适用于我自己。离婚仿佛是一场恶梦，那种痛苦太深了，以至于我想蜷缩起来或是死掉，我不知道自己能不能独自振作起来。但是，难道孩子们不也正依靠我吗？难道我不能与痛苦作斗争，并度过这个难关吗？当我将脸靠在夏安的鼻子旁边时，眼泪顺着脸颊流了下来。她的呼吸是么轻柔，使我的皮肤感到很舒服。呼吸让我想起生命是多么珍贵啊。

"小可爱，我要和你做一个交易，"我说道，"如果你拼搏并度过这个难关，我也将会为自己而奋斗。我们都将学到如何依靠自己一路走好。"

从那天起，事情有规律地发生了改变。夏安看起来更加警惕和舒适，勇敢地迈出了她的第一步，而我也开始哭得越少，笑得越多了。开始复原了，感觉真好。一天一点，一步一点，我和夏安一起努力着。

"看啊，妈妈！她做到了！夏安自己走起来了！"一周之后，当夏安在院子里漫步的时候，凯蒂指着她喊道。尽管她的前肢没有了，但是她走得非常好。事实上，她看起来好像并没有失去什么。

玛丽开心地鼓起掌来："就像原来的她！"

我想了想并不同意："很明显，宝贝，我认为现在的夏安比以前还要好，她会更加强壮的，因为她现在获得了重生。就像我们……比以前更好。"

这一刻，夏安停下来，望着我。那金色的眼睛闪烁着光芒。我们都获得了期许未来的新生命，每一次都是珍贵的一步。

In Her Golden Eyes

Diane Nichols

My six–year–old daughter, Mary, held on to my hand as we walked through the animal shelter. We wanted to pick just the right puppy for her sister Kitty's twelfth birthday. I scanned each cage, noticing all the pairs of needy brown eyes staring back at us.It was neediness for love and a happy home—things the girls and I also hungered for since their father and I had divorced.

"Here are our newest arrivals," the volunteer said. He led us to a cage where three puppies were sleeping. They were the size of small bear cubs with beautiful fur.

"What kind are they?" I asked, stooping down to take a closer look.

"They're chow mixes," the boy said, "I've never seen such awesome–looking dogs."

My heart quickened as the pup in the middle suddenly yawned and looked up at us. She was breathtaking, with oversized paws and silvery–black wolf markings on her face. Most of all, it was her eyes that struck me. They were so gentle and sweet. As golden as her fur. Something told me that she was the one.

As long as I live, I'll never forget Kitty's face when we surprised her with her new companion.

"I'm going to name her Cheyenne." Kitty beamed.

In the coming days, Cheyenne accomplished exactly what I was hoping for.Instead of the children feeling homesick for the life we'd lost, they spent time playing with their new puppy. Instead of feeling depressed over missing their daddy, they romped and laughed for hours. It gave me hope that they would make this very difficult transi-tion a bit better—if only something would help me do the same.

It was on a late April afternoon that things took a horrible turn. The girls were in the backyard playing with Cheyenne while I went to the store. When I got back home and pulled into the driveway, a pickup truck came speeding down our street. I got out of my car, keys in hand, and saw that Cheyenne had gotten loose. She ran past me in a blur.

"Cheyenne !" I called out. "No! Get back here!" But it was too late. She chased after the truck, caught up to the front tires, and was flipped in the air before landing with a thud on the side of the road.

Luckily, the vet was still open and they took her right in. I kept watching Cheyenne's side, willing her to keep breathing as the vet put her on the examining table.

"The front leg appears to be the worst of her injuries," he said, pinching between her toes with a silver clamp. "The nerves have been damaged and she doesn't have any feeling. I'm afraid we'll have to amputate."

The day of Cheyenne's surgery was the longest day of my life. Nothing prepared us for what we would see once we went to pick her up. In the bottom cage, Cheyenne lay panting and blinking sleepy eyes, the entire right side of her body shaved clean from her stomach to her neck. A white bandage was wrapped around the shoulder area where her leg used to be. A plastic tube was also taped to the area to help the surgical site drain. She looked totally miserable. Tears slid from my eyes as I saw Cheyenne's tail give a faint wag.

That night we all camped on the floor to sleep next to Cheyenne. As she moaned in agony and lay on her side unable to move, I kept trying to picture her as she used to be: running, playing, jumping up on the bed to snuggle down next to me. I felt frightened and uncertain, wondering how she would ever be that same carefree pup again. In a way, I understood the kind of trauma she was going through. One day you were happy, then life just shattered, leaving you in a world of pain.

Kitty and I took shifts for the first few nights. We'd keep watch, try to comfort her, give her pain pills and feed her vanilla ice cream from a spoon. She'd doze, but usually she was too uncomfortable to sleep. Every few hours, we'd carry her outside and help her stand so she could go to the bathroom. We were exhausted, but nothing was more important than Cheyenne coming back to us—even if she would never be the same again.

On Monday I had to take care of her myself when Kitty went to school. Mary kept busy with her coloring books while I constantly hovered over Cheyenne. I changed her bandages and made sure she wasn't trying to bite at them. I stroked her head and kept telling her how strong she was. Seeing her so miserable and watching the blood ooze from her drainage tube broke my heart over and over again. I missed her sweet eyes looking at me with love instead of so much suffering.

"You're a survivor," I whispered in her ear. "We need you, so you have to get better. Those children are depending on you, so please...don't give up. Fight and get through this."

As I said these things to her, something struck me deep inside. The same words applied to me. It had been a night−mare since the divorce, the pain so deep that I want−ed to curl up and die; I didn't see myself able to stand on my own. But weren't the children depending on me,too? Didn't I have to fight and get through this? Tears ran down my cheeks as I lay my face against Cheyenne's muzzle. It was so soft and her breath fanned my skin. Breath that reminded me how precious life was.

"I'll make a deal with you,girl,"I said. "If you fight and get through this, I'll fight my way back,too.We'll learn how to walk on our own together."

From that day on, things steadily improved. Cheyenne looked more alert and comfortable, daring to take her first steps, while I started crying less and smiling more. A healing was beginning to take place and it felt so very good. One day at a time, one step at a time, Cheyenne and I were making it together.

"Look,Mom! She's doing it! Cheyenne's walking on her own ! " Kitty pointed as Cheyenne wandered about the yard one week later. She managed just fine with the front leg missing. In fact, it seemed as if she didn't miss it much at all.

Mary clapped happily. "Just like her old self! "

I thought about that a moment and had to disagree. "Actually, sweetheart, I think Cheyenne's going to be better than she used to be. She'll be stronger because she's a survivor now. Just like us...better than ever."

In that instant, Cheyenne stopped and looked at me. The gleam was back in those golden eyes. We both had a new life to look forward to, one precious step at a time.

丑 丑

侠名

当你贫困时，你的狗在身边；当你痛苦时，你的狗在身边；当你伤心时，你的狗依然在身边。所以，当你的狗遭遇不幸时，你要守候着它，因为它是你唯一忠诚不变的朋友。

——狗迷

住在这座人员混杂的公寓中的每一个人都知道丑丑。丑丑是一只常驻于此的公狗。在这个世界上，丑丑最欢做三件事：打架、吃剩菜，还有就是我们将要说到的——爱。

这几件事交织在一起，再加上丑丑常年在外流浪，极大地影响了他的生活。从头说起吧，他只有一只眼睛，剩下的那只也只是一个黑洞洞了，耳朵也只剩下一只了。他的左腿看起来曾经严重扭伤过，虽然现在已经痊愈了，但是走起来还是很不自然，好像在转弯。他的尾巴早就不见了，只留下一个残根，还不停地扭动着。

丑丑本来是一只有着黑灰色斑纹的小狗——除了他的头顶、脖子，甚至肩上都有着厚厚的、黄色的疤痕。人们看见丑丑都会有同样的反应："那真是一只丑陋的狗啊！"

所有的孩子都被警告不要去摸他，大人们总是朝他扔石头、用水浇他，当他试图进入他们房子的时候就用水冲他，如果他不离开，就把他的爪子挤在门缝里。丑丑总是做出同样的反应：如果你打开水龙头用水冲他，他就会一动不动地站在那里，浑身上下湿漉漉的，直到你放弃。如果你朝他扔东西，他就会蜷缩着他那瘦长的身体趴在那里，没有丝毫反抗。

无论他什么时候看到那些孩子，他总是跑过去，汪汪地狂叫着，用头去拱那些孩子的手，请求他们的爱抚。如果你将他抱起来，他就会马上舔你的衣服、耳环，碰到什么就舔什么。

一天，丑丑跑到邻居家向他们的爱斯基摩狗示爱。那些狗儿们却没有做出友善的回应，丑丑被咬伤了，伤势严重。我在公寓里听到他的尖叫，于是马上冲出去救他。当我到达那里时，看见他躺在地上。很显然，丑丑悲惨的生活就要走到尽头了。

丑丑躺在一片湿地上，他的后腿和后背扭曲得变了形，前胸白色的条纹有一条撕裂的伤口。我将他抱在怀里，打算带他回家，这时我能听到他艰难地喘息着，能够感觉到他在颤抖。我想他一定伤得很重。

随后，我感到耳边有一种很熟悉的被舔吮的感觉。丑丑，尽管忍受着剧痛和苦楚，又面临着死亡，他仍然试图舔吮着我的耳朵。我将他抱得更紧了，他用头蹭着我的手掌，然后转过头用他那仅剩的一只金色的眼睛看着我，我能够清楚地听到他发出的咕噜咕噜声。尽管忍受着剧痛，这只浑身上下布满了丑陋伤疤的狗依旧只是在寻求一丝爱意，也许是同情吧。

此刻，我觉得丑丑是我所见过的最漂亮、最可爱的动物了。因为他从未咬过或是抓伤过我，甚至试图离开我，或者是做任何挣扎。丑丑只是看着我，他完全相信我可以减轻他的痛苦。

在我还没有走到家的时候，丑丑就死在了我的怀抱里，但是我抱着他坐了很久，一直在思索着：这样一只伤痕累累、丑陋而又到处流浪的小狗，是怎样改变了我的看法的，到底什么是真正的纯洁心灵，怎样才能爱得那么深、那么真。丑丑教会了我比任何书籍、讲座或访谈节目所学到的更多的给予和同情，为此，我将永远感激他。他的伤疤裸露在外，而我的却在内心深处。我要继续前行，学会如何爱得真切、爱得深沉，我会将我的一切都献给我所关爱的人。

许多人都希望自己能够更加富有、更加成功，哦，还有更加讨人喜欢、更加漂亮，对我来说，我只希望做丑丑。

The Integrity of "Ugly"

Anonymous

Everyone in the apartment complex I lived in knew who Ugly was. Ugly was the resident tom dog. Ugly loved three things in this world: fighting, eating garbage, and , shall we say, love.

The combination of these things combined with a life spent outside had their effect on Ugly. To start with, he had only one eye and the other should have been was a gaping hole. He was also missing his ear on the same side, his left foot appeared to have been baby broken at one time, and had healed at an unnatural angle, making him look like he was always turning the corner. His tail has long age been lost, leaving only the smallest stub, which he would constantly jerk and twitch.

Ugly would have been a dark grey tabby, stripeb –type, except for the sores covering his head, neck, even his shoulders with thick, yellowing scabs. Every time someone saw Ugly there was the same reaction, "That's one UGLY dog. "

All the children were warned not to touch him, the adults threw rocks at him, hosed him down, and squirted him when he tried to come in their homes, or shut his paws in the door when he would not leave. Ugly always had the same reaction. If you turned the hose on him, he would stand there, getting soaked until you gave up and quit. If you threw things at him, he would curl his lanky body around feet in forgiveness.

Whenever he spied children, he would come running, barking frantically and bump his head against their hands, begging for their love. If you ever picked him up, he would immediately begin suckling on your shirt, earrings, whatever he could find.

One day Ugly shared his love with the neighbor's Huskies. They did not respond kindly and Ugly was badly mauled. From my apartment I could hear his screams, and

I tried to rush to his aid. By the time I got to where he was laying, it was apparent that Ugly's sad life was almost at an end.

Ugly lay in a wet circle, his back legs and lower back twisted grossly out of shape, a gaping tear in the white strip of fur that ran down his front. As I picked him up and tried to carry him home, I could hear him wheezing and gasping, and could feel him struggling. It must be hurting him terribly, I thought.

Then I felt a familiar tugging, sucking sensation on my ear. Ugly, in so much pain, suffering and obviously dying, was trying to suckle my ear. I pulled him closer to me, and he bumped the palm of my hand with his head, then he turned his one golden eye towards me, and I could hear the distinct sound of purring. Even in the greatest pain, that ugly battled–scarred dog was asking only for a little affection, perhaps some compassion.

At that moment I thought Ugly was the most beautiful, loving creature I had ever seen. Never once did he try to bite or scratch me, or even try to get away from me, or struggle in any way. Ugly just looked up at me completely trusting in me to relieve his pain.

Ugly died in my arms before I could get inside, but I sat and held him for a long time afterwards, thinking about how one scarred, deformed little stray could so alter my opinion about what it means to have true pureness of spirit, to love so totally and truly. Ugly taught me more about giving and compassion than a thousand books, lectures, or talk show specials ever could, and for that I will always be thankful. He had been scarred on the outside, but I was scarred on the inside, and it was time for me to move on and learn to love truly and deeply, to give my total to those I cared for.

Many people want to be richer, more successful, well–liked, beautiful, but for me, I will always try to be Ugly.

杰克和猫

佚名

> 养狗是唯一一种金钱能买到的爱。
>
> ——史塔克

一开始,杰克就很清楚地表现出他对猫的看法:她们最适合作为一道菜放在盘中。杰克是我们的一条居家狗,他是一条身形高大、盛气凌人的公狗,他的身上有着博德牧羊犬、拉布拉多猎犬以及一点德国牧羊犬的血统。在他两岁的时候,我们从当地的一家动物避难所收养了他。我心爱的玛撒因一场意外的疾病死去了,后来杰克走进了我们的生活。一天,我们去避难所原本想再找一条像玛撒一样的皮毛乱蓬蓬的母狗,但是在湖边我们发现了一条短毛的公狗,他高傲地、静静地坐在那些狂吠不止的狗中间。我们告诉避难所的管理员,我们要带杰克回家,因为我们能感觉到他的身上有一种神奇的魔力。"这样太好了,"管理员说道,"当他把那种神奇的魔力展现在你面前的时候,请不要再将他送回来了!"

杰克很快就成了我们珍爱的家庭成员。他很喜欢看我们用无数的喂食器和鸟盆来吸引院子里的小鸟。他和邻居家的小狗还有附近其他的狗在公园里一起做游戏,但是他有非常明确的表示:猫是不允许到他的领地上来的。如果有任何猫走得太近了,他就会穷追不舍地将她们撵走。

有一天,我发现我们的柴堆房里有几只很小的野猫。尽管我是一个养狗人,也从来没有想过要和一只猫共同生活,但是我的内心深处还是对这3只小猫充满了怜悯。她们大概有4个星期大,灰色斑纹皮毛十分漂亮,大大的眼睛充满了恐惧,她们的妈妈不见了。我将她们放进一只箱子,并拿到屋里。杰克听见猫叫的声音,就立刻开始分泌唾液,流着口水,并喘着粗气。兽医告诉我们:"有些狗在任何情况下都是不会接受猫的。"

那次小猫事件已经过去一年了,有一天我向外望去,目光落在一张桌子上,看见杰克的耳朵竖着,头歪向一边,盯着地面。在他的脚下有一只小猫咪,静静地坐着。我试图用温和的话语安抚杰克，使他平静下来，我又往前走得近些，希望能阻止那种我确信即将发生的悲惨攻击。那只小猫的眼睛受到了严重感染，可能已经看不见了，不知道自己在哪里或是还不知道自己即将面临危险。但是杰克只是盯着那只小猫，然后又看看我，再转过去看看小猫。我听见了猫叫声，发现桌子底下还有一只小猫。于是我把这两只猫都放进盒子里，将这个盒子作为她们临时的家。我把盒子放在车库，然后开始给我所知道的那些动物收养所打电话，不厌其烦地向他们说着同样的故事——我的狗从来不允许那些猫进入我们家，我需要立刻将这两只小猫重新安置好。

第二天早晨，我们又发现 3 只小猫躺在门口的柴堆旁，蜷缩在一起取暖。于是我把她们也带了进来，并放在盒子里。

我的心情异常沉重。现在，我们已经有 5 只小猫了，她们的眼睛都感染得很厉害。她们都将被送到一个挤满了被遗弃的动物的家庭里。一整天，我都在不停地打电话，只是一遍又一遍地被告知已经没有足够的地方再收养更多的动物了。我知道现在我已经无从选择了。我的眼中噙着泪，拨通了兽医院的电话，希望他们把小猫永远带出我的生活。与此同时，我又看了看杰克，静静地观察着身边的一切。没有流口水，也没有喘息声，他看起来没有一点不安与急躁。我感觉有些事情发生了改变。

于是，我平静地坐着，而且心中有一个声音告诉我该怎么做。我给兽医打了电话，预约检查小猫的眼睛。从兽医院回家的路上，我去了一家宠物店，买了第一箱猫食。回到家中，我将放小猫的盒子拿到屋里。杰克在旁边等着。时间到了，于是我小心翼翼地将那几只小猫放在厨房的地板上，屏住呼吸，时刻准备在必要时刻去拯救那几只小猫。

杰克走了过来，用鼻子挨个闻了闻那几只小猫，接着就坐在了她们的中间，看着我。那几只小猫蜂拥而上，很高兴能够找到这么大的可以依偎的既温暖又毛茸茸的身体来取暖。那是杰克打开他的心扉接受这 5 只小猫咪的时刻，我不知道他是不是也想起了当时自己也需要一个家。我蹲下来感谢他的爱心和怜悯之心，告诉他，我是多么感激他走进了我的生活。但是这些感激的话语等到以后再告诉他吧——杰克和他的小猫咪们已经睡着了。

Jack And Cat

Anonymous

From the beginning, Jake made his feelings clear about the subject of cats: they were best served on a plate.

Jake was our resident dog, a large dominant male, part Border collie and part Labrador retriever, with a little German shepherd thrown in. Jake was about two years old when he was adopted by us from the local animal shelter. He came into our lives shortly after I lost my beloved dog Martha to an unexpected illness. One day we went to the shelter, searching for a shaggy-haired female (like Martha) to bring into our home. Instead, we found Jake, a short-haired male, proud and silent in the middle of all that barking. We told the shelter worker that we wanted Jake to come home with us because we could sense he had a lot of magic inside of him "That's great, " she said, "Just don't bring him back when he shows you that magic! "

Jake immediately became a cherished member of our family. He loved watching the birds we attracted to our yard with **numerous**[1] feeders and birdbaths. He played with the puppy next door and other dogs in the park, but made it extremely clear that cats would never be allowed on his property, chasing any feline that came too close.

One day, I found a litter of wild kittens in our woodpile. Although I had been a "dog person" all my life and had never had the **privilege**[2] of sharing my life with a cat, my heart went out to these little fur balls. They were only about four weeks old, and had beautiful gray-**striped**[3] bodies and large, frightened eyes. Their mother was nowhere in sight. I put them into a box and brought them inside. Jake heard the meowing and immediately began to salivate, drool, and pant. Our veterinarian told us, "Some dogs just don't accept cats under any condition."

A year after the kitty experience, one day I looked outside onto the deck and saw Jake with his ears up and his head **cocked**[4] sideways, staring at the ground. There at his feet was a tiny kitten, sitting very still. Using soothing words to try and keep Jake calm, I moved in closer, hoping to prevent the ugly attack I felt sure was coming. The kitten had badly infected eyes, and it probably couldn't see where it was or what was looming over it. But Jake just looked at the little creature, then looked up at me, and then back at the kitten. I heard some meowing, and discovered another kitten under the deck. So I scooped them both up into a box that would be their temporary home. I put the box in the garage and started making calls to all the animal people I knew, telling each the same story—my dog would never allow these cats into our home, and I need to relocate them right away.

The next morning, we found three more kittens lying in a pile outside the door, huddled together for warmth. So I took them in and added them to the box.

My heart was very heavy. Now we had five little kittens, all with infected eyes, which would be sent out into a world already crowded with unwanted little creatures. I spent the day making phone calls, only to be told over and over that no one had room for more critters. I knew I'd run out of options, so with tears in my eyes, I picked up the phone to make the call to the vet that would take the kittens out of my life forever. At the same moment, my eyes fell on Jake, calmly observing everything going on around him. There was no drooling, no panting, he didn't seem upset or anxious. I felt something was different.

So I became still and I sat. And I heard a voice in my heart telling me what to do. I called our veterinarian and made an appointment to bring the kittens in and get their eyes checked. On the way home from the doctor, I went to a pet store and bought my first litter box. I came home and brought the box of kittens back into the house. Jake was waiting. The time had come, so I carefully put the babies on the floor of the kitchen and held my breath, ready to come to the rescue if necessary.

Jake walked over and sniffed each of the kittens. Then he sat down in the middle of them and looked up at me. The kittens swarmed over him, happy to find a big, warm body of fur to curl up next to. That's when Jake opened his heart to the five little kittens and adopted them as his own. I wondered if he remembered a time when he, too, had needed a home. I went down to thank him for his love and compassion and tell him how grateful I was he'd come into my life. But it would have to wait until later——Jake and his kittens were fast asleep.

1. numerous ['nju:mərəs] *adj.* 众多的；许多的；无数的
2. privilege ['privilidʒ] *n.* 特权；特别待遇
3. striped [straipt] *adj.* 有斑纹的
4. cock [kɔk] *v.* 使耸立；使竖起

献给聪明顽皮的诺拉

金·西莉亚

> 狗可能是上帝派来的天使,他让人快乐,让人幸福,如果你一无所有,只要拥有一只狗,你也会感到无比幸福和快乐。
>
> ——狗迷

我的小狗诺拉,在一年零五个月之前被诊断患了纤维瘤。在过去的一年半中,我们给她进行了 6 次外科手术,还有许多药物治疗,甚至为她泣不成声。令人悲痛的是,病魔最终降临,诺拉那龟甲色的身体完全被癌细胞所充斥。她的左前腿上又长出了新的肿瘤,看起来每天都会有所增长,这使她成了一个跛子。看着癌细胞在她的身上扩散,痛苦真是不言而喻,然而最心痛的还是我已经无能为力了,我什么都做不了,只能坐在那里眼睁睁地看着病魔把她从我这里带走。

8 年来,诺拉已经成了我生命中的一部分。她跟着我穿过屋子里的每一个房间;在浴盆前耐心地等待我沐浴;每晚与我同眠;四肢伸开卧在我的怀里看电视;在以往的这个时候,在我打字时,她会坐在我的膝上,脑袋静静地靠在键盘的边上。我与诺拉共同经历了我的人生中的沟沟坎坎——关系破裂、工作调动、搬迁,她那让我安心的咕噜声以及盯着我看时的双眼,都是我的精神支柱,拯救我于水火之中。

今天早上,我痛哭不已。这种哭泣我从未经历过,这使我全身疼痛,好像永远不会停止。在痛苦至极时,我跪在诺拉面前,她正卧在床上她最喜欢的那个地方。我的头倚着床,我抱起她那毛绒绒的身体,我哽咽了。透过泪水,我可以看到她盯着我正在思考着什么,眨着她那猫头鹰似的眼睛,好像有些东西她不太明白似的。她从未见过我这样。她一直望着我,吻着我的手,很显然,她明白了,于是有了这样一些动作。

你们这些善良、温柔的动物爱好者,或许会猜想,她会蜷缩在我的身旁,一边蹭着我的身体,一边咕噜咕噜地叫着来安慰我。或许你们会预料,她会舔去我的泪水。

这应该是一个很令人满意、非常温情的结果，然而故事并非如此。

这只狗咬了我！

起初，我很震惊，我停止了哭泣，望着她说："为什么你现在会这样？"

然而这只是开始。她用她那尖尖的牙齿咬住我的手，并开始啃了起来。还用她那毛绒绒的小脚踢我的胳膊，她的眼睛中迸发出一种凶狠的神情。

我泪流满面，带着怨恨对她说："你忘了我给你的肚皮挠痒痒了吗？忘了在餐桌上我喂你食物了吗？忘了我在暴风雨中保护你了吗？忘了我跳到卡车前避免你的毛茸茸的小屁股惨遭压扁了吗？忘了当你把隔壁店铺里的那只波斯猫咬得狼狈至极时，我并未吼你吗？你忘了，是吗？我彻底崩溃了，你竟然这样对待我？"

可是我的恼怒好像更刺激了她。不一会儿，我发现自己笑了，并开始回应她，我弯着手指，模仿成一个爪子模样，像飞机俯冲轰炸似地冲下来攻击她。在这个过程中，我明白了她这样做的用意——她想让我跟她一起玩耍。她好像在对我说："是呀，我知道我们最近的感觉都很差，可是，让它见鬼去吧，我们来玩吧！"

她很机灵，所以我采纳了她的建议。我们就这样玩闹着，即使这样翻滚很有可能会使她的腿受伤，即使这几天她很容易感到疲劳；我们就这样玩闹着，即使我淌着鼻涕，即使我知道我所处的这个世界正在坍塌；我们就这样玩闹着，即使事实上，我与这个珍爱的小生灵即将结束我们相依相伴的人生旅程。

Tribute to a Wise
And Playful Soul

A year and five months ago, my dog, Norah was diagnosed with Fibrous Sarcoma. Over the last year and a half, we've been through six surgeries, a lot of medication, and even more tears. Sadly, it finally caught up to us, and the cancer has spread through Norah, tortoise shell–colored body. She developed a new tumor just above her left front leg, which appears to be growing in size each day and has caused her to develop a limp. The pain of watching the cancer spread through her body is excruciating, but not as painful as knowing that there was nothing I can do to help her. Nothing to do but sit back and watch this disease take her away from me.

Norah has been a constant in my life for eight years. She follows me through every room of the house, waits patiently in front of the tub while I shower, sleeps with me each night, sprawls on my stomach to watch television, and is, at this moment, sitting on my lap with her head resting on the edge of the keyboard as I type. Through all of my problems, broken relationships, jobs, and moves, Norah has been with me through it all. The reassuring rumble of her purring against my ear and the steadiness of her eyes when she gazes at me has anchored me and brought me, back from some pretty terrible places.

This morning, I broke down. It wasn't the type of crying that I've experienced in the past, but the kind that leaves your entire body sore and seems like it may never stop. In the middle of the jag, I kneeled in front of Norah where she was laying in her favorite spot on the bed. Placing my head against the bed, I clasped on to her fur, and sobbed. Through my tears, I could see that she was staring at me quite thoughtfully,

27 <<<<*The Soul of the Dogs*

blinking her large, owl-like eyes in confusion. She had never seen me carry on like this. After some time of watching and sniffing my hand, she apparently came to an assessment and a course of action.

You kinder, gentler animal lovers would probably guess that she curled up next me, rubbing and purring to comfort me. Or perhaps you've anticipating that she licked my tears away. And while that would be a satisfying, endearing conclusion to my story that was not what happened.

That dog bit me!

I was shocked at first. I stopped crying, looked at her, and said," Now why did you go and do that?"

But that was just the beginning. She grabbed hold of my hand with her pointy little teeth and started gnawing. Then putting her furry little feet against my arm, started to kick me; and this wild, devil-may-care look in her eye.

Through accusing, tear-stained eyes, I said to her, " What about the entire belly rubs and table food I've given you? What about all the thunder storms I've protected you from? Have you forgotten the time when I jumped in front of that truck to save your furry little butt from being run over? Or the time I didn't yell at you for beating the crap out of that snotty Persian cat next store? You forgot about that, didn't you? I am going through some kind of breakdown and this is what I get?"

But my indignant outrage just seemed to spur her on. In time, I found myself laughing as I batted back at her paws and curled my hand, mimicing a claw, to dive-bomb her belly with a playful attack. And some where in the middle of it all, I saw her reaction for what it was: Norah wanted me to play with her. It was as if she were saying to me, "Yeah, I know both of us haven't been feeling well lately, but let's just say to hell with it and play! "

She had a point, so I took her advice. We played despite the fact that rolling around must of made her leg hurt and that she tired easily these days. We played despite the fact that my nose was running and what I knew of the world was crashing around me. We played despite the fact that the time I had left with this precious creature was running out.

家

俟名

当万物共同的结局来临，死神夺走了主人的生命，尸体埋藏在寒冷的地下，纵使所有的亲友都各奔前程，这只高贵的狗依然会独自守护着忠诚，直到死亡。

——佛斯特

冰冷的倾盆大雨冲刷着小城酒吧前面的柏油马路。与往常一样，我孤零零地坐在那里，凝望着雨中的昏暗。穿过积满雨水的马路就是小城的公园，那里有 5 英亩的草坪，还有巨大的榆树，今晚，又增添了一片到脚踝那么高的冰冷雨水。

我在那间破旧的酒吧里停留了半个小时，一口一口地品着酒。我沉思的目光终于停留在 100 英尺以外一个绿色的水坑里的一团东西上。有 10 分钟的时间，我一直穿过落满雨水的窗户向外看，我想看看那究竟是一只动物还是一堆被雨打湿的没有生命的东西。

前一天晚上，一只看上去很像德国牧羊犬的狗来到酒吧里讨土豆片吃。他的身上长满了疥癣，肚子饿得咕咕叫，从大小来看，和那团湿乎乎的东西很相像。我心想，这只狗为什么会冒着寒冷的雨水躺在冰冷的水坑里呢？很显然，或者他不是一只狗，要是狗的话，他一定是虚弱得没有力气站起来了。

榴弹在我的右肩留下的伤口隐隐作痛，一直延伸到手指。我不想冒着暴风雨走出去。再加上他不属于我，也不属于任何人。他只是一只流浪狗，在一个寒冷的夜晚独自飘泊的狗。然而我感觉自己和他的处境相同，我把剩下的酒一口喝光，起身向门外走去。

他在 3 英寸深的水里躺着。我碰了碰他，他却一动不动。我感觉他已经死了。我用双手抓着他的胸部，将他扶了起来。他摇摇晃晃地站在水里，耷拉着脑袋，仿佛吊在他的脖子上的重物。他的半边身体全是疥癣，耷拉着的耳朵简直就像长满烂疮的、没有毛的两片肉。

"跟我来。"我对他说道，但愿我不用抱着他长满疮的身体去寻找避雨的地方。他摇了摇尾巴，拖着虚弱的身体，迈着沉重的脚步跟在我的身后。我带着他走到酒吧的吧台旁边，他在冰凉的水泥地上躺了下来，闭上了眼睛。

我看到隔着一个街区的一家便利店的灯还亮着，尚未关门。我买了三罐狗粮，把它们全部塞进皮衣口袋。我浑身湿透了，样子丑陋，在我离开的时候，售货员仿佛松了口气。我骑上我的哈雷·戴维森摩托车回到酒吧，酒吧的玻璃窗被赛车用的排气管震得咔哒直响。

酒吧女招待替我把罐头打开，并告诉我这只狗叫谢普，大概一岁左右，他的主人去德国了，他就被扔到了街上。那只狗专心致志地吃光了所有狗粮。我想摸摸他，然而他的身上散发出死狗的恶臭味，模样更是令人恐惧。"祝你好运。"我对他说道，接着跨上摩托车走了。

第二天，我找到一份工作——为一家小筑路公司开卸料卡车。正当我拉着一车砾石穿过小城中心时，我看到谢普站在离酒吧很近的人行道上。我对着他大叫，仿佛看到他摇了摇尾巴。我为他的反应感到高兴。

下班后，我又买了三罐狗粮和一块奶酪汉堡包。我和我的"新朋友"在人行道上共进晚餐，他先吃完了自己的那份。

第二天晚上，当我给他带来食物时，他用极大的热情欢迎我。因为缺乏营养，他的腿支撑不住身体而不时地跌倒在地上。别人抛弃了他，虐待他，然而如今他有了朋友，他对我的感激难以言表。

第三天，我拉着一辆车子沿着主干道途经酒吧时，却并没有看见那只狗。我猜测或许有人将他带回家了。

下班之后，我把我的那辆黑色摩托车停在街上，沿着人行道寻找他。我害怕我找到的谢普不知会变成什么模样。在附近的小巷里，他身体的一侧倒在地上，舌头被尘土淹没了，他看到我时只动了一下尾巴尖。

当地的兽医尚未下班，因此我从雇主那里借来了客货两用车，将这只瘸拐的狗装进驾驶室。在为躺在桌子上有气无力、令人心生怜爱的狗检查完之后，兽医问道："这是你的狗吗？"

"不是，"我回答说，"他是只野狗。"

"他已经开始出现犬热病的症状了，"兽医忧伤地说，"假如他没有家，最好的办法就是结束他的生命，让他摆脱痛苦。"

我把手搭在他的肩上，他那长满疥癣的尾巴有气无力地拍了拍不锈钢检查桌。我长叹了一口气，说："他有家。"

之后的三个晚上、两个白天，这只狗(我称他为谢普)就侧卧在我的公寓的地板上。我和室友利用几个小时的时间给他喂水，试图让他吃一点炒鸡蛋。尽管他无法下咽，但是每当我碰他的时候，他都会轻轻地动一下尾巴尖。

在他来到我家的第三天早上10点左右，我返回家中为装电话的人开门。一进门，差一点被那只又蹦又跳的野狗撞倒在地。谢普康复了！

时间一天天过去，那浑身疥癣、肚子饿得咕咕叫、差点死在我面前的野狗，现在可是肌肉健壮，重达80磅。他有着宽大的胸脯，身上的黑毛浓密而有光泽。有好几次，当我的身心被孤独和沮丧快要摧垮的时候，谢普为了报答我的恩情，都会把他那无拘无束的友情传达给我，直至我别无选择，重新露出笑脸，和他玩起"丢棒拾棒"的游戏。

回首往夕，我与谢普相识时，我们都处于生活的低谷，但是如今我们不会感到孤单，也不再流浪。我想说的是：我们两个都回家了。

Home

Anonymous

A freezing downpour washed che black asphalt street in front of the small town bar. I sat gazing into the watery darkness, alone as usual. Across the rain−drenched roadway was the town park:five acres of grass, giant elm trces and, tonight, an ankle-deep covering of cold water.

I had been in that battered old pub for half an hour, quietly nursing a drink, when my thoughtful stare finally focused on a medium−sized lump in a grassy puddle a hundred feet away. For another ten minutes, I looked out through the tear−streaked windowpane trying to decide if the lump was an animal or just a wet and inanimate something.

The night before, a German shepherd looking mongrel had come into the bar begging for potato chips. He was mangy and starving and just the size of the lump in question. Why would a dog lie in a cold puddle in the freezing rain? I asked myself. The answer was simple: either it wasn't a dog, or if it was, he was too weak to get up.

The shrapnel wound in my right shoulder ached all the way down to my fingers. I didn't want to go out in that storm. Hey, it wasn't my dog, it wasn't anybody's dog. It was just a stray on a cold night in the rain, a lonely drifter. So was I, I thought, as I tossed down what was left of my drink and headed out the door.

He was lying in three inches of water. When I touched him, he didn't move. I thought he was dead. I put my hands around his chest and hoisted him to his feet. He stood unsteadily in the puddle, his head hung like a weight at the end of his neck. Half his body was covered with mange. His floppy ears were just hairless pieces of flesh dotted with open sores.

"Come on." I said, hoping I wouldn't have to carry his infected carcass to shelter. His tail wagged once and he plodded weakly after me. I led him to an alcove next to the bar, where he lay on the cold cement and closed his eyes.

A block away I could see the lights of a late night convenience store. It was still open. I bought three cans of Alpo and stuffed them into my leather coat. I was wet and ugly and the clerk looked relieved as I left. The race–type exhausts on my old Harley Davidson rattled the windows in the bar as I rode back to the bar.

The barmaid opened the cans for me and said the dog's name was Shep. She told me he was about a year old and that his owner had gone to Germany and left him on the street. He ate all three cans of dog food with an awe–inspiring singleness. of purpose. I wanted to pet him, but he smelled like death and looked even worse. "Good luck." I said. Then got on my bike and rode away.

The next day I got a job driving a dump truck for a small paving company. As I hauled a load of gravel through the center of town, I saw Shep standing on the sidewalk near the bar. I yelled to him and thought I saw his tail wag. His reaction made me feel good.

After work I bought three more cans of Alpo and a cheeseburger. My new friend and I ate dinner together on the sidewalk. He finished his first.

The next night, when I brought his food, he welcomed me with wild enthusiasm. Now and then, his malnourished legs buckled and he fell to the pavement. Other humans had deserted him and mistreated him, but now he had a friend and his appreciation was more than obvious.

I didn't see him the next day as I hauled load after load up the main street past the bar. I wondered if someone had taken him home.

After work I parked my black Harley on the street and walked down the sidewalk looking for him. I was afraid of what I would find. He was lying on his side in an alley nearby. His tongue hung out in the dirt and only the tip of his tail moved when he saw me.

The local veterinarian was still at his office, so I borrowed a pickup truck from my employer and loaded the limp mongrel into the cab. "Is this your dog?" the vet asked after checking the pitiful specimen that lay helplessly on his examining table.

"No, "I said, "he's just a stray. "

"He's got the beginnings of distemper, "the vet said sadly, "If he doesn't have a home, the kindest thing we can do is put him out of his misery. "

I put my hand on the dog's shoulder. His mangy tail thumped weakly against the stainless steel table. I sighed loudly. "He's got a home. "I said.

For the next three nights and two days, the dog—I named him Shep—lay on his side in my apartment. My roommate and I spent hours putting water in his mouth and trying to get him to swallow a few scrambled eggs. He couldn't do it, but whenever I touched him, his tail wagged slightly at the very tip.

At about 10:00 a. m. on the third day, I went home to open the apartment for the telephone installer. As I stepped through the door, I was nearly flattened by a jumping, wiggling mass of euphoric mutt. Shep had recovered.

With time, the mangy starving dog that nearly died in my living room grew into an eighty-pound block of solid muscle, with a massive chest and a super thick coat of shiny black fur. Many times, when loneliness and depression have nearly gotten the best of me, Shep has returned my favor by showering me with his unbridled friendship until I had no choice but to smile and trade my melancholy for a fast game of fetch-the-stick.

When I look back, I can see that Shep and I met at the low point of both of our lives. But we aren't lonely drifters anymore. I'd say we've both come home.

阳 光

佚名

对狗而言，每个主人都是拿破仑，因此狗这么受人喜爱。

——赫胥黎

他那闪闪发光的金色毛发就像灿烂绚丽的阳光，于是他有了阳光这个名字。而这也使他更加区别于其他的狗狗。他的头发很柔滑，就像光滑的上等天鹅绒。

他的腿上覆盖着雪白的茸毛，蓬松地垂下来。他看着其他的狗狗们，昂着头大摇大摆地跟在我的身后，而最后他却成了"领导人"。

阳光咕噜咕噜地叫着，用他那金绿色的眼睛凝视着我。他领着我向他的狗食盘子走去，还没有走到他就停了下来，转过脑袋认真地看着我，我跟了过去。

他用鼻子嗅着昨天的食物，我将新鲜的食物放到他的盘子里。他看着我，当我打开一罐鸡肝放到他的食物中时，他转了过去，吃了起来。我将他的水碗倒满了清水，又加了一些冰块。他已经将我训练得很好了。

当他想出去玩的时候，会告诉我他会选择哪扇门通过。当他决定回来的时候，就会用爪子在那扇门上抓个不停，于是我就从椅子上跳起来为他开门。他走了进来，昂着头，尾巴还一直翘翘着，他已经将我牢牢地控制在他那利爪之下了。

当我的丈夫格伦下班回家的时候，阳光总是毫不吝啬地将他的爱意转移到格伦的身上。他不失时机地跟着格伦一直走到衣柜旁。他闻来闻去，直冲着格伦在家穿的鞋子走过去，然后用爪子将它们拖到格伦的面前。

当格伦坐在椅子上读报纸的时候，阳光就会蜷缩在椅背旁打起盹来。白天，当我对着电脑工作的时候，他就会静静地蜷缩在我的大腿上。

当格伦从南边的窗户向外望去的时候，我有好多次都能听到他的笑声。于是我就问他："你笑什么呢？"

格伦会说："阳光正在小山上检查格伦医生和玛丽家的菜单呢。"或者他会这样说:"阳光正在从山上下来呢,他已经检查完医生的家了。"而阳光的这些游历又给自己增添了一个新的昵称——伴侣狗。

当阳光感到冷落的时候,他就会伸出雪白的爪子抓住我的裙摆。我就将他抱起来,抚摸着他那天鹅绒般的毛发,这会使他非常满意。

阳光有自己的爱好。他喜欢坐车,喜欢睡在车库里的汽车顶上,还喜欢看电视,尤其爱看那些狗狗们在电视里跳来跳去的有关狗食的广告节目。

一天,阳光和我在后院漫步,这个后院与马克·吐温国家森林公园相连。我提着色拉桶,打算去摘一些青菜。

阳光停了下来,从喉咙里发出一声沉沉的令人害怕的叫声。我停了下来,看着他。噢!他那天鹅绒般的毛发都竖了起来,他的眼睛斜视着。他在看什么呢?

我静静地站着,向树林深处望去。我立刻看到两只山狗站在篱笆的外面。我大声喊着,将手中的色拉桶扔到篱笆上。他们不见了。

"噢,阳光,"我把他抱了起来,"你今天真是好样的!没有白养你。"

他咕噜咕噜地叫着,将脑袋靠在我的肩上。

格伦突发心脏病离开了我们。这场噩耗将我打垮了,我吃不下也睡不着。虽然我已经精疲力竭,但是日子还要继续。晚上我躺在床上希望能够入睡。

我很清楚地听到了呼吸和咕噜咕噜的声音。阳光躺在床上,靠着我的头。他从未在我们的床上睡过觉。他用爪子抚摸着我的头发。格伦在睡前总会抚摸我的头发。阳光是怎么知道这个的呢?

自从格伦去世之后,阳光看起来也发生了一些变化。他知道怎样帮助他人,他会走到一边,将狗食留下给另一只狗;他知道怎么抚慰其他的动物,他让一只小狗依偎在他的身边睡觉。他对我也表现出了很大的耐心,不会因为我给他喂食太慢而感到不耐烦。

我不理解,阳光怎么会如此了解我,了解人类的生活,但是他帮助了我,使我可以在那些孤单的日子里支撑下来。

从阳光的身上,我也学到了更多的尊重,尊重他,尊重所有的狗狗们,不管他们是不幸被遗弃的,还是深受宠爱的。我和阳光之间有一条看不见的纽带。我们爱着彼此,也将爱给予他人。

Sunshine

Anonymous

His gleaming, golden fur as sunny as sunlight gave Sunshine his name. It also sets him apart from other dogs. His hair has a silky soft feel like lush plush velvet.

His **fleecy**[1] milk white feet are **fluffy**[2] like down. He looks at the other dogs, cocks his head sideways, and then follows me. Follows until he becomes the boss.

Sunshine purrs then peers at me through golden green eyes. He leads me towards his dog pan, stops before he gets there, turns his head and scrutinizes me. I follow.

He turns up his nose at yesterday's food. I put fresh food in his pan. He eyes me, and then turns as I open him a can of chicken and liver to fill his dish. He eats. I fill his water bowl with fresh water and add a couple of ice **cubes**[3]. He has me well trained.

Sunshine tells me to whichever door he chooses to pass through when he wants to go outside. He scratches on the French Doors when he decides to come in. I spring from my chair and open the door. He walks in, head held high, tail straight up. He has me under his paw.

When Glenn, my husband, would come home from work, Sunshine would then transfer his affections to him. He never failed to accompany him into the walk–in closet. He smelled, then walked to Glenn's house shoes, and pulled them forward with his paw.

When Glenn would settle down in his chair to read, Sunshine would curl up on the back of his chair, and nap. During the day, when 1 worked at my computer, he always quietly curled in my lap.

Many times I have heard Glenn laugh as he looked out the south window. I asked, "Why are you laughing?"

Glenn would say, "There goes Sunshine up the hill to check the menu at Doctor Gene and Mary's house. " Or he would say, "Sunshine's coming down the hill. He's checked out Doctor's place." These travels of Sunshine brought about a nickname, The Partnership Dog.

When Sunshine feels left out, he reaches a white paw out and grabs my skirt. I take him in my arms and stroke his **velvety**[4] fur. That satisfies him.

Sunshine has hobbies. He likes to ride in the car, sleep on the car's roof in the garage, and watch television, especially the dog food commercials where the dogs swish across the screen.

One day, Sunshine and I strolled across our backyard, which joins the Mark Twain National Forest. I carried my **salad**[5] bucket planning to pick greens.

Sunshine stopped and made a blood curdling noise deep in his throat. I stopped and looked at him. Oh! The velvet fur stood straight outward from his body. His eyes slanted. What was he looking at?

I stood still and looked toward the woods. A second later, I saw two coyotes just outside the fence. I yelled and threw my salad bucket at the fence. They disappeared.

"Oh, Sunshine," I picked him up and hugged him, "You sure paid for your keeps today. "

He purred then laid his head on my shoulders.

Glenn suddenly passed away with a heart attack. A stunned shock gripped me. I couldn't sleep; I couldn't eat. Exhausted, but I had to carry on. I lay on the bed at night hoping to rest.

I would become aware of breathing, purring by my pillow. Sunshine would be lying on the bed near my head. He had never slept on our bed before. He stroked my hair with his paw. Glenn always stroked my hair before he went to sleep. How did Sunshine know to do this?

Sunshine seems to have changes since Glenn's passing. He doesn't take all. He knows how to give by walking away from his dog food in favor of another dog. He shows how to comfort by letting a **pup**[6] snuggle up to him to sleep. He grants patience with me by not prancing when I'm slow to feed him.

I don't understand how Sunshine knows so much about me, a human life, but he has helped make my lonely days more bearable.

Through Sunshine, I've learned to have more respect, respect for him, respect for all dogs, both the unfortunate discarded ones, and the loved ones. There's a bond between Sunshine and me. We love each other. We give our love to others.

1. fleecy ['fliːsi] *adj.* 以羊毛盖上的;蓬松的;羊毛似的
2. fluffy ['flʌfi] *adj.* 绒毛似的;披着绒毛的;蓬松的
3. cube [kjuːb] *n.* 立方体;立方
4. velvety ['veiviti] *adj.* 像天鹅绒的;柔软的
5. salad ['sæləd] *n.* 色拉
6. pup [pʌp] *n.* 小狗

遵从

洛里·乔·奥斯瓦尔德

　　我的父亲已经退休了,可是他还没有到退休的年龄,7年来,他一直在和结肠癌做斗争。现在,他已经病得很严重了,不能吃饭,也喝不下水,又因为感染被迫住进了医院。我意识到他讨厌住院,可是他几乎没有埋怨,这不是他的风格。

　　一天晚上,很不幸,他没有找到护士,自己试着进浴室时摔倒了,头部碰在了床头的小桌子上,划了一条很深的口子。第二天,当我看到他受伤的头时,我感到万分沮丧,无助的愤怒感油然而生。在我等电梯的时候,我在想,为什么我不能做点什么呢? 我的祷告好像有了回应,电梯门开了,是两只狗。

　　狗? 在医院里? 就我个人而言,想不出哪个地方更适合有狗,然而令我感到震惊的是,城市法规和医院规章居然允许狗进入医院。

　　"你怎么把狗带到这里啊?"我边往电梯里走,边问狗的主人。

　　"他们是治疗狗。我每个星期都会带他们去六楼一趟,去见那些接受康复治疗的患者。"

　　当我从医院出来,走向我的汽车时,我的脑海中浮现出一个想法,而且越来越强烈。几年前,父亲买了一只名叫布茨的猎犬作为圣诞节礼物送给了母亲。母亲一直都想要一只狗,而且必须是猎犬。当父亲要我跟他一起开车去找一只小狗的时候,他做了如下解释。

　　当他精心挑选了一只身体扭来扭去、喜欢舔别人的小狗时,我看到父亲脸上的表情由紧张渐渐放松下来。我马上明白了母亲的意思。这只狗不是为她自己买的,而是为父亲。很明显,她要这只狗是因为父亲年幼时就一直想要那种狗,可是从未实现过。

　　那时,我们这几个孩子都已经离开了家,于是布茨就成了父亲从未有过的理想孩子，他是父亲热爱、钟情、顺从的挚友。

我心想布茨实在是太听话了。不让他上床或是爬到任何其他的家具上，他从未违背过。有时候，我想告诉父亲，他在家卧床休息时，叫布茨过来！他会给您爱，吻您，爱抚你，我有点不太适合做这些了……然而，您需要。

可是我并未开口。父亲没有叫布茨来，布茨也没有来给他安慰。但是，时光流逝，布茨一直坐在他的床边，看护着他。父亲的身体日渐衰弱，布茨一直守着他，表达着他的爱，直到他不能独自行走。有几次，他病情加重，被送进了医院，布茨焦虑地等待着他，一旦有车在房子前停下，他都会期盼地跳起来。

我决定，如果我没有什么东西可以给父亲，就让他和他心爱的狗待几分钟。所以我回到医院，就此事询问了护士。她告诉我说，如果我带狗来医院，她会"什么都看不见"，我知道这就算同意了。

当天晚些时候，我带着布茨再次来到医院。我告诉父亲，车里有一份惊喜在等待着他。我去带布茨时，发生了最奇怪的事情。

布茨是一只完美的狗，拴上项圈时也像服从其他命令时一样听话。可是，这次几乎是冲出汽车，猛拖着我穿过被雪覆盖的停车场来到了前门，又拽着我穿过医院大厅。不知道他是如何知道该停在哪个电梯前面（我从未找对过）。虽然布茨从未来过这所医院附近的任何地方，可是当电梯门在四楼打开时，他跑过走廊，拐了两个弯，跑进另一条走廊，进入了父亲的病房，他都快把我的手臂拽脱臼了。当时，他毫不犹豫地顺势跳上了病床！他是如此温柔地爬进父亲张开的双臂，并没有碰到他疼痛的身体侧部或肚子，他把脸贴近了父亲的脸。

这是布茨第一次上父亲的床，这是属于他的地方。也是很久以来，我第一次看到父亲的灿烂微笑。我知道我们都应该感激布茨，因为他违反了规定，最终遵从了自己的心愿。

Obedience

Lori Jo Oswald

For seven years my father, who was not yet old to retire, had been battling colon cancer. Now he was dying. He could no longer eat or drink water, and an infection had forced him into the hospital. I sensed that he hated being in the hospital, but he hardly complained. That wasn't his way.

One night when he had no luck summoning a nurse, and tried to reach the bathroom on his own, he fell and gashed his head on the nightstand. When I saw his wounded head the next day, I felt my frustration and helpless anger rise. Why isn't there anything I can do? I thought, as I waited for the elevator. As if in answer to my prayers, when the elevator opened, two dogs greeted me.

Dogs? In a hospital? Personally, I couldn't think of a better place for dogs, but I was shocked that the city laws and hospital codes allowed it.

"How did you get to bring dogs here?" I asked the owner, as I stepped in.

"They're therapy dogs. I take them up to the sixth floor once a week, to meet with the patients in rehab."

An idea grew stronger and stronger as I walked out of the hospital and to my car. My dad had bought a springer spaniel named Boots for my mom for a Christmas present a few years ago. My mother had insisted that she wanted a dog, and it had to be a spaniel. My dad had explained this to me when he asked me to go for a ride with him to pick out a puppy.

When he picked up, a wriggly kissy puppy, I saw the tension ease from my father's face. I realized the genius of my mother's plan immediately. The dog was not for her, it was for him. Brilliantly, she asked for a spaniel so he could have the breed of a dog he'd always wanted, and never had, when he was a boy.

By then, all of us kids had moved away from home. So Boots also became the perfect child my father never had. She was an eager, loving and obedient pal for him.

Personally, I thought she was a little too obedient. Boots was not allowed on the bed or any other furniture, and she never broke this rule. Sometimes I wanted to tell my dad when he was at home lying on his sickbed, "Call Boots up here! She'll give you love and kisses and touch you like I'm too restrained to do... and you need it."

But I didn't. And he didn't. And Boots didn't.

Instead, she sat near his bed, watching him protectively, as the months rolled by. She was always there, a loving presence as his strength ebbed away, till he could no longer walk or even sit up without help. Once in a while, he got very sick, and went to the hospital, and she awaited his return anxiously, jumping up expectantly every time a car pulled up to the house.

I decided that if I could give my dad nothing else, I was going to give him a few minutes with his beloved dog. So I went back to the hospital and asked a nurse about it. She told me that if I were to bring his dog, she would not "see anything." I took that as a yes.

Later that day, I came back for another visit, bringing Boots. I told my dad I had a surprise for him in my car. I went to get her, and the strangest thing happened.

Boots, the perfect dog, who was as impeccably leash –trained as she was obedient, practically flew out of the car, yanked me across that snowy parking lot to the front door and dragged me through the hospital lobby. She somehow knew to stop directly in front of the appropriate elevator (I could never find the right one myself). And even though she had never been anywhere near that hospital before, when the elevator door opened at the fourth floor, she nearly pulled my arm off its socket as she ran down the hall, around two corners, down another hall and into his room. Then, without a moment of hesitation, she jumped straight up onto his bed! Ever so gently, she crawled into my father's open arms, not touching his pain–filled sides or stomach, and laid her face next to his.

For the first time, Boots was on my dad's bed, just where she belonged. And for the first time in a long time, I saw my father's broad smile. I knew we were both grateful Boots had broken the rules and finally obeyed her own heart.

两个失落的灵魂

谢利·圭多蒂

"你们听到声音了吗？"老狗呼喊道。

其他的狗都跑到狗屋门口，以便确认是否有什么人来"领养他们"。

"对不起，"老狗对他们说，就在说话的时候，老狗的耳朵耷拉了下来。"我甚至可以发誓我确实听到有人说：'瞧它多聪明伶俐啊！现在是圣诞节了，咱们把它带回家好不好？'"

"你一定又是在做白日梦了，老东西。"旁边狗屋里的狗说，"不管怎么说，让人家当作圣诞礼物带走，没有什么值得高兴的。我们都体验过这样的事情，看看我们现在，不还是这个样子吗。"

"哪怕只有一次，我想体验一下一只温暖的手来触摸我的头，"老狗说。"我想吻去一张写满伤心的脸上的泪水。我想依偎在炉火旁，而不是待在这冷冰冰的水泥地板上，待在这里使我的骨头酸痛。"

其他的狗对他说："老东西，你只能在梦里找到那个你想象的地方。"听到他们这么说，老狗把身子蜷缩起来，叹了口气。

汉克的妻子刚刚去世一年，那种思念的痛苦丝毫没有减退，好像时间都静止了。

现在，他年纪大了，孤零零一个人，期盼得到安慰，而他明白不会有人能够再次给他安慰。妻子不在身边陪伴，他的生活会是什么样子呢？

汉克的食品橱里差不多空无一物了，虽然他不想外出，可他明白最起码也要去买一些最基本的物品……他在便道上慢悠悠地开着车，要是在高速公路上开车，对他而言可是一件很有挑战性的事情。

忽然，车子发出嘎嚓声，后来是劈啪声，最终发动机停了下来。他连汽车行驶所必需的燃料都忘记了！因此，他把车停在路边，看到附近有一幢建筑物，他走着就能过去。他满怀希望地走过去，希望他们能让他打个电话。

他来到一个办公区域，于是他按了服务铃，但是没有人出来。他向外走时，看到另一扇门，可是没有看到门上挂着的牌子——"员工专用"。

正当汉克刚要走出来的时候，不同种类、活蹦乱跳的狗发出了狂吠声。他这才明白自己不经意间来到了狗的收容所。

他慢慢地沿着水泥路面走廊向前走，想找到一位工作人员。

老狗就安静地坐在汉克右边的第三个狗屋里。老狗为什么会兴奋呢？任何人都不会要他。可他感觉到一种需求，情不自禁地给出一个友好的目光，轻轻地摆了摆尾巴。

汉克接近老狗的窝，停了下来，为了站稳，他抓住狗屋的钢丝网。这时，他感到一只湿润的鼻子，蹭着他患有关节炎的手指，他立刻感觉到了一种慰藉，这是他一年来第一次体会到的。

正在这时，一个威严的声音突然传到汉克的耳朵里，他被吓了一跳。

"先生，对不起，您不可以到这个地方来。"她说。

幸运的是，汉克不清楚他已经到达了"终点区"——被抛弃的狗集中在这里，等候结束生命。

老狗又一次轻靠和亲舔着汉克，汉克低头看到他平生见到的最让人心碎的乞求的目光。

汉克不顾工作人员让他离开的要求，他问工作人员他能否更近些看看这只狗。工作人员的态度发生了很大的转变，严厉的表情不见了。她强迫自己装出那种面孔，只是为了这份她讨厌的工作。

她把老狗拿了出来，刹那间——曾无比失落的两个灵魂，发现了点燃希望之火的动力。

汉克的食品橱里现在满是食物，壁炉里温暖的炉火噼里啪啦地响着，一想到同伴们说的"只能是在你的梦中"的那句话，老狗就开心地微笑着。老狗合上眼睛，享受着汉克一边小声吟唱"在天堂般的宁静中睡吧"，一边轻抚他的头。

毕竟是圣诞节呀。

Two Lost Souls

Shelly Guidotti

"Did you hear that?" the old dog shouted.

They all ran to the front of their kennel doors to see if someone was coming to "pick them."

"Sorry," he said to the other dogs as his ears fell down from their perked position."I could have sworn I heard voices saying, 'Isn't he cute? It's Christmas, can't we take him home with us?"

"You must have been dreaming again old man," said the dog in the cage next to him. "Anyway, what's the big deal about getting picked up as a Christmas gift. We've all been through that routine and look where it got us."

"Just once, I' d like to feel the warmth of a hand stroking my head," said the old dog. "I'd like to be the one who kisses the tears off a sad face. I'd like to curl up next to a fire instead of this cold concrete. It hurts my bones."

He curled up and sighed as the others said, "The only place you're going to find that is in your dreams, old man."

Hank' s wife had only been gone a year but the pain was as fresh as if time had stood still.

He was an old man now, alone and longed for the comfort that he knew no other person would ever be able to give to him again. What would his life become without her by his side?

Hank' s cupboards were close to bare now and, although he didn't want to go out, he knew he should at least pick up the basics... He drove slowly down the side streets for freeway driving had become too challenging.

Suddenly, the car started chugging and sputtering until finally the engine quit altogether. One of the basic needs he forgot was fuel for the car! So he coasted over next to the curb, spotting a building within walking distance. Hopefully, they'd let him use their phone.

He walked into an office area and rang the bell for service but no one came. He spotted another door going outside, failing to notice the sign posted "Employees Only."

As Hank walked out, he was overwhelmed by yaps, barks and insane jumping from dogs all sizes and shapes. He then realized he had unintentionally gone to the dog shelter.

Slowly he walked down the concrete aisle looking for an attendant.

Three kennels down on the right, the old dog calmly sat there. Why should the old dog get excited? No one would want him. But, he sensed a need and couldn't resist offering a kind look and a gentle wag of the tail.

As Hank neared the old dog's cage, he laced his fingers through the chain link to steady his gait and the first feeling of comfort he'd remembered in over a year came from a wet nose and lick across his arthritic fingers.

Just then a voice of authority sounded, and Hank jumped.

"I'm sorry sir, you aren't supposed to be in this area! " she said.

Luckily Hank didn't know he had walked into the "final area" where unclaimed dogs were scheduled to be put down.

There went the nudge and lick thing again. Hank looked down to the most pleading eyes he'd ever seen.

Ignoring the attendant's order to leave, Hank asked if he could see the dog closer. Her demeanor changed completely and her sternness melted away. She had forced herself to be this way so she could do the part of her job she despised.

She brought the old dog out and instantly the two souls—once so lost—found reason to hope.

Hank's cupboards were now filled, a warm fire crackled and the old dog smiled inside as he remembered "only in your dreams." Closing his eyes he felt Hank's hand stroking his head whispering "sleep in heavenly peace."

It was Christmas after all.

永恒的友谊

佚名

21年前,我的丈夫将桑姆送给了我,以慰籍失去女儿的痛苦。桑姆是一只8个星期大的德国猎狗。在接下来的14年里,我和桑姆的关系非常融洽,而且看起来好像没有什么事情会改变我们的关系。

有一年,我和丈夫决定从纽约的公寓搬到新泽西的新家。我们到了那里不久,邻居家的猫刚生了好几只小猫,他问我们是否要一只。我们有点担心桑姆会嫉妒,他会怎么处理自己的地盘被别人入侵这件事呢,不过我们还是决定冒险试一试,于是同意收养一只小猫。

我们选了一只毛绒球似的爱玩的小灰猫。屋子里就像添了一只走鹃。她在屋子里的家具中间来回穿梭,追逐想象中的老鼠和松鼠,从桌子上跳到椅子上,一只眼睛还闪烁着光芒,于是我们给她取名为闪电。

起初,桑姆和闪电都很谨慎,彼此之间保持着一定距离。但是慢慢地,随着日子一天天过去,闪电开始跟随在桑姆的后面上楼、下楼、走到厨房看他吃饭、在起居室观察他睡觉。睡觉的时间到了,他们就一起睡觉;吃饭的时候,他们就挨着一起吃饭;当我与他们其中的一个做游戏的时候,另一个一定也会加入进来。如果桑姆朝着一些东西狂吠时,闪电就会跑过去看看。当我领着其中一个出去的时候,回家时总会看到另一个站在门口等着。多年来始终如此。

不久,没有任何先兆,桑姆浑身抽搐,并被诊断出患了心脏衰竭。我别无选择,只能让他离开。做出这样的决定是很痛苦的,然而,当我将桑姆留在兽医院独自回家的那种经历是任何事情都无法与之相比的。这一次,闪电再也等不到桑姆了,我也不知该如何向她解释为什么再也见不到她的朋友了。

在接下来的日子里,闪电的心好像碎了。她不能用言语向我倾诉她的痛苦,但是每当前门打开,我可以从她的眼睛里看出那种痛苦和失望,或是当她听到其他的狗叫声时眼中流露出的希望。

时光荏苒,闪电的痛苦好像也减轻了。有一天,当我走进我们的起居室,我下意识地向沙发旁边的地板瞥了一眼,那里摆放着几年前做的桑姆的石膏像,闪电躺在雕像的旁边,前腿搂着雕像的脖子,仍然和她最好的朋友睡在一起。

Friendship Lasts Forever

Anonymous

Twenty–one years ago, my husband gave me Sam, an eight–week–old schnauzer, to help ease the loss of our daughter. Sam and I developed a very special **bond**[1] over the next fourteen years. It seemed nothing that happened could ever change that.

At one point, my husband and I decided to relocate from our New York apartment to a new home in New Jersey. After we were there a while, our neighbor, whose cat had recently had **kittens**[2], asked us if we would like one. We were a little apprehensive about Sam's jealousy and how he would handle his turf being invaded, but we decided to risk it and agreed to take a kitten.

We picked a little, gray, playful ball of Fur. It was like having a roadrunner in the house. She raced around chasing imaginary mice and **squirrels**[3] and vaulted from table to chair in the blink of an eye, so we named her Lightning.

At first, Sam and Lightning were very cautious with each other and kept their distance. But slowly, as the days went on, Lightning started following Sam—up the stairs, down the stairs, into the kitchen to watch him eat, into the living room to watch him sleep. As time slept, it was always together, when they ate, it was always next to each other, when I played with one, the other joined in. If Sam barked at something, Lightning ran to see what it was. When I took either one out of the house, the other was always waiting by the door when we returned. That was the way it was for years.

Then, without any warning, Sam began suffering from convulsions and was **diagnosed**[4] as having a weak heart. I had no other choice but to have him put down. The pain of making that decision, however, was nothing compared with what I experienced when I had to leave Sam at the vet and walk into our house alone. This time, there was no Sam for Lightning to greet and no way to explain why she would never see her friend again.

In the days that followed, Lightning seemed heart–broken. She could not tell me in words that she was suffering, but I could see the pain and disappointment in her eyes whenever anyone opened the front door, or the hope whenever she heard a dog bark.

The weeks wore on and the cat's sorrow seemed to be lifting. One day as I walked into our living room, I happened to glance down on the floor next to our sofa where we had a sculptured **replica**[5] of Sam that we had bought a few years before. Lying next to the statue, one arm wrapped around the statue's neck, was Lightning, contentedly sleeping with her best friend.

1. bond [bɔnd] v. 结合
2. kitten ['kitn] n. 小猫；小动物
3. squirrel ['skwirəl] n. 松鼠
4. diagnose ['dailəgnəuz] v. 诊断
5. replica ['replikə] n. 复制品

"渔夫"佩德罗

鲍勃·特伦

　　这是我曾经听到过的最触动人心的一则有关狗狗的故事。

　　故事发生在西班牙群岛东部的马略卡岛的一个小峡谷。那里有一个英国人，他是一名职业潜水员，以开潜艇为生，并与一只西班牙猎犬生活在一起。他将潜艇固定在一个码头，那里是潜水的最佳位置。每当那个英国人潜水时，那只狗就会坐在码头焦急地等着主人回来。有一天，那个英国人在水中消失了，那只狗非常关心主人，于是跟在主人的后面也跳入水中。

　　在水下，那只狗看到一群鱼游了过去。他抓住一条鱼并把它带上码头。那个英国人既惊奇又高兴，并表扬了他。从那以后，那只狗总会随着主人一起潜水。在潜水的过程中，那只狗展现出他卓越的捕鱼技巧，给他的主人带来了相当大的乐趣。那个英国人将那只狗的技艺告诉了岛上的居民，他们都来到那个码头观看，并对那只狗赞不绝口，还根据那个英国人的名字彼得，给他起了个名字——佩德罗。

　　有一天，那个英国人病了，没过多久就离开了人世。镇里的人都试图收养佩德罗，但是那只狗从不离开那片海滩，因为他害怕他的主人回来会找不到他。无论是烈日炎炎还是大雨倾盆，他始终在那片海滩上等着。人们试着去喂他，但最终都放弃了。除了主人，他不接受任何人的食物。最后，为了养活自己，佩德罗回去捕鱼了。

　　在同一座岛屿上还有一群流浪猫。他们贪婪地聚在一起看着佩德罗捕鱼，佩德罗把他想要的鱼挑出来带回海滩上吃掉，然后那群猫就会争夺他不吃的鱼。佩德罗一定也注意到了这一点，因为一天早晨，当佩德罗吃完他的鱼之后，又潜入水中，上来的时候带着一条大鱼，他将鱼放在沙滩上的那群猫的面前。然后他走开了，观察着那群猫。有一只黑猫显然比其他猫有勇气靠近那条鱼，于是他叼起来就跑。从那以后，除了给主人守夜，那只狗好像认为喂养那些不幸者是自己的责任。因为从那以后的每一天早晨，"渔夫"佩德罗都会将自己抓到的鱼与那群饥饿的马略卡岛上的猫共同分享。

Pedro the Fisherman

Bob Toren

The most touching dog story I've ever heard.

The setting of the story is a little cove on the east side of the Spanish island of Mallorca. It was there that an Englishman, a professional diver, lived on his yacht with his dog, a springer spaniel. He had tied his yacht to a pier where diving conditions were ideal. Each time the Englishman made a dive, the dog sat anxiously on the pier, awaiting his return. One day the dog became so concerned when the Englishman disappeared into the water that he dove in after him.

Underwater, the dog saw a school of fish swim past. He grabbed a fish and carried it back to the pier. The Englishman, surprised and pleased, praised him. After that, the dog followed the man on his dives. In the course of the shared diving, the dog developed excellent fishing skills, to the man's considerable amusement. The Englishman told the island's residents of his dog's accomplishments, and they came to the pier to watch. Delighted, they began calling the dog Pedro, after Peter, the fisherman.

One day the Englishman became ill, and shortly thereafter, he died. Townspeople tried to adopt Pedro, but the dog would never leave the beach for fear he would miss his master's return. He waited on the beach through hot sun and driving rain. People tried to feed him, but eventually they gave up. He wouldn't accept food from anyone other than his master. Finally, to feed himself, Pedro went back to fishing.

It happened that on this same island there were a number of stray cats. Ravenous, they would gather to watch Pedro dive into the schools of fish, select the fish he wanted and bring it back to eat on the shore. Then the cats would fight over what the dog had left uneaten. The dog must have observed this, for one morning when Pedro had eaten his fish, he dove into the water again and came back up with a large fish, which he placed on the sand before the group of cats. Then he backed off and watched. One black cat, with greater courage than the others, approached the fish, grabbed it and ran. After that, in addition to keeping vigil for his master, the dog also seemed to consider it his duty to feed those less fortunate. For every morning thereafter, Pedro the fisherman shared his catch with the hungry cats of Mallorca.

一起走过的日子
Friends Like Us

在每个漫长的夜晚，都有无数永不熄灭的壁炉，那些燃烧的木柴一根根卷曲起来，闪烁着火焰的光芒，我们倦怠地打着盹，进入甜蜜的梦乡。

"坚持"的回报

赫斯特·蒙迪斯

彼得的狗名叫哈里,6岁了,是一只活力四射的牧羊犬。他每天都会在电车站等待彼得下班。这已经成为习惯了,当哈里还是一只小狗的时候就开始了。哈里对去车站的路线了如指掌,而且走在那条路上是他一天之中最快乐的时候。所以当彼得调换工作,并搬到了加利弗尼亚时,他认为最好将哈里留在费城的家中与亲戚住在一起。他对哈里解释了离开的原因,并告诉他,他们两个都应该学着去适应新的家庭。

但是哈里并不想要一个新家,也不愿意待在那个家庭里。于是他回到了彼得的老房子,尽管那里都被木板钉住了,他还是在门廊下的那把被遗弃的椅子旁边度过了他孤独的日子。但是每天傍晚,他都会摇着尾巴,一路小跑到电车站。因为从哈里很小的时候,彼得总是乘坐那辆电车下班回家,而哈里总会在那里迎接他。但是一个个晚上过去了,这只深情的狗狗的主人还是没有出现,他既迷惑又悲伤,独自回到那个被遗弃的房子。

哈里的沮丧感与日俱增,他开始绝食了。时光荏苒,他日渐消瘦,身上的肋骨透过他那厚厚的金色皮毛清晰可见。但是每天傍晚,他总是满怀希望地走到车站去迎接那辆电车。然而,每天晚上,他都会比以前更加沮丧地回到门廊下。

没有人知道为什么哈里的新家没有联系彼得,但是哈里日益恶化的状况引起了人们的注意。一个住在附近的朋友对这种情况感到非常不安,于是他给在加利福尼亚的彼得发去了电报,通知了他这只狗的状况。

彼得立刻买了返程的火车票,他知道自己该做些什么了。在抵达费城的时候,他等了几个小时,仅仅是为了能够乘坐他以前回家时总是搭乘的那辆电车。当电车到达车站的时候,很确定,那就是哈里,等待着并看着乘客们走下来。观望着、盼望着。然后,彼得突然出来了,他深爱的主人。他的主人终于回来了!哈里的世界再一次圆满了,彼得也是一样。

不久,彼得告诉他的朋友:"哈里就像一个小孩那样哭泣着,他浑身颤抖着,就好像得病了一样。而我也擦着鼻涕,快速地眨着眼睛。"

彼得带着他深爱的哈里,回到了加利福尼亚,从此,他们再也没有分开过。

Patience Rewarded

Hester Mundis

Peter 's dog, Harry, was an **energetic**[1], six-year-old collie that would meet him every day at the **trolley**[2] station when Peter returned from work. This was a ritual that had begun when Harry was a pup. The dog knew the route to and from the station like the back of his paw—and following that route was the highlight of his day. So when Peter changed jobs and had to move to California, he thought it best to leave Harry on his home turf in Philadelphia with a relative. He explained all this to the dog upon leaving and told him that they both would have to adjust to new homes.

But Harry didn't want a new home. He would not stay with the family he'd been left with. He returned to Peter 's old house, even though it was boarded up, and there he passed his solitary days beside an abandoned chair beneath the **portico**[3]. But every evening, tail wagging, he trotted off to the trolley station. For as long as Harry had been in the world, Peter had always taken the same trolley home from work, and Harry had been there to greet him. But evening after evening, there was no sign of the devoted dog's master. Confused and sad, he would return alone to the deserted house. The dog's depression grew. He refused the food left for him, and as the days passed, he became thinner and thinner, his ribs noticeable even through his thick blond coat. But every evening, ever hopeful, he'd go to the station to meet the trolley. And every evening, he'd return to the porch more despondent than before.

No one knows why Harry's new family didn't contact Peter , but Harry's deteriorating condition did not go unnoticed. A friend who lived nearby was so upset by it that he took it upon himself to send a telegram to Peter in California informing him of the dog's situation.

Peter bought a return train ticket immediately; he knew what he had to do. Upon arriving in Philadelphia, he waited several hours just so that he could take the same trolley that he always did when coming home. When it arrived at the station, sure enough, there was Harry, waiting and watching as the passengers got off. Looking and hoping. And then suddenly there he was, his beloved owner. His master had returned at last! Harry's world was whole once more—and so was Peter 's.

Peter later told his friend, "Harry was sobbing almost like a child might **sob**⁴. He was shivering all over as if he had a chill. And I? Well blew my nose and did a lot of fast winking."

Peter took his devoted dog, Harry, back to California with him. They were never separated again.

1. energetic [enə'dʒetik] *adj.* 精力充沛的；积极的
2. trolley ['trɔli] *n.* 电车；(电车)滚轮；手推车
3. portico ['pɔːtikəu] *n.* [建](有圆柱的)门廊；柱廊
4. sob [sɔb] *v.* 哭诉；哭泣

一见如故

黛安娜·威廉森

> 有时候我会思索狗为什么这么短命的真正原因,我想那必定是因为它们体恤人类,因为如果一只狗只有十年或十二年的生命,失去它就让我们痛苦,那么假如狗的寿命再加一倍,怎么得了!

> ——史考特爵士

我们拥有的一切都很完美—— 一座占地 40 英亩的漂亮的圆木房子、美满的婚姻以及一只忠心耿耿的狗。唯一的缺憾就是我们没有孩子。我们尝试了很多年,想拥有一个孩子,却一直没能如愿,因此我和丈夫艾尔想领养一个孩子。基于各种原因,我们决定领养一个年龄大一些的。不仅因为我们两个人都要工作,照顾孩子会成问题,而且我们目前唯一的"孩子"科尔比—— 一只斯伯林格斯班尼种犬,它的精力太旺盛了,小孩子根本控制不了它。坦率地说,我们从未抚养过孩子,一想到照看婴儿就有一些紧张。领养机构让我们回去耐心等待,几个月后会有学龄儿童可以被领养。谁知刚过几个星期,也就是在圣诞节的前几周,他们就给我们打了电话,问我们是否愿意先领养一个名叫卡莱布的两岁半的孩子,试着照看他几个月。这使我们措手不及,他们说那个孩子急需一个能照顾他的人家。

情况并不符合我们几周前经过一番理性的讨论后提出的要求。困难很多——通知得那么急,我们已经有了度假计划,最重要的是,那个孩子才刚刚学会走路! 我们在房间里踱来踱去,深思熟虑后还是接受了。

"只有几个月而已。"丈夫劝我说。我们互相安慰说不会有问题,但私底下我却满腹狐疑。

卡莱布来我们家的日子确定了。那天,一辆汽车停在我家门口,透过车窗,我看到了他。在现实面前,我觉得头一下子大了。我们做了些什么?这个孩子要和我们共处了,我们却对他一无所知!对于他的到来,我们真的做好准备了吗?我看了一下丈夫,知道他心里也在犯嘀咕。

我们出去迎接这位小客人。还没走到孩子面前,就听到背后传来一个声音。我转过身来,看见科尔比冲下台阶,直奔小男孩。一定是我们太匆忙了,没有关好门。我屏住了呼吸,科尔比如此激动,肯定会吓着卡莱布的,甚至会把他撞倒在地。哦,不!我想,我们第一次见面怎么就是这样啊!卡莱布肯定会很害怕,不愿跟我们一起进屋,整件事情就要化为泡影了。

在我们拦住科尔比之前,它已经冲到卡莱布面前了。它蹦跳着奔向他,开始欢喜地舔他的脸。同时,这个可爱的小男孩抱住狗的脖子,向我们转过头,欣喜若狂地叫起来:"这是给我的狗吗?"

我和丈夫站在那里,相互对望了一下,笑了。那一刻,我们的紧张感一下子跑到了九霄云外,心想,一切都会如愿的。

卡莱布原本只会和我们待几个月,但是八年半之后,他仍然和我们生活在一起。是的,我们收养了卡莱布。他成了我们的儿子,还有科尔比……哦,它高兴极了,它最终成了卡莱布的狗。

The Ice Breaker

Diane Williamson

It was the perfect setting—a beautiful log house on forty acres of land. We had a solid marriage; we even had the loyal family dog. All that was missing was kids. We had tried for many years to have children, but it just never happened. So my husband, Al, and I applied to be foster parents. We decided we should start with an older child for a number of good reasons. Since we both worked, child care might be a problem. Corby, our springer spaniel—and our only "child"thus far might be a bit too energetic for a young child to handle. And frankly, we **novices**¹ were a little nervous about taking on an infant. We sat back to wait the few months they thought it might take to get a school–age child—which was why we were floored when the agency called us within weeks, just before Christmas, and asked if we would take Kaleb, a two–and–a–half–year old boy, for a few months. It was an emergency, and he needed a home right away.

This wasn't what we had discussed so **rationally**² a few weeks before. There were so many difficulties—it was such short notice, we had made holiday plans and most of all, the boy was a **toddler**³! We went back and forth, and in the end, we just couldn't say no.

"It's only for a couple of months," my husband assured me. It would all work out, we told each other, but privately I was full of doubts.

The day was set for Kaleb to arrive. The car pulled up to our house and I saw Kaleb through the car window. The reality of the situation hit me and I felt my stom—ach tighten. What were we doing? This child we didn't know anything about was coming to live with us. Were we really ready to take this on? Glancing at my hus—band, I knew the same thoughts were going through his mind.

We went outside to greet our little guest. But before we could even reach the child, I heard a noise from behind me. Turning, I saw Corby **tearing down**[4] the steps and heading straight for the little boy. In our hurry, we must not have closed the door completely. I gasped. Corby, in all her excitement, would frighten Kaleb—probably even knock him down. Oh no, I thought, what a way to start our first meeting! Kaleb will be so terrified he won't even want to go into the house with us. This whole thing's just not going to work out!

Corby reached Kaleb before either of us could grab her. She bounded up to the boy and immediately began licking his face in a frenzy of joy. In response, this darling little boy threw his arms around the dog's neck and turned toward us. His face alight with **ecstasy**[5], he cried, "Can this be my dog?"

My eyes met my husband's and we stood there, smiling at each other. In that moment, our nervousness disappeared, and we knew everything would be just fine.

Kaleb came to stay those few months. Eight and a half years later, he is still with us. Yes, we adopted Kaleb. He became our son, and Corby... well, she couldn't have been happier. She turned out to be Kaleb's dog, after all.

1. novice ['nɔvis] *n.* 生手；初学者
2. rationally ['ræʃənəli] *adv.* 合理化；基于理性地
3. toddler ['tɔdlə] *n.* 初学走路的孩子
4. tear down *v.* 向……猛扑
5. ecstasy ['ekstəsi] *n.* 狂喜

小狗蒂皮

佚名

一只狗带给人的最大快乐就是，当你对它装疯的时候，它不会取笑你，反而会跟你一起疯。

——山姆·巴特勒

上学快迟到了，我打算冲过去赶校车。而我的狗，蒂皮，也冲到了我的前面。我恼怒地想，你着什么急？你又不会像我这样来不及赶校车。当她跑到前门时，就顺势躺在了那里，这是她要求亲昵的一种方式。对于她这种不知羞耻、乞求怜爱的动作，我没有回应，而是跳过她，用尽全力跑向等待着的黄色校车。

下午，我跳下车，跑到车道上。我觉得有些古怪。蒂皮以往都会在外面，一看到我回来就会一直狂吠着跟我说"哈罗"。于是我急忙进门，屋里很安静。我把外套和背包扔到地板上。此时母亲默不作声地走了出来，让我坐在厨房桌子的旁边。

母亲说："亲爱的，我有一个坏消息要告诉你。今天早上你在学校的时候，蒂皮出车祸了，当场死亡，没有什么痛苦。很抱歉，我知道你多么在乎她。"

"不，不可能！"我遭到了沉痛地打击。我根本无法相信母亲的话。"蒂皮，过来！快点，宝贝！"我反复地叫着她。我等着，可她没来。我感到很失望，迷迷糊糊地走进了起居室。她没在沙发上，那我以后看动画片的时候就没有可以靠着的枕头了。母亲叫我吃晚餐，我磨磨蹭蹭地来到了位子上。她也没有在桌子底下藏着，因此我不得不吃掉所有的饭。晚上睡觉时，我没有哭，因为我仍然不相信她已经走了。

第二天下车回家后，屋里的寂静让我感到窒息。最终，我控制不住自己的泪水，犹如火山爆发似地哭了出来。我感觉自己就要因内脏破裂而死。我无法控制泪水，也不能停止胡思乱想。我本应该更好地训练她。如果我在家，就可以让她远离马路。我离开的时候都没有爱抚她。我怎么会知道那就是最后的机会？我哭得筋疲力尽。

我不喜欢父母给我买的那只名叫廷克·贝尔的新狗。我经常怒视那些开着车飞驰而过的司机。他们不应该以这么快的速度驾驶，以至于当他们看到路上的狗时无法立即停车。我对我的父母仍然很冷淡。为什么他们没有把蒂皮拴紧？蒂皮的死让我很愤怒，也为整个"狗王国"不懂得远离马路而愤怒。

　　我不让新狗品尝我的晚餐。她太小了，我看电视的时候都不能把她当枕头，她的叫声又是那么尖利。当她乞求我的怜爱时，我推开了她。很长时间，我都独自待着，感到自己可怜又疑惑。为什么这种事会发生在我的身上？怎么办？为什么蒂皮一定要死？时光飞逝，在挣扎中，我也渐渐明白了一些事情。我忽然间感觉清醒了。我意识到没有谁能控制狗身上发生的事。当然，我们能训练和拴紧她们，安排好一切，但不如人意的事还是会发生。尽管如此，还是会有好事降临。生活就是这样。度过困难时期的最有效的方法，就是明白我们怎样做才能征服它，还要坚信困难一定会过去。

　　我也发现，我并没有因蒂皮的死而失去爱的能力。当我试着将心灵尘封起来的时候，却感到很寂寞。我开始意识到廷克·贝尔的优点是不同于蒂皮的。虽然我不能靠着她的小身体休息，或假装像骑蒂皮那样对待她，但我可以把她放在背包里带着她到处游玩。

　　我懂得了要真正地跟她一起享受美好的时光，只要有机会，就要爱护我的狗！如今，一有机会我就会慢慢地和她亲昵，匆忙时，我会加快速度，每次我离开家前，都记得和她亲昵一下。

　　此时，我深刻地体会到了"生命的循环"。每个人有生也有死，这就是生活。如果狗永远都不死，那就没有像廷克·贝尔那样的狗以及她的5只狗宝宝生活的空间了！

　　最幸运的是，我意识到蒂皮给我留下了许多美好的记忆，而且它们时时刻刻都会随着我的召唤而来！

Tippy

Anonymous

I was late for the school bus and rushing to get ready. My dog, Tippy, ran past me. What's your big hurry? I wondered, annoyed. It wasn't like he was late for the school bus like I was. When he got to the front door, he lay down in front of it—his way of asking to be petted. I ignored his shameless begging for affection, hurdled over him and sprinted for the waiting yellow bus.

That afternoon, I jumped out of the bus and dashed up the driveway. That's odd, I thought. Tippy was usually outside, barking an entire paragraph of "hellos" as soon as he saw me come home. When I burst through the door, the house was quiet and still. I dumped my coat and backpack on the floor. Mom silently appeared. She asked me to sit down at the kitchen table.

"Honey, I have some sad news that I need to tell you. This morning, while you were at school, Tippy was hit by a car and killed. He died instantly, so he didn't suffer. I know how much he meant to you. I'm so sorry." said Mom.

"No! It's not true! " I was in shock. I couldn't believe her. "Tippy, come here! Come on, boy! " I called and called for him. I waited. He didn't come. Feeling lost, I wandered into the living room. He wasn't on the couch, so I had no pillow for my head while I watched cartoons. Mom called me for dinner and I rambled to my place. He wasn't hiding under the table, so I had to eat all of my dinner. I went to sleep that night, but I didn't cry. I still couldn't believe that he was gone.

When I got off the bus the next day, the silence grew deafening. Finally, my sobs bubbled up and erupted like lava from a volcano. I felt like I was going to die from having my inside shaken apart, and I couldn't stop crying or end the thought that kept going through my head. I should have trained him better. If I had been home, I could have called him away from the road. I didn't even pet him when I left. How could I have known that was my last chance? I cried until I felt hollow inside.

My parents brought a new dog named Tinker Belle. I didn't care. I was busy giving hate looks to people speeding in their cars. They shouldn't drive so fast that they couldn't stop when they see a dog in the road. My parents still got the silent treatment from me. Why hadn't they made sure that Tippy was tied up? I was mad at Tippy for getting killed, and I was mad at the entire "dog kingdom" for not knowing enough to stay out of the road.

I didn't share my dinner with our new dog. She was too small to be my pillow for television, and her bark was squeaky. When she begged for attention, I pushed her away. I spent a lot of time alone, feeling sorry for myself and wondering: Why did this have to happen to me? What am I going to do now? Why did Tippy have to die?

Time passed, and against my will, I started to understand some things. It felt like waking up a little at a time. I realized what little control any of us have over what happens to a dog. Sure, we can train them and tie them up and do everything right, but bad things can still happen. And, in spite of us, good things can happen too. That's life. The best way to deal with the hard times is to figure out what I need to do for myself to get through them when they come, and to remember that hard times would pass.

I also discovered that my capacity to love didn't die with Tippy. I became awfully lonely when I was trying to harden my heart. I began to realize that there were good things about Tinker Belle that were different from the good things about Tippy. I couldn't rest my head on her little body, or pretend to ride Tinker Belle the way I had done with Tippy, but I could fit Tinker Belle into my backpack and carry her around.

I learned that I need to pet my dog whenever I can—and to really enjoy my time with her! Now I pet my dog slowly when I have the chance and quickly when I'm in a hurry, but I never leave the house without petting her.

I now deeply understand the "Circle of Life". Everyone is born, everyone dies, and that's the way it is. If dogs never died, there would be no room for others like Tinker Belle... and her five cute puppies!

Best of all, I realized that Tippy left behind all of my good memories of him. And they come to me every time I call!

今天我偷了你的狗

吉姆·维利斯

> 洪荒时代，人类从大自然中选择了狗，而它终究也没叫人失望，成了自然界中最善解"人"意的动物。

> ——嘉贝丽·文生

今天，我偷了你的狗。请不要误解，我并未踏上你的领地，只是从你的狗狗的状态中，想象那是一个什么样的地方……我的脑海中突然闪现出"垃圾场"这个词。

我是在一条马路上发现她的，那个时候，她的脖子上拴着一条铁链，后面拖着一截狗屋上的烂木板，还有几根露在外面已经生锈的钉子。从发现她的地方来判断，我不仅知道这个城镇大部分人都已经不再理睬她了，而且还知道如果她钻进树林，拖着的那个"十字架"一定会缠到树干上，直到她被饿死或是渴死。而在通常情况下，当地的居民对这些急需帮助的动物都是熟视无睹、不闻不问，可是当这些动物做错事时，他们就会立刻将其射杀掉。

她的肋骨露在外面、耳朵很脏，总体条件不是很好，皮毛暗淡无光、眼神呆滞，这一切都显示出你不值得拥有她。不过为了证明这一点，我去了当地的几家机构，核实是否有丢失狗的报道，看是否有和她的特征一致的描述。

你应该在当地的报纸上刊登一则"寻狗启示"的广告。而你没有，我就能猜测到你并不想念她。而且这样为你提供了方便，因为事实上她还没有被阉割，也没有注射过狂犬疫苗，可能有犬恶丝虫病，而这些都意味着如果要把她治好，可能会花费一千美圆呢。

如果你知道她也不想你的话，是不是就会感到欣慰一些。事实上，她的出逃已经清晰地表明她受够你的监护了。花了一天时间才让她明白我不是你，而且我不会伤害她，尽管我们相识的时间很短，但是我爱她。用了两天的时间她才意识到这里的其他动物已经接受了她，才意识到她前所未有的快乐就是有朋友的陪伴。她用了3天的时间才享受起家里做的饭菜的狂喜，才开始享受躺在睡椅上的舒适感觉，而且她再也不用睡在外面了——事实上，响雷的时候，她还会得到一个温暖的拥抱，为她搓揉耳朵。而且我还会像小孩子那样与她交谈。

她现在有了一个漂亮的名字。而且在她来到这里的第一周，她已经恢复了原貌，很漂亮。她的眼睛闪闪发光，还学会了摇尾巴打招呼。当我突然移动的时候，她也不会再畏缩害怕了，因为她现在知道我不会打她，事实上，她总是待在我的身边。她甚至变得勇敢起来，敢于冲着猫狂吠。今天我透过窗户看到，她已经开始和其他的狗狗们玩游戏了。哦，不，很显然，她现在已经不再想你或是回想以前那种备受忽视的铁链生活了。

虽然和她相处的时间不长，但是我懂了许多事情，例如，狗狗天性宽容大度，她们拥有神奇的自我恢复能力，信赖他人，我相信爱能创造奇迹，而我最明白的事情是：你很愚蠢。她也许是你人生中最值得信赖、最忠诚于你的挚爱，而你却让她生活在一个肮脏和孤寂的环境里，直到她做出最好的选择——离开你。也许是她的守护天使帮助她逃脱的。以免其他人误解我原来就是这个天使，我将承诺有一天我会像她的守护天使那样好好地照顾她；我相信在她过上新生活的第一个24小时之后她就原谅了你，原谅了你对她大约4年的冷落对待。而且我试着压制自己的那个念头——总有一天，你会受到地狱般的煎熬。

我现在还不是很确定是否要将她留在这里或是为她找到一个更温馨的家，一个比我还可以给她更多关注的家，但是有一件事情可以确定，这份偷来的"财产"，我绝对不会再归还给你。所以你可以起诉我、告发我，请求法院归还你的所有权……我深信偷走你的狗是我毕生中犯的最出色的"罪行"，偷走你的狗是我一生中最快乐的事情。我只需要看着她那美丽的棕色眼睛就知道她会终其一生地捍卫我的决定。如果我们有一个愿望，那就是希望你不要带走她；如果我们有一个特殊的日子来纪念我们在一起的时光，那就是我偷走你的狗狗的那一天，而在那一天，她也偷走了我的心。

I Stole Your Dog Today

Jim Willis

I stole your dog today. No, I didn't set a foot on your property, but from the condition of your dog, I can imagine what it looks like... the word "junkyard" comes to mind.

I found her along a road, with a heavy chain wrapped around her neck, still at-tached to rotten boards from her doghouse, with rusty six-penny nails protruding. Not only did I know that most of the town had already ignored her, judging by where I found her, but I knew that if she had gotten into the woods the "cross" that she dragged behind her would have wrapped around a tree until starvation or thirst killed her. The local populace is usually deaf to the sound or blind to the sight of an animal in need, unless they decide to shoot one for trespassing.

That her ribs showed, that her ears were filthy, that her overall condition was poor and that her coat and eyes were dull, were good indications that you didn't de-serve her. But just to make sure, I checked with the local authorities for a report of a missing dog matching her description and to see if you'd placed a "lost dog" adver-tisement in the local newspaper. You hadn't, which I can only surmise means that you do not miss her. That's rather convenient, because the fact that she is not spayed, probably unvaccinated, and possibly heartworm positive, means that restoring her health could cost me around a thousand dollars.

Perhaps it may be some small comfort to know that she doesn't miss you. In fact, her very act of escape made it clear that she'd had enough of your brand of pet guardianship. It took her about a day to realize that I'm not you, that I won't hurt her, that despite our brief acquaintanceship. I love her. It took two days for her to re-alize that the other animals who live here accept her and that one of the joys she has been missing has been the companionship of other dogs. It took three days for her to appreciate the ecstasy of a homecooked meal and that a couch is meant to be reclined on, and that she no longer has to sleep outside—in fact, when the thunder starts, she'll get a hug and her ears rubbed, and I'll make a fool of myself with baby talk.

She has a beautiful name now. Already in the first week she has come to look more like she should. Her eyes sparkle and she has learned to wag her tail in greeting. She has stopped flinching when I make a sudden movement, because she knows now that I won't beat her, in fact, she rarely leaves my side. She's even become brave enough to bark at a cat and today I watched from the window as she initiated play with the other dogs. No, it's clear she does not miss you or her former life of neglect on a chain.

Of all the things that have become apparent from my brief relationship with her—such as the forgiving nature of the dog, their wonderful ability to heal and to trust, the fact that love can work miracles—one of the most apparent is what a fool you are. She was possibly the most trusting, loyal and loving being in your life, and you consigned her to a life of filth and loneliness until she made the best choice she's ever made when she broke free. Perhaps her guardian angel helped her escape. Lest anyone should mistake me for a angel, I will admit that one day I hope to be as good as she; I believe she forgave you within the first twenty-four hours of her new life for the about four years of her previous "life", while I still try wrestle with the part of me that hopes that one day you will burn in Hell.

It's not clear yet whether she'll remain here or whether I'll find her a loving home where she can count on more individual attention than I can give her, but one thing is certain, this is one bit of stolen "property" who is never returning to you. So sue me, prosecute me, plead with the courts that she is rightfully yours... I'm convinced this is the best "crime" I've ever committed. Hardly anything has pleased me more than the day I stole your dog. I need only look into her beautiful brown eyes to know that she'd defend my decision with her life. If we have one prayer, it is that you will not replace her, and if we have one special day to commemorate together, it is the day I stole your dog and the day she stole my heart.

你信任谁

朱丽叶·米德

狗爱他们的朋友,咬他们的敌人;和人不同,后者无法纯粹地爱,在客观关系中,总是爱恨交织。

——佛洛伊德

以我的个人经验,仅仅是喜欢一个人,并不能成为向他倾诉心底秘密的理由。最崇拜的亲戚、最珍视的爱人以及最亲密的友人,或许会激起我们的强烈爱意,可是并不一定是值得信赖的。

一个完美的挚友应该具备以下几个要素:

其一,他们应该是一个很好的倾听者;

其二,他们应该关心你和你的生活。理想的是,他们能够公正地向你提出建议;

其三,你需要确定一点,无论你说什么,他们都会爱你。他们必须判断正确,守口如瓶。

让我们首先考虑一下母亲们吧。我的母亲一直是一个极好的红颜知己。我已经记不清有多少次她会整夜地陪伴我,听我讲述着我的秘密,从小伙伴偷走我的悠悠球到数不清的爱情危机。她善于倾听、心胸宽广,而且非常聪慧,但还是不符合要求。在与别人谈起我时,她并不会口无遮拦,而是经心思考,打心底里地想要维护我的最大利益。可是这就是问题所在。

作为母亲的本能,她不是担心我,就是夸耀我,会把我的芥微失败或成功全部公之于众。我上一次去探望母亲时,她的邻居叙述着我目前生活中的每一个细节,从我去掉一颗黑痣到遇到前男友时的尴尬。还好,这些都不是我最大的秘密,可是我有些疑惑:关于隐私,母亲是如何看待的呢?

我很幸运地拥有两个好姐妹。我们经常在一起玩"三个火枪手"的游戏——我为人人，人人为我，所以，如果我想把我不愿对家里其他人说的事情告诉了我的姐妹的话，那我就是在玩俄式轮盘赌。曾经告诉她的秘密反过来会给我带来多少麻烦啊！很久之前，我犯了一个错误，那就是告诉我的妹妹我曾经在校长办公室尿湿了短裤，于是就把责任推给了校长的狗。

无论你是否已经结婚，交朋友时应该将爱人排除在外。他们很擅于倾听人们的秘密。举个例子，如果一个朋友在告诉你秘密之前会警告一句："你可不要告诉别人啊！"这时，我并未将我的丈夫考虑在内。我或许并不会将这个秘密告诉他，认为他会对此毫无兴趣，不过我在听到这个秘密之前可不会做任何承诺。我的丈夫是一个优秀的保密者，一个真正守口如瓶的人，可是在大多数情况下，我想要说出的秘密正巧是关于他的，所以一开始他就被排除在外。

那就只剩下苏西和其他几个朋友可以考虑了。如今，苏西已经成了我的"铁哥们"。我还有一些好朋友也有一点"大嘴巴"，另有一些是完全不可信任的。信赖一个尚未证明靠得住的人是很天真的。莫尼卡·莱温斯基从痛苦的经历中懂得了这个道理。提到美国总统，我时常想起本杰明·富兰克林的一句名言："如果让三个人保守一个秘密，只有其中两个人死去。"

以我个人而言，我信任的是我的狗，我有一只拉布拉多猎犬。10年来，她一直忠诚地听我诉说秘密，而且从未背叛过我。正巧有一天，我低声地告诉了我的小狗一个天大的秘密。一切都很好，直到黄昏狗叫的时候，我看见她正在向栅栏那边邻居家的猎狗疯狂地叫个不停。从那之后，邻居家的猎狗总会有意地瞥我一眼。

所以，如果你在列车上曾经看到有人在向一只陌生的狗低语时，你就会明白，那就是我。

Who Do You Trust

Juliette Mead

In my experience, just liking someone is not a justification for telling them the secrets of your heart. The most adored relative, the cherished lover, the dearest friend may inspire devotion, yet remain untrustworthy.

The perfect confidant is one who combines several factors: they need to be a good listener.

They need to care about you and your life. Ideally, they should have some impartiality to be able to offer you sound advice.

You need to feel sure they will love you whatever you say. And they must be the soul of discretion—oystertight.

Let's consider mothers first. My mother has always been an excellent confidante; I have lost track of the times she has stayed up until the wee hours listening to me babble on about almost everything, from the playmate who stole my yo-yo through countless romantic crises. Her ears are elephantine, her heart is immeasurable, and she is an inordinately wise woman, but she falls down on the mollusc requirement. She doesn't blab in a careless way, she blabs in a fully calculated way... with my best interests at heart. And there's the rub.

Her maternal instinct either to worry or boast puts my slightest failing or smallest triumph on the public stage. The last time I visited, her neighbour recounted every detail of my recent life, from the mole I'd had removed, to an embarrassing encounter with an ex-boyfriend. Ok, these aren't my biggest secrets, but it made me wonder what my mother considers pnvate.

I'm fortunate to have two very fine sisters. We generally play The Three Mus-keteers game—one for all and all for one—so if I confide something I'd rather the rest of the family didn't know, I'm playing Russian roulette in telling my sister. And how those former confidences can come back to haunt you! A very long time ago, I made the mistake of confessing to one sister that I had wet my pants while standing in our headmistress's office, and then blamed her dog.

Lovers we can dispense with very quickly, whether you're married to them or not. They are tremendous at hearing other people's secrets. For instance, if a friend flags a secret with the warning, "You mustn't tell anyone", I do not include my hus-band in that instruction. I may not pass it on to him, because I don't think he'd be interested, but I'm not prepared to make that commitment until I've heard the subject matter. My husband is an excellent secret-keeper, a veritable clam, but most matters where I would want the secrets of the confessional observed happen to concern him, so he's ruled out from the start.

That leaves us with friends—Susie, plus a few others. Susie is now a rock-solid confidante; some of my best friends remain a little leaky, while others are positively incontinent. It is naive to trust anyone until they have proven themselves trustworthy, a lesson Monica Lewinsky learnt painfully. Talking of American presidents, I often remember Benjamin Franklin's wise words: "Three can keep a secret, so long as two of them are dead. "

Personally, I turn to my dogs. I have a Labrador who has listened faithfully for ten years and never betrayed my trust. Just the other day, I whispered a major secret to my puppy. All went well until the Twilight Barking, when I spotted her yapping animatedly to the neighbour's terrier across a fenee. The terrier has leered at me knowingly ever since.

So if you ever spot someone whispering to a strange dog on a train, you'll know it's me.

老黑狗

基姆·格尔登

这个世界若是少了它们,将会变得多么孤寂和冷清啊!

——A.Y.

在我的生命里,我曾遇到一个居住在这座大山上的老农夫。这个老人既没有奶牛、马匹、猪,也没有鸡群。实际上,这个农夫甚至没有一个老农妇来照料他。镇上的每一个人都知道这个老人是个很吝啬的家伙。雨还没停,他就迫不及待地跑出去驱赶那些在他的农场上唱歌、吃谷粒的小鸟。你看,这个老农夫是多么吝啬啊。

"我无法全部射中你们,因为你们是一大群。"农夫说着放下了他的枪。接着,他把手伸到那只被吓坏的老母狗的脖子后面,把她一路侧身拖到他那辆小型运货卡车的旁边。那只老狗发出阵阵哀嚎。然而那个吝啬的老农夫对这些不管不顾,只是拖着这只老黑狗,使出全身的力气,将她扔到那辆破旧的货车上。接着,他用枪托在她的屁股上打了几下,让她躺下。然后,他跳上卡车,以最快的速度在曲折泥泞的路上朝树林冲去。

农夫越开越快,嘴里不停地唠叨,时不时地高声咒骂几句。那辆破旧的老卡车在肮脏而泥泞的路上滑行颠簸着。最初在这条路上滑行,不一会又滑到那条路上。突然之间,卡车向路边滑去,完全滑出了泥泞的大路,一下撞在了排水沟上,接连翻滚了好几下。那里全是灌木丛、树叶、烂泥和各式各样的被扔掉的垃圾。最后,一切都异常安静,只有那辆破旧货车底部的那一小团火焰发出了劈啪的声响。

"有没有人呀? 谁来帮帮我!"老农夫大声地喊叫着。然而没有一个人过来帮他,甚至连那只老黑狗为了活命也跑掉了。

老人再一次完全孤独了,就像他在农场度过的 30 年。那团火变得越来越大,离他越来越近。最终,老人一头倒在泥泞中,无力地咒骂着,叫喊着,试着用手指抓些小泥块扔向火团。大火烧到了他的双手，变得异常肮脏，他的外衣也被烧焦了，冒着烟。最终，他只好放弃了，他最后咳了一下，缓缓地把脸埋入烂泥和灰土中。

突然，他听到身后的路上传来了声音。他极其缓慢地抬起他那污黑的脸，尽力撑起来向身后的那条路望去。不远的地方，那只老黑狗正一瘸一拐地尽快向他跑过来。那只狗的后面还跟着五六个人，也向燃烧的卡车跑来。

我不太清楚后来发生了什么事情，因为没过几天，我就从那里搬走了。因为我在佐治亚州布伦斯威克的小服装店多次遭窃，只好关门停业。然而3年后，我回到里兹尔赫斯特地区——我的销售点就在那里，我决定停下，在当地路边的小餐馆喝一杯咖啡。当我静静地坐在那里，向窗外望去时，我看到这辆被烧过的又黑又旧的运货卡车，此时它就停在当地饮料商店前的街上，一侧已经塌陷坏掉。两个小伙子正在往它的后部装载成捆的干草。我顺着长长的木制装载坡道看去，那里有三四把破旧的椅子，经过风吹日晒，已经摇摆不定。令我倍感吃惊的是，我看到了那个只有一条腿、满脸笑容的老农夫，他的拐杖靠在墙上，他则紧紧地抱着那只剩下三条腿、一只耳朵的肮脏的老黑狗，老黑狗正舔着他的脸，仿佛很喜欢他似的！

That Old Black Dog

Jim Golden

Once upon a time in my life, way up on this great big hill there lived this really old farmer. That old man didn't have any cows, horses, pigs or chickens, in fact, that old famer didn't even have an old farm wife to help take care of him. Everyone around town knew that this old guy was a very mean person. He was so mean that he could hardly wait for the rain to stop so he could run outside and chase all the birds away who were coming out to sing and eat grain on his farm. That is just how mean this old farmer really was.

"Ain't gonna shoot you right here because it's too big a mess, "said the farmer, as he lowered his shot gun. Then he reached down and grabbed the scared old female dog by the back of the neck and drug her on her side all the way over to his pick–up truck. The old dog was just a–crying and a–whining the whole time. But that did not matter to that mean old farmer. He just took the old black dog and flung her, as hard as he could, into the back of his old run down pick–up. Then hit her in the rump a couple of times with the butt of his shot gun until she laid down. Then he jumped in the truck and headed as fast as he could down the long winding dirt road, towards the woods.

Faster and faster the old farmer drove, just a talking and cursing out loud the en–tire time. That beat up old truck was a–slipping and a–sliding all over the wet dirt road. First sliding this a–way and then sliding that a–way. Then all of a sudden the truck slid sideways and ran completely off the dirt road, hit the ditch and began rolling over and over. There were bushs, leaves, dirt and all kinds of stuff being flung everywhere. Finally everything became very still and quiet, except for the crackle of a small fire that was coming out from underneath the old pick–up truck.

"Please, somebody help me! " yelled the old farmer. But there was nobody to help him, not even that old black dog who had now ran away in order to save her-self.

Once again, the old man was all alone, just like he had been for the past thirty years on his farm. The fire was getting hotter and hotter and closer and closer. The old man finally laid his head back down into the dirt, softly cursing, crying to himself and trying to fling a little dirt with his fingers onto the fire. His hands were burnt and dirty and his overalls were singed and smoking. Finally he just gave up, gave one last cough and slowly lowered his face into the dirt and ash.

All of a sudden he heard voices coming from the road behind him. Very slowly he raised his blackened face and looked back towards the road, as best he could being up side down. Here came that old black dog hobbling as fast as she could towards him. Behind that dog were five or six people running towards the burning truck.

I really do not know much about what happened after that because I moved away several days later because my small clothing store in Brunswick, Georgia, had been broken into so many times that I had to shut it down. But as I was in the Hazlehurst area, where my distributor was located and after being gone for three years, I decided to stop at the local diner for a cup of coffee. As I sat there quietly, looking out the window, I noticed this burnt old black pick–up truck with it's side caved in sitting across the street at the local feed store. Two young boys were loading bales of hay into the back. I looked down the long wooden loading ramp to where there were three or four old weather beaten rocking chairs and to my surprise I saw this one legged, laughing old farmer man, his crutches leaning against the wall, hugging this three legged, one eared, dirty old black dog who was licking him in the face, as though she liked him!

最爱小狗

佚名

我非常喜欢动物，和一只狗说话的时候，它从来不会要求你闭嘴！

——玛丽莲·梦露

"丹妮尔经常到这家动物收容所来，至少来过5次了。从第一次到现在，算算也有几个星期了。"丹妮尔的母亲对义工说。

"她想要什么呢？"义工问。"小狗！"母亲答道。"我们这里有很多小狗，看有没有她中意的。""我知道……我们已经看过很多狗了。"她沮丧地说道。

就在那时，丹妮尔走进了办公室。"有喜欢的吗？"母亲问她。"还没有，"丹妮尔失望地说，"周末还能来吗？"两个大人相互对视着，摇了摇头，笑了起来。"很遗憾，你们不知道我们什么时候来新狗，但始终会有提供。"义工说。

丹妮尔拉起母亲的手，向门口走去。"不要紧，这个周末我们会找到一只的。"她说。接下来的几天，父母亲都找她长谈，他们觉得女儿太挑剔了。"如果这个周末再挑不出一只中意的，我们就不要了。"最后，父亲灰心地说。"我们希望你不要太在意小狗的大小。"母亲补充道。

周六早上，不用说，来收容所最早的就是他们。丹妮尔已经对这里很熟悉了，她直接跑到关小狗的地方。对此母亲已经感到厌倦了，于是她就坐在第一排笼子末端的一间小休息室里。在顾客禁止入内时，可以透过这间房屋的窗户看到那些动物。

丹妮尔慢慢地从一个笼子走到另一个笼子，不时地跪下来仔细看看，抱抱摸摸每只狗。

每次她都说："对不起，你不是我想要的。"最后一个笼子预示着她选小狗的日子的终结。义工打开最后一个笼子，丹妮尔小心翼翼地抱起狗，紧紧地搂在怀里。

这次，她抱的时间长了点，"妈妈，就是她了！我找到想要的狗了！"

"就是她了！"她兴奋地大叫起来，"就是这样的叹息！"

"她和你之前抱的狗一样大啊，"母亲说。"不是大小的问题——是叹息声。我抱着她时，她叹息了。"丹妮尔说。

"您还记得吗？有一天我问您爱是什么，您告诉我，爱取决于心灵深处的叹息，爱得越深，叹息越长！"母女俩对视了片刻。母亲蹲下身来抱起女儿，又是哭又是笑。

"妈妈，您每次抱我时，我都会叹息。您和爸爸工作回来彼此拥抱时也会叹息。我在挑选小狗的过程中，如果抱起她时，她叹息了，那她就是我想要的。"她说着，便把小狗紧贴在脸上说："妈妈，她爱我，我听到她内心的叹息声了！"

闭上眼睛，感受值得你叹息的爱。我不仅能在爱人的手臂上找到爱，也可以在夕阳的爱抚、月光的亲吻和热天里凉风的微拂中发现爱。

那里有上帝的叹息。腾出点时间静心聆听，你会大为吃惊。"我们不能把呼吸简单地看做是生命的标志，它也是衡量情感的标准。"

拥抱，叹息……

Puppy Love

Anonymous

"Danielle keeps repeating it over and over again. We've been back to this animal shelter at least five times. It has been weeks now since we started all of this," the mother told the volunteer.

"What is it she keeps asking for?" the volunteer asked. "Puppy size! " replied the mother. "Well, we have plenty of puppies, if that's what she's looking for." "I know... we have seen most of them," the mom said in frustration.

Just then Danielle came walking into the office. "Well, did you find one?" asked her mom. "No, not this time," Danielle said with sadness in her voice. "Can we come back on the weekend?" The two women looked at each other, shook their heads and laughed. "You never know when we will get more dogs. Unfortunately, there's always a supply," the volunteer said.

"Danielle took her mother by the hand and headed to the door. "Don't worry, I'll find one this weekend," she said. Over the next few days both mom and dad had long conversations with her. They both felt she was being too particular. "It's this weekend or we're not looking any more," Dad finally said in frustration. "We don't want to hear anything more about puppy size either," Mom added.

Sure enough, they were the first ones in the shelter on Saturday morning. By now Danielle knew her way around, so she ran right for the section that housed the smaller dogs. Tired of the routine, mom sat in the small waiting room at the end of the first row of cages. There was an observation window so you could see the animals during times when visitors weren't permitted.

Danielle walked slowly from cage to cage, kneeling periodically to take a closer look. One by one the dogs were brought out and she held each one.

One by one she said, "Sorry, you're not the one." It was the last cage on this last day in search of the perfect pup. The volunteer opened the cage door and the child carefully picked up the dog and held it closely.

This time she took a little longer. "Mom, that's it! I found the right puppy! "

"He's the one! I know it! " she screamed with joy. "It's the puppy sighs! "

"But it's the same size as all the other puppies you held over the last few weeks," Mom said. "No, not size–the sighs. When I held him in my arms, he sighed," she said.

"Don't you remember? When I asked you one day what love is, you told me love depends on the sighs of your heart. The more you love, the bigger the sigh is! " The two women looked at each other for a moment. Mom didn't know whether to laugh or cry. As she stooped down to hug the child, she did a little of both.

"Mom, every time you hold me, I sigh. When you and Daddy come home fromwork and hug each other, you both sigh. I knew I would find the right puppy if it sighed when I held it in my arms," she said. Then holding the puppy up close to her face, she said, "Mom, he loves me. I heard the sighs of his heart! "

Close your eyes for a moment and think about the love that makes you sigh. I not only find it in the arms of my loved ones, but in the caress of a sunset, the kiss of the moonlight and the gentle brush of cool air on a hot day.

They are the sighs of God. Take the time to stop and listen; you will be surprised at what you hear. "Life is not measured by the breaths we take, but by the moments that take our breath away."

Hugs and sighs...

小狗待售

佚名

农夫要卖几只小狗。他做了一个广告牌,钉在院子里的一根柱子上。钉最后一根钉子时,他忽然感到有人在扯他的裤脚。他低下头,看到了一个小男孩。

"先生,"小男孩说,"我想买一只小狗。"

"哦,"农夫边擦脖子后面的汗边说,"这些都是纯种小狗,价格很高的。"

小男孩低下了头。一会儿,他把手伸进口袋,摸出一把零钱,举到农夫眼前,说道:"我有 39 美分,可以让我看一眼小狗吗?"

"当然可以。"农夫说。

农夫说完,吹了一声口哨,喊道:"过来,多利!"

只见多利从窝里跑了出来,越过斜坡,后面紧跟着 4 只小狗。小男孩的脸贴紧在铁丝网上,眼里闪烁着喜悦。

5 只狗跑过来时,小男孩注意到狗窝里隐隐约约还有些动静。又一个小家伙慢腾腾地跑了出来。显然,和其他小家伙相比,她瘦弱了许多,她从斜坡上跌跌撞撞地滑了下来,使劲地追赶着同伴……

"我想要那只。"小男孩指着那只弱小的小狗说道。

农夫蹲下身对小男孩说:"小家伙,你不能要那只。她永远都不会跑,不会陪你玩,而别的狗却可以。"

听到这些话,小男孩后退了一步,坐了下来,把一只裤脚卷了起来。只见他小腿的两侧用一只钢制的支架护着,脚下穿着一只特制的鞋子。小男孩转过身,抬头望着农夫,说道:"先生,你看,我自己跑得也不快,那只小狗需要人理解。"

这个世界还有许多人需要我们理解。

Puppies for Sale

Anonymous

A farmer had some puppies he needed to sell. He painted a sign advertising the pups and set about nailing it to a post on the edge of his yard. As he was driving the last nail into the post, he felt a tug on his overalls. He looked down into the eyes of a little boy.

"Mister," he said, "I want to buy one of your puppies."

"Well," said the farmer, as he **rubbed**[1] the sweat off the back of his neck, "these puppies come from fine parents and cost a good deal of money."

The boy dropped his head for a moment. Then reaching deep into his pocket, he pulled out a handful of change and held it up to the farmer. "I've got thirty –nine cents. Is that enough to take a look?"

"Sure," said the farmer.

And with that he let out a whistle, "Here, Dolly! " he called.

Out from the doghouse and down the ramp ran Dolly followed by four little balls of fur. The little boy pressed his face against the chain link fence. His eyes danced with delight.

As the dogs made their way to the fence, the little boy noticed something else **stirring**[2] inside the doghouse. Slowly another little ball appeared; this one noticeably smaller. Down the ramp it slid. Then in a somewhat **awkward**[3] manner the little pup began **hobbling**[4] toward the others, doing its best to catch up...

"I want that one," the little boy said, pointing to the runt.

The farmer knelt down at the boy's side and said, "Son, you don't want that puppy. He will never be able to run and play with you like these other dogs would."

With that the little boy stepped back from the fence, reached down, and began rolling up one leg of his trousers. In doing so he **revealed**[5] a steel brace running down both sides of his leg attaching itself to a specially made shoe. Looking back up at the farmer, he said, "You see sir, I don't run too well myself, and he will need someone who understands."

The world is full of people who need someone who understands.

1. rub [rʌb] v. 擦；摩擦
2. stir [stɜː] v. 动；移动；摇动；激起
3. awkward ['ɔːkwəd] a. 难使用的；笨拙的
4. hobble ['hɔbl] v. 蹒跚
5. reveal [ri'viːl] v. 展现；显示；揭示；暴露

两件善事

罗斯玛的·米勒

一天，我正在花园里种花，发现了一只伤痕累累的老拳师犬，他的脖子上拴着一条破旧的铁链，正摇摇晃晃地在路上走着，一幅受虐待的样子。他，毫不犹豫地朝我的车道走来，并挨着车卧了下来。他筋疲力尽，只是卧在那里，我跑回屋里给他倒水时，他的目光一直停留在我的身上。在取回水盘时，我看见了他那双深沉、热情的双眼，我顿时震惊了：我认识这只狗。

大约在8年前，一天上午，我正在镇子中心，这时一只漂亮的、浅黄褐色的小拳师犬向我跑来，我俯下身去抚摸他，注意到他那双漂亮的眼睛，还有他脖子上印有身份证明的标签。标签上写着他的主人的名字叫雷诺兹夫人，还有当地的一个电话号码。雷诺兹夫人住得并不远，很快就会把他接走。他用湿乎乎的舌头舔了我几下，之后就回家了。那是我最后一次看见那只狗。

我的丈夫从屋里出来，我告诉他，我确定这只狗是我几年前在镇上见过的那只。他认为我疯了。"你是如何确定的呢？他既没有带项圈，也没有任何辨认他的方法。他可能是另外一只狗。这只狗也遭到了虐待，主人一定不是个善良的人。除此之外，你还能想起他的主人的名字吗？"

不知道为什么，我如此确定。"是雷诺兹家，"我说，"我知道这听起来很疯狂，可是我确定这就是他家的狗！"

我跑进屋里，拿起电话簿，给雷诺兹先生打了电话，是他接的电话，并告诉我他没有养过拳师犬。然而，就在他准备挂电话的那一刻，他说他的哥哥曾经养过一只拳师犬，并告诉了我他哥哥的电话号码。

我给雷诺兹先生的哥哥打了电话，他说那不可能是他的狗，因为早在6年前他的狗就被偷走了。我说服他允许我带着拳师犬过去，让他看一看是不是他的。我把狗放进车里，他虚脱了似的静静地趴在后座上。当车穿过主干道，进入镇子后，他开始在后座上又蹦又跳。

当我将车驶入雷诺兹先生的车道时，没有什么能抑制住他的激动情绪了。三个小伙子从屋里跑了出来，我打开车门，拳师犬立刻窜出来奔向他们，兴奋地狂吠着。

在返回的路上，我又想起了多年前第一次帮助这只迷路的拳师犬找到了他的家。我高兴地回家了，并且知道自己已经是奇迹的一部分了——因为我在一只狗的生命中再一次出现。

Two Good Deeds

Rosemarie Miele

I was planting flowers in my garden one day, when I spotted a **battered**[1] old boxer with a broken chain around his neck, staggering up the road. He had the look of a dog who had been abused. Without any **hesitation**[2], he proceeded to walk down my driveway and lie down next to me. Exhausted, he just lay there, his eyes following me as I ran inside to get him a dish of water. Returning with the water, I looked into his dark, soulful eyes. A ripple of shock ran through my body: I knew this dog!

About eight years earlier I'd been in the center of town one morning, when a beautiful, fawn–colored boxer puppy ran up to me. Bending down to pet him, I noticed his beautiful eyes—and the ID tag around his collar. The tag said he belonged to Mrs. Reynolds and gave a local telephone number. She lived not too far away and came to pick him up in a matter of minutes. After a few wet kisses, the boxer went home. That was the last time I had seen the dog.

My husband came out of the house. I told him I was sure this dog was the one I'd found in town years ago. He thought I was crazy. "How can you be certain? He doesn't have a collar on and there's no way to identify him. It has to be another dog. This one is so abused; it couldn't belong to that nice family. Besides, do you even remember the name of the family?"

Somehow, I did. "It was Reynolds," I said. "I know it sounds crazy, but I'm sure this is their dog! "

Running inside, I grabbed the telephone book and called Reynolds listed. Mr. Reynolds answered and told me he didn't have a boxer. However, just as he was about to hang up, he said that his brother once had a boxer, and gave me his brother's number.

When I called the first Mr. Reynolds's brother, he said it couldn't be his dog because his dog had been stolen six years before. I convinced him to let me bring the dog over so he could look at him. I put the dog into my car. He **collapsed**² in the backseat and lay very still. Crossing over the main highway going into the town, he started to move around. As we passed through the center of town, he started jumping and **bouncing**³ around in the backseat.

When I pulled into the Reynolds' driveway, there was no containing him. Three teenagers ran out of the house, and when I opened the car door, the dog **bounded**⁴ out and raced to them, whining and yelping in his excitement.

Backing out of the driveway, I thought again of that morning so many years ago when I had first helped the lost boxer find his family. I went home happy, knowing I had been part of a miracle—for the second time in one dog's life.

1. battered ['bætəd] *adj.* 打扁了的；敲碎的
2. hesitation [ˌhezi'teiʃən] *n.* 犹豫；踌躇
3. bounce [bauns] *v.* （使）反跳；弹起；弹跳
4. bound [baund] *v.* 跳跃

我的快乐中有你
You Are in My Happiness

在这个自私的世界上，一个人唯一不自私的朋友，唯一不抛弃他的朋友，唯一不忘恩负义的朋友，就是他的狗。

第三卷

好一只服务犬

布伦达·莫斯利

它并不要求受到极大的关注,只是默默地把爱和安慰送给人们。

——狗迷

有什么东西在戳我的脸,又冷又湿的。"不要再戳了,托比。"我晕晕乎乎地低吟着,伸手把狗鼻子推到了一边,并翻了个身。在我又要睡着的时候,他咬住了我的袖子。"停下,托比!"我命令道。他猛地趴在了我的床边,很快就发出了鼾声。我对这种鼾声并不在意。也许我还能再睡上一觉。我又睡着了。

有什么东西在拖我的脚。现在又是什么呢? 我勉强睁开眼睛。托比正试图拽掉我的袜子。我用肘把他推开,并盯着他。他竖着脑袋,刺探似地看着我。我的闹钟还没有响,现在刚刚早上 5 点钟。虽然我计划今天要早起去看医生,可是也不用这么早啊。这只狗会知道吗?

几个星期以来,他总是在早晨的这个时间把我叫醒。已经不止一次了,是经常性的。我已经记不清上次睡过的好觉是在哪一天了。上帝知道,我是需要睡眠的人啊。大脑性麻痹和多发性硬化这两种疾病使我很衰弱。如果我原来的那只服务犬还活着,我还能处理一些其他的事情,但是托比呢? 我能训练他的只是衔来我的拖鞋,仅此而已。什么服务犬! 我需要比这更多的帮助。

我原来的狗是一只拾獚,叫法利,他刚和我住到一起的时候只接受过一些最基本的服从训练。我以前从来没有训练过狗,但是他很聪明,我并未花费太长的时间来教他做各种家务活。法利可以帮我拿电话,从冰箱里取苏打水,从烘干机里取出衣服。他驮着购物袋,帮助我从轮椅上站起来,如果我走路摇摇晃晃,他就会扶稳我。在我不得不坐轮椅的那些日子里,他甚至可以拉着我走。

10 年来,他是我的伙伴、我的搭档。我们一起帮助其他残疾人训练他们的服务犬。感谢法利,如果没有他,我就不能逃离我所恐惧的那种命运——住进生活辅助中心,在我病情恶化不得不辞去幼儿园的教学工作,继续过着残疾的生活时,他是解决问题的真正帮手,我的法利—— 一只优秀的服务犬。

他死的时候我很伤心。还能有什么样的狗可以取代他的位置呢? 但是我知道,如果我还想继续过独立的生活,就必须再去寻找一只新的服务犬。所以我去了养狗场,希望能够找到一个帮我解决问题的帮手。然而,就连我自己也不能相信,我在一个户外饲养场发现了一只拾獚。他和法利长得一模一样! 长长的腿,淡红色的毛发,一切都是那么像。场主说他的名字叫托比。

我带着托比在一条沙砾小路上试走。这条小路的路面对我来说难以应付。他在我的身边慢慢地、小心翼翼地走着,好像知道我的犹豫似的。好脾气,我想到。唯一的缺点就是:一只理想的服务犬在两岁的时候就应该开始训练了,而托比已经四岁了。

但是托比与法利又是离奇的相似……他除了是一个解决问题的帮手,还能是其他别的什么吗?我想,我可以保证我能够把他训练得和法利一样优秀。训练一只服务犬,我是有一系列优秀纪录的。

我把托比带回家。他做的第一件事情就是在房间里来回飞奔。"停!"我命令道。他停了下来,看着我,然后穿过狗门跑到院子里去了。

托比自小就在户外饲养场度过。他需要时间来适应房间里的生活。我只是不希望这个时间太长。每一件事情都使他感到恐惧。当电话响的时候,他嚎叫着并蜷缩在角落里。当烘干机嗡嗡响的时候,他跑开躲了起来。当送货员敲门时,托比跳起一米高,狂暴地乱叫着。

看起来,托比唯一的本领就是睡觉了。他在训练的过程中就能睡着。有一次,我用了整整一个上午的时间在地板上滚网球。"接住。"我说。有时候,托比把球衔在嘴里,但是他就是不把球还给我。难道一只拾獚就只能做这些了吗? 我决定再试着用一些更软的东西来训练他。也许这对他来说会容易一些。

在他的身边,我扔下一只细绒毛的拖鞋。"托比,把拖鞋拿过来。"托比不理睬那只拖鞋,只是向我走来,把脑袋放在我的腿上,打哈欠。"走开,"我说着把他的脑袋轻轻地推向地板。"把拖鞋拿过来。"托比在我的脚边蜷缩着,打起了盹。

我心里突然火冒三丈。"托比,"我喊道,声音很大,他猛地醒了过来,看着我。我弯下身来。"这是拖鞋！"我大声喊着。我把鞋塞进了他的嘴里。"我当时怎么会认为你是一个解决问题的好帮手呢！"我站起来，跌跌撞撞地走进浴室，砰地一声关上门。

看着镜子中的自己，很憔悴。多发性硬化症使我越来越虚弱。我提醒自己，狗对生气的反应并不灵敏。你还要再接着训练托比。你已经没有精力再去重新训练另一只狗了。

我打开门，托比还坐在我走时他待的地方。他摇着尾巴，嘴里仍然衔着那只拖鞋。我真是哭笑不得。"放下，"我说，他立刻放下了。"好样的！"我拍了拍他的脑袋。在这一天剩下的时间里，他都快活地衔着我的拖鞋。

不过，这就是他两个月的训练中学会的全部任务了。我不能天天指望着托比为我做些什么了。当然，紧急情况是不可能的。真的，他除了在晚上总是把我叫醒之外，事实上，每天晚上都是如此，什么都不能指望他了。

而我已经受够了这样的日子，我一边想着，一边把腿移到床边，坐了起来。我看了一眼那只所谓的服务犬。托比趴在地板上，显然非常满意，他又一次成功地把我从睡眠中叫醒。上帝呀，你不会故意把这样的狗派到我的身边吧。

我穿上拖鞋，站了起来。还是准备一下去赴医生的预约吧。准备好去告诉她我已经决定换个活法，我真害怕再这样活下去了。我打算放弃我的狗、我的房子和我的独立生活。她能帮我在生活辅助中心找个位置吗？

那天上午的晚些时候，我的医生把我领进了她的检查室。"你还好吗，布伦达？"她担忧地问道。"你看起来很疲惫。"

"那是因为我没有睡觉。"

"为什么不睡呢？"她问道。

我给她讲了托比的问题。"也许他那样做是因为我对他要求太严厉了，"我说道，"但是如果他好好学，我也不会那样对他的。"

医生听了听我的肺部，然后又检查了我的鼻子和喉咙。"托比把你叫醒可能对你来说是件好事。"

"好事？"

"你有睡眠间歇呼吸的征兆。有这种情况的人在夜间睡觉时会停止呼吸。如果不及时治疗，就会引起心脏疾病或是中风。"她给我安排了一家睡眠诊所，预约了下个星期的检查。

我和托比一起去了那个诊所。因为他是一只服务犬,所以他们同意让他陪着我。晚上,我的睡房和一间控制室连着,在我睡觉的时候可以对我进行监控。在通常情况下,那会影响我的睡眠。但是我太累了,也就没有时间在意这些了。一个护士将电极粘在我的头上、胸口和腿上。我四肢伸开地躺在床上,托比蜷缩在地板上挨着我。就像平常一样,他不一会儿就睡着了,比我睡得早很多。

如往常一样,托比只是让我睡了一小会儿。他站起来舔着我的手,往我的脸上喷气。他已经无药可救了,我想着,不过至少现在我的医生知道我面临着什么样的困境了。我带着托比去取睡眠检测报告单。"看来我的推测是正确的,布伦达,"我的医生说,"你在夜间停止呼吸 15 次。你的狗每次都把你唤醒。"

就是那样,一切都清楚了。难怪可怜的托比会那么爱睡觉,我想着。他那么疲倦是因为要挽救我的生命!他和那些我所读过的具有非凡天赋的狗一样。当他们的主人即将突发疾病或是心脏病的时候,他们能提醒主人。

我看着托比,在我的椅子旁打着盹。我倾身抚摸他耳旁的淡红色毛发。他睁开了眼睛,站了起来。"不,你睡吧,托比,你该休息的。"我告诉他,"你愿意再给我一次机会吗? 我会像你对我那样地耐心对待你,我保证。"

托比舔着我的手,躺下了。

医生给我配备了一根氧气管,在我晚上睡觉的时候能够调节我的呼吸。现在托比只会在管子滑落的时候叫醒我。我们俩一旦都能有充足的睡眠,就会合作得非常好,这太令人惊奇了。不久,法利可以做的每一件事情,托比都学会了。这些日子,我和托比一起训练其他的狗来帮助残疾人。他很爱示范怎样从冰箱里取出一罐苏打水,怎样背一袋东西,当然了,还有衔拖鞋。我的托比是一只不起的服务犬,确实如此。一个真正能解决问题的好帮手,一个我甚至不知道自己需要,然而生活中却离不开的帮手。

Some Service Dog

Brenda Mosley

Something poked me in the face. Something cold and wet. "Not again, Toby," I moaned groggily, pushing my dog's nose away from mine. I rolled over. Just as I was falling asleep again, he nipped at my sleeve. "Toby, stop!" I commanded. He flopped down next to my bed and promptly started snoring. I didn't even care about the noise. Maybe I'd finally be able to get some sleep myself. I drifted off.

A tug on my foot. What now? I forced my eyes open. Toby was trying to pull off my sock. I **nudged**[1] him away, glaring at him. He cocked his head and looked at me quizzically. My alarm clock hadn't gone off yet. It was only 5:00 A. M. I'd been planning to get up early for my doctor's appointment, but not this early. Would this dog ever learn?

Every night for weeks now he'd been waking me up. Not just once or twice. Constantly. I couldn't remember the last time I got a good night's rest. And, Lord knows, I needed it. Living with both cerebral palsy and **multiple**[2] sclerosis was debilitating. If my old service dog were still around, I might have coped, but Toby? All I'd been able to train him to do so far was fetch my slippers. Some service dog! I needed help with a lot more than that.

My old dog, a retriever named Farley, had only taken basic obedience lessons when he came to live with me. I'd never trained a dog before, but he was so smart it didn't take long for me to teach him to do all kinds of things around the house. Farley would bring me the phone, get a can of soda from the fridge, take clothes out of the dryer. He carried grocery sacks, helped me up from chairs, steadied me if my walk got wobbly. He even pulled me in a wheelchair those times I had to use one.

For 10 years he was my companion, my partner. Together we helped other people with disabilities train their service dogs. Thanks to Farley, I'd been able to avoid the fate I dreaded—moving into an assisted-living center—even after my condition deteriorated so much that I had to quit my job teaching preschool and go on disability. He was a real answer to prayer, my Farley. A champion service dog.

I was inconsolable when he died. What dog could ever replace him? But I knew that if I wanted to continue living on my own, I'd have to get a new service dog. So I went to a kennel, hoping I would find another answer to prayer. Yet even I couldn't quite believe the **retriever**[3] I spotted in an outdoor run. He looks just like Farley! Long legs, reddish fur and all. Toby was his name, the kennel owner said.

I took Toby for a test walk on a gravel path, a tricky surface for me. He walked beside me slowly and deliberately, seeming to sense my hesitation. Good temperament, I thought. The only drawback: Ideally, a service dog is fully trained by age two, and Toby was already four.

But Toby's uncanny resemblance to Farley... what else could he be but another answer to prayer? I bet I can teach him to act like Farley too, I thought. I had a good track record when it came to training service dogs.

I brought Toby home. The first thing he did was to tear through every room in the house. "Stop!" I ordered. He paused, looked at me, then bolted through the doggy door to the backyard.

Toby had been kenneled outdoors his whole life. It would take time for him to adjust to living in my house. I just didn't expect it to take this long. Everything scared him. When the phone rang, he howled and cowered in a corner. When the dryer buzzed, he ran for cover. When the deliveryman knocked on the door, Toby jumped a mile high, barking frantically.

Toby's sole talent seemed to be napping. He would drop off right in the middle of a training session. Once I spent an entire morning rolling a tennis ball across the floor. "Fetch." I said. Sometimes Toby grabbed the tennis ball in his mouth, but he wouldn't bring it back to me. Aren't retrievers bred to do this? I decided to try something softer. Maybe it would be easier for him.

I dropped one of my fuzzy slippers near him. "Get the slipper, Toby." Toby ignored the slipper, walked over to me, put his head on my leg and yawned. "Off, "I said, pushing his head gently toward the floor. "Get the slipper. "Toby curled up at my feet and dozed off.

Something in me just snapped. "Toby, " I called. Loudly. He jolted awake and looked at me. I bent down. "This is a slipper! " I yelled. I pushed it into his mouth. "How could I have ever thought you were an answer to prayer! "I got up, stumbled into the bathroom and slammed the door.

I stared at my reflection in the mirror. I looked drained. The MS was making me weaker and weaker. Dogs don't respond well to anger, I reminded myself. You've got to try again with Toby. You don't have the strength to start over with another dog.

I opened the door. Toby sat in the exact spot I'd left him. His tail wagged. He still had the slipper in his mouth. I didn't know whether to laugh or cry. "Drop, "I said. Right away he did. "Good dog! "I patted his head. He spent the rest of the day happily retrieving my slipper.

But that was all he learned in two months of training. I couldn't count on Toby day-to-day. Certainly not in an emergency. I couldn't count on him for anything, really, except waking me up at night, practically every night.

And I've had enough of that, I thought, swinging my legs over the edge of my bed and sitting up. I eyed my so-called service dos. Toby **sprawled**[4] on the floor, apparently satisfied that he'd successfully kept me from yet another night's rest. Lord, you couldn't have meant this dog for me.

I stuck my feet into my slippers and stood. Might as well get ready for my doctors appointment. Prepare myself to tell her I'd made the decision I had dreaded my whole adult life. I was going to give up my dog, my house, my independence. Could she help me find a place in an assisted-living center?

Later that morning my doctor ushered me into her examination room. "Are you okay, Brenda?"She said with concern. "You look tired. "

"That's because I'm not sleeping. "

"Why not?" She asked.

I told her about my problems with Toby. "Maybe he's just acting out because I've been working him so hard, "I said. "But I wouldn't have to if he'd just learn."

My doctor listened to my lungs, then checked my nose and throat. "It might be good that Toby's been waking you. "

"Good?"

"You're showing signs of sleep apnea. People with this condition stop breathing during the night. Left untreated, it could lead to a heart attack or stroke." She set up an appointment for me at a sleep clinic the following week.

Toby and I went to the clinic together. They said it was okay since he was a service dog. My bedroom for the night was connected to a control room, where observers would monitor me whilet I slept. Normally that would've bothered me. But I was too tired to care. A nurse attached electrodes to my head, chest and legs. I stretched out on the bed and Toby curled up on the floor beside me. As usual, he conked out right away. Well before I did.

And as usual, Toby barely let me sleep a wink. He'd get up to lick my hands and snort in my face. He's hopeless. **Incorrigible**[5], I thought. At least now my doctor will know what I'm up against.

I took Toby with me to get the sleep–test results. "Looks like my suspicion was on target, Brenda," my doctor said. "You stopped breathing fifteen times during the night. Your dog woke you every time. "

Just like that, everything came into focus. No wonder poor Toby naps so much, I thought. He's wron out from trying to save my life! He was like those dogs I'd read about who have a remarkable talent. They can sense when a seizure or a cardiac episode is about to hit their owner and alert the person.

I looked at Toby, dozing beside my chair. I leaned over and stroked the soft red–dish fur behind one of his ears. He opened his eyes and started to his feet. "No, you rest, Toby, you've earned it, "I told him. "Will you give me another chance? I'll be as patient with you as you've been with me. I promise. "

Toby licked my hand and lay down.

My doctor **outfitted**[6] me with an oxygen tube to regulate my breathing while I sleep. Now Toby wakes me only if the tube slips off. It's pretty amazing how well we learned to work together once we both got enough rest. Before long Toby could do everthings Farley had done. These days Toby and I train other dogs to help people with disabilities. He loves to demonstrate how to get a call of soda from the fridge, carry a bag and, of course, fetch slippers. My Toby is some service dos, all right. A real answer to prayer, one I didn't even know I needed, yet I couldn't live without.

1. nudge [nʌdʒ] *n.* 用肘轻推；轻推为引起注意
2. multiple ['mʌltipl] *adj.* 多样的；多重的
3. retriever [ri'tri:və] *n.* 取回的人；能把猎物找回来的猎狗的一种
4. sprawl [sprɔ:l] *v.* 四肢伸开地坐(或卧)；爬行；蔓生；蔓延
5. incorrigible [in'kɔridʒəbl] *adj.* 无药可救的；不能被纠正的
6. outfit ['autfit] *v.* 配备；装备

我们并不狐单

玛丽·L. 米莱尔

我们有家人、朋友和学业，但它们，只有你一个。它们用自己的全部换你一个拥抱、一个"热吻"、一个玩具和一顿丰盛的午饭，它们的一生虽然只有 15 年左右，但它们愿做你永远的朋友，给你依赖和信任。

——狗迷

我的丈夫因为突发心脏病猝死在网球场之后，我的世界在一夜之间坍塌了。我那 6 个孩子却只有 10 岁、9 岁、8 岁、6 岁、3 岁和 18 个月大。我要养家糊口、照顾孩子，还要凑合着过下去，生活的重担完全落在了我的肩上，压得我喘不过气来。

幸运的是，我找到了一个出色的管家来帮我照顾孩子，但是从星期五的晚上到星期一的早晨，孩子和我都孤孤单单地在一起。坦率地说，我真的很不安。房间里每一次吱吱作响，每一次听到不寻常的声音，任何深夜里的电话铃声都会让我感到恐惧。我感到难以想象的孤单。

一个星期五的晚上，我下班回到家，发现了一只漂亮的、身材魁梧的德国牧羊犬坐在我的门前。而这只神奇的、强壮的动物给了我一种暗示，那就是他要进入房子，并将房子当做他的家。可是我还是很机警。这条明显受过良好训练的狗是从哪里来的？让孩子和这只陌生的狗在一起玩耍安全吗？尽管他看起来是那么温顺，但他仍然充满力量，让人感到敬畏。孩子们马上就喜欢上了这只"德国犬"，请求我让他进入房间。我同意让他睡在地下室直到第二天，这样我们就有时间去找邻居们打听他的主人。而那天晚上是我数周以来第一次睡得如此安稳的一个晚上。

第二天上午，我们开始打电话寻找那只德国犬的主人，并查看失物招领广告，但是毫无结果。与此同时，那只德国牧羊犬已经将自己当作我们这个家庭的一员了，温和地与我们拥抱在一起，和孩子们在院子里摔打着、玩耍着。到了星期六，他还和我们在一起，于是他再次得到允许睡在地下室。

星期日，我计划和孩子们去野餐。我想最好还是将那只德国牧羊犬留下来，以免他的主人找来,所以我们就没有带着他一起出发。当我们停在一家加油站的时候,我们很奇怪地看见德国牧羊犬紧随我们身后也到了加油站。他不只是跑过来,还跳到车蓬上,把鼻子贴在挡风玻璃上,直直地盯着我的眼睛。这回无论如何都不可能把他甩下了。于是他跳进旅行车,坐在车后和我们一起去野餐。星期日他又一次留了下来。

星期一的早晨,孩子们准备去学校了,我放他到外面跑跑。可是他没有回来。到了晚上,那只德国牧羊犬还是没有出现。我们感到很失望。我们确信他已经回到家中或是找到了他的主人,因此我们再也见不到他了。可是我们想错了。在第二个星期五的晚上,他又出现在我们家的门前。我们再一次让他进了家门,而他再一次待到星期一的早晨,直到我们的管家回来。

这种情况在每个周末都会重复一次,持续了大概10个月之久。我们越来越喜爱这只德国牧羊犬了,每个星期都期待他的到来。我们不再想他来自哪里——他是属于我们的。他身材魁梧、性情温和,有他在身边,我们感到很安全。每当我们看见德国牧羊犬那聚精会神的神情,竖起的耳朵,听到从他的喉咙中发出的沉沉的咆哮声时,我们知道他正在保护我们。

这只德国牧羊犬已经成为我们家中的一份子,他将每晚检查每间卧室以确保每个孩子都舒适地躺在床上看作是自己的责任了。当他满意地看着最后一个孩子盖好被子之后,他就站在前门坚守他的岗位,直到第二天的早晨。

每个星期,在德国牧羊犬来之前,我感到自己变得更加坚强、更加勇敢,更有处理问题的能力了,我享受着他在每个周末陪伴我们时的乐趣。在一个星期一的早晨,我们拍拍他的脑袋,让他跑出去,然而这却成了最后一次。他再也没有回来。我们再也没有看见过或是听说过那只德国牧羊犬。

我经常会想起他。在我最需要他的时候他来到我的身边,一直陪伴着我,直到我能坚强地面对生活。也许他的到来有一个全面的、普通的解释——也许他的主人周末的时候不在家,也许吧。我相信他的到来是因为我们需要他,因为不管我们感到被抛弃,还是感到孤单,无论怎样,总会在某一个地方,有某一个人知道并关心着我们。我们并不孤单。

We Are Not Alone

Mary L. Miler

After my husband died suddenly from a heart attack on the tennis court, my world crashed around me. My six children were ten, nine, eight, six, three and eighteen months, and I was overwhelmed with the responsibilities of earning a living, caring for the children and just plain keeping my head above the water.

I was fortunate to find a wonderful housekeeper to care for the children during the week, but from Friday nights to Monday mornings, the children and I were alone, and frankly I was uneasy. Every creak of the house, every unusual noise, any late-night phone call—all filled me with dread. I felt incredibly alone.

One Friday evening I came home from work to find a big beautiful German shepherd on our doorstep. This wonderful strong animal gave every indication that he intended to enter the house and make it his home. I, however, was wary. Where did this obviously well-cared-for dog come from? Was it safe to let the children play with a strange dog? Even though he seemed gentle, he still was powerful and commanded respect. The children took an instant liking to "German" and begged me to let it in. I agreed to let him sleep in the basement until the next day, when we could inquire around the neighborhood for his owner. That night I slept peacefully for the first time in many weeks.

The following morning we made phone calls and checked lost-and-found ads for German's owner, but with no results. German, meanwhile, made himself part of the family and good-naturedly put up with hugs, wrestling and playing in the yard. Saturday he was still with us, so again he was allowed to sleep in the basement.

On Sunday I had planned to take the children on a picnic. Since I thought it best to leave German behind in case his owner came by, we drove off without him. When we stopped to get gas at a local station, we were amazed to see German racing to the gas station after us. He not only raced to the car, he leaped onto the hood and put his nose on the windshield, looking directly into my eyes. No way was he going to be left behind. So into the station wagon he jumped and settled down in the back for the ride to the picnic. He stayed again Sunday.

Monday morning I let him out for a run while the children got ready for school. He didn't come back. As evening came and German didn't appear, we were all disappointed. We were convinced that he had gone home or been found by his owner, and that we would never see him again. We were wrong. The next Friday evening, German was back on our doorstep. Again we took him in. and again he stayed until Monday morning. when our housekeeper arrived.

This pattern repeated itself every weekend for almost 10 months. We grew more and more fond of German and we looked forward to his coming. We stopped thinking about where he belonged—he belonged to us. We took comfort in his strong, warm presence, and we felt safe with him near us. When we saw German come to attention and perk up his ears, and heard that low growl begin deep in his throat, we knew we were protected.

As German became part of the family, he considered it his duty to check every bedroom to be sure each child was snug in bed. When he was satisfied that the last person was tucked in, he took upon his position by the front door and remained there until the morning.

Each week, between German's visits, I grew a little stronger, a little braver and more able to cope; every weekend I enjoyed his company. Then one Monday morning we patted his head and let him out for what turned out to be the last time. He never came back. We never saw or heard from German again.

I think of him often. He came when I needed him the most and stayed until I was strong enough to go on alone. Maybe there is a perfectly natural explanation for German's visits to our house—maybe his owner went away on weekends—maybe. I believe German was sent because he was needed, and because no matter how abandoned and alone we feel, somehow, somewhere, someone knows and cares. We are never really alone.

班卓

大卫·C.胡普斯

只要一看到它们那充满爱意和神采飞扬的眼睛,我就懂得,眼神能够拯救一个人,而它们用自己的眼神拯救了我。

——狗迷

我发现班卓的时候,他被装在一只纸袋子里,就放在我家门前的台阶上。很显然,他是一窝德国牧羊犬中最小的一只,因此惨遭遗弃。那时,我住在乡村,30岁,还是单身,容易冲动,所以我还是可以负担起养一只宠物的责任的。可是我真的想要一只吗?我愿意花费一些时间来好好训练一只狗吗?

当我把这只黑棕相间的小球抱入怀中的时候,这些问题都烟消云散了。而在接下来的日子里,我也从来没有为此后悔过。

不久,我结婚了。我的妻子桑迪却没有我对班卓那样的感情。她明确地表明她并不喜欢狗。对她来说,班卓是制造床上的毛发和地毯上的泥的元凶,还是无论我们什么时候出去,都要先安排好的讨厌鬼。

但是过了一段时间,我发现了一些变化。她坚持说只是偶尔在她的麦片中添加了过多的牛奶,为了不浪费,就把剩下的麦片粥给班卓喝了。

桑迪对班卓的爱是在我们婚后的第二年真正发展开来的,当时,由于工作原因,我不得不离开家10个星期,而照顾班卓就完全成了她的责任。班卓从来没有享受过如此舒适的生活。她们不管做什么都在一起,他成了桑迪做梦都没有想到的好朋友。

我们和班卓一起快乐地生活了10年。不久,班卓的健康开始恶化。当他被诊断出患有癌症的时候,桑迪和我都痛苦地意识到班卓就要离开我们了。

在接下来的几个星期里,我们为还能再和班卓在一起的每一刻而感到高兴,但是我们仍然无法摆脱心中的悲痛。当班卓那可爱的脸告诉我们他很不舒服的时候,我们就会对他关心备至。然而在那个时候,我们又不能做出任何决定来帮助他。尽管我们对一定会发生的事有所准备,但是当这件事真正出现在面前的时候,我们还是那么痛苦,感到难以接受。

班卓去逝的那天,当我穿上大衣时,他摇摇晃晃地朝我走来。我相信他是想让我等他。我知道为什么,因此我最后一次帮他来到外面,把他带到火炉旁,让他的脑袋靠在我的大腿上。就像我们10年前相遇的时候一样,我们静静地说了好多话。而这一切就仿佛是在昨天,班卓蜷缩在我的双臂中,满足地打着呼噜,那是只有小狗才会发出的声音。如果说我有什么遗憾的话,我想我应该把一切做得更好,如果我能够再多了解一下幼小的、毛躁的小狗,那该多好啊,然而现在这一切都已经无关紧要了,因为班卓和我就要以我们最初相遇的方式结束我们的关系了,我们只能紧紧地抱着彼此。

他很痛苦,当壁炉的热气将我们笼罩在一起的时候,我不停地告诉他放心走吧。最终他还是去了,我感到起居室是如此孤寂,很难想象10年的时间已经转眼即逝。

当桑迪回到家,穿过前门时,她从我的脸上知道一切都结束了。我相信她的心碎了,甚至比我还痛苦。

我们和班卓在一起待了很长时间,直到我们平静下来,把他抱到他喜欢奔跑的小树林里,埋葬了他。用松树枝铺在他的坟墓上,将花放在匆匆做好的十字架上。

这个时候,除了冬日穿过树林的寒风之外,树林变得静悄悄的。最终,我们转过身走了出去,班卓的墓地显得那么小,而对于在我们的心目中那么高大的班卓而言,实在是太小了。

我喜欢认为我和班卓之间有着一种非同寻常的血缘关系,是一种值得记录和铭记的关系。但是坦白地说,我们之间并没有什么独特的,这个世界不会因为我们而停止旋转。这个简单的事实就是我们彼此喜欢,而这才是最重要的。

Banjo

David C. Hoopes

Banjo came to me by way of a paper bag deposited on my doorstep, apparently the unwanted runt of a litter of German shepherd puppies. At the time, I was single, pushing thirty and living in the country, so I was able to take on the responsibility of a new pet. But did I want one? Was I willing to spend the time it takes to properly train a dog?

These questions disappeared the moment I lifted that black and brown furball into my arms. And in the years that followed, I never regretted my decision.

Later when I married, my wife Sandy didn't share my feelings about Banjo. She made it abundantly clear that she wasn't fond of dogs. To her, Banjo was simply the cause of hair on the couch and mud in the carpet, and a nuisance to make arrangement for whenever we went away.

But in time, I noticed a change. She insisted that she had accidentally added too much milk to her cereal, and instead of wasting it, she might as well give it to Banjo.

Sandy's love for Banjo truly blossomed during the second year of our marriage when my work took me away from home for ten weeks and Banjo became entirely her responsibility. Banjo never had it so good. The two of them did everything together, becoming better friends than Sandy ever dreamed.

Our life together with Banjo continued for ten happy years. Then Banjo's health began to deteriorate. When he was diagnosed with cancer, Sandy and I reached the painful realization that Banjo was leaving us.

In the weeks that followed, we were glad for every extra moment we had with Banjo, but we couldn't shake the sadness we felt. We were concerned when Banjo's dear face told us he wasn't feeling well. yet we were unable to make the decision that the time had come to help him along. And although we prepared ourselves for the in-evitable, the end was no less painful, no easier to accept.

The day Banjo died, he walked unsteadily over to me as I was pulling on my coat. I believed he was asking me to stay. I knew why. So I helped him outside one last time, then took him next to the fire and held his head on my lap. We talked about a lot of things, alone in the quiet, just as we had in the beginning, ten short years ago. After all, it seemed like only yesterday Banjo was curled up in the crook of my arm making contented little grunts, a sound only a puppy can make. If I had any regret, if I thought I could have done certain things better, if I wished I'd been a little more understanding with a young, rambunctious puppy, none of this mattered now as Banjo and I were ending our relationship the same way we started it: just the two of us hold-ing each other close.

He was in pain, and as the glow of the fireplace enveloped us I kept telling him it was okay to let go. And he finally died, leaving me feeling very alone in the mid-dle of the living room, wondering how the last ten years could have possibly gone so quickly.

When Sandy came home and walked through the front door, she knew by the expression on my face that it was over. I believed her heart broke even more deeply than mine.

We stayed with Banjo for a long while before composing ourselves and carrying him into the woods where he so loved to run. We buried him. covered his grave with pine bows and placed flowers against a hastily made cross.

And then the forest grew silent, except for the wind that pushed through the win-ter trees. When we finally turned to walk away, Banjo's gravesite seemed small, so small for a dog so large in our hearts.

I'd like to think Banjo and I shared an extraordinary kinship, one worthy of be-ing recorded and remembered. But frankly, there was nothing unique about it. The world didn't spin differently because of us. The simple truth is we liked each other, and that's all that really mattered.

一只聪明的狗

佚名

一个肉店老板正在照看店铺,这时一只狗走了进来,吓了他一跳,他把狗轰跑了。可是没过多久,那只狗又回来了。

他走近一看,发现那只狗的嘴里衔着一张纸条,他拿过那张纸条,上面写着:"请给我十二根香肠和一条羊腿,好吗? 狗的嘴里衔着钱。"

老板又往狗的嘴里看了看,发现还有一张十美圆的钞票,于是他把钱取走,把香肠和羊腿装进一个袋子,并放入狗的嘴里。这件事给老板留下了深刻的印象,反正也快下班了,于是他决定关门,跟着这只狗。

于是他动身了。那只狗沿着马路走到了一个十字路口,他放下袋子,跳起来去按过街的按钮,然后又衔起袋子,耐心地等待绿灯。他们两个都站在那里,后来那只狗过了马路,老板紧随其后。

这只狗走到了一个公共汽车站,看着汽车时刻表。

老板十分惊奇,那只狗看完时刻表之后,就坐在了旁边的座位上。有一辆车驶来了,那只狗绕到车前看了看号码,又坐了回去。

又有一辆车驶来了,那只狗又起来去看了看号码,看到是要乘坐的那一辆,便走上车去。此时的老板目瞪口呆,也跟着他上了车。

汽车驶出城镇,开到了郊外,那只狗欣赏着窗外的风景。最后,他站起来,走到前面,两条后腿撑着,前爪按下了停车的铃,他下了车,嘴里还衔着袋子。

狗和老板沿着马路往前走,后来那只狗拐进了一座房子,在一条小路上走着,然后他把袋子放在了台阶上。

随后那只狗又走了回来,冲着门猛地跑过去,并撞在了上面,然后又走回来,又跑了过去,撞在门上。没有人回应,于是那只狗走到小路上,跳上一堵矮墙,顺着花园边走,走到一个窗口时,用头碰了几下窗户,又走回来,跳下墙,在门口等着。

老板看见一个强壮的男人开了门,接着便对那只狗拳脚相加,嘴里还不停地骂着。

老板跑上前去阻止:"你要干什么?这只狗简直是个天才。他简直可以上电视!"可是那个男人回答说:"你把这叫做聪明? 这已经是这只蠢狗在这个礼拜里第二次忘记带钥匙了。"

A Clever Dog

Anonymous

A **butcher**[1] watching over his shop is really surprised when he saw a dog coming inside the shop. He shoos him away. But later, the dog is back again.

So, he goes over to the dog and notices he has a note in his mouth. He takes the note and it reads "Can I have 12 **sausages**[2] and a leg of lamb, please. The dog has money in his mouth, as well. "

The butcher looks inside and finds out that there is a ten—dollar Note. So he takes the money and puts the sausages and lamb in a bag, placing it in the dog's mouth. The butcher is so impressed, and since it's about closing time, he decides to shut up shop and follow the dog.

So off he goes. The dog is walking down the street when he comes to a level crossing. The dog puts down the bag, jumps up and presses the button. Then he waits patiently, bag in mouth, for the lights to turn. They do, and he walks across the road, with the butcher following him all the way.

The dog then comes to a bus stop, and starts looking at the timetable.

The butcher is in awe at this stage. The dog checks out the times, and then sits on one of the seats provided. Along comes a bus. The dog walks around to the front, looks at the number, and goes back to his seat.

Another bus comes. Again the dog goes and looks at the number, notices it's the right bus, and climbs on. The butcher, by now, open—mouthed, follows him onto the bus.

The bus travels through the town and out into the **suburbs**[3], the dog looking at the scenery. Eventually he gets up, and moves to the front of the bus. He stands on two back paws and pushes the button to stop the bus. Then he gets off, his **groceries**⁴ still in his mouth.

Well, dog and butcher are walking along the road, and then the dog turns into a house. He walks up the path, and drops the groceries on the step.

Then he walks back down the path, takes a big run, and throws himself against the door. He goes back down the path, runs up to the door and again, it throws him—self against it. There's no answer at the house, so the dog goes back down the path, jumps up on a narrow wall, and walks along the perimeter of the garden. He gets to the window, and beats his head against it several times, walks back, jumps off, and waits at the door.

The butcher watches as a big guy opens the door, and starts abusing the dog, kicking him and punching him, and swearing at him.

The butcher runs up, and stops the guy."What the hell are you doing? The dog is a genius. He could be on TV, for the life of me! " to which the guy responds, "You call this clever? This is the second time this week that this stupid dog's forgotten his key."

1. butcher ['butʃə] *n.* 屠夫；屠户
2. sausage ['sɔsidʒ] *n.* 香肠；腊肠
3. suburb ['sʌbə:b] *n.* 市郊；郊区
4. grocery ['grəusəri] *n.* <美>食品杂货店；食品；杂货

杰 里

哈里特·L.奈

如果当初它离开人世时,我有选择的机会,我一定会陪它走到生命的最后一刻。

——狗迷

亨利·威廉姆斯和他的妻子开车到大树林里给杰里扫墓。他将几枝常青藤放在杰里的墓碑前,垂下头,默默地为他祈祷着。

墓碑前长时间的沉默令亨利感到极度悲痛。而这使他清晰地回想起一桩桩往事。虽然往事已过,一切都已变得暗淡,但是亨利却不愿让它从脑海中消失。就像杰里墓前的那束常青藤一样,永远鲜活地活在他的记忆里。他年年都要来这里看望杰里……已经太多年了,数也数不过来了……

在这昏暗阴沉的冰雨中,亨利的妻子仔细地观察着他在坟墓周围的一举一动。丈夫脸上那沉重的表情使她感到很痛苦,她一次又一次地要求丈夫讲有关杰里的故事。而他却什么也没有说——只是说那是杰里的坟墓,杰里是一只狗的名字,是一只他所知道的最机警、最伶俐的狗。亨利的妻子莱拉对这些并不满足,她想知道杰里到底发生了什么事情。

她感到去墓地的路途变得越来越艰难。她的丈夫所经受的痛苦似乎太强烈了,而他的举动又显示出他好像犯过什么可怕的错误,也好像是还没有还清他的债务……即使已经过去这么多年了。

当他们驾车回到城里,亨利的妻子想起来这可能又是一次从丈夫那里得到一些答案的好机会。她想帮助丈夫,分担他的痛苦。她不能再置身事外,看着丈夫那样悲伤下去。他必须彻底地将烦恼他太久的负担消除掉。

"亨利,"她以他从未听到过的坚定的语气说道,"我想知道杰里到底发生了什么事情……请你把发生的一切告诉我……这一次你必须说清楚。我再也不想听你那否定的回答了。"

听到这里,他吃了一惊,沉默了一会儿。他看起来那么紧张不安,对自己没有信心,起初他只是干巴巴地低语着。最终,他可以比较清晰地说出来了。"莱拉……我亲爱的莱拉……我不知道该从何说起。你和我一起过着圆满的生活,这一点我深信不疑。我们养育了几个好孩子,一起看着他们成长、结婚。我们在一起过得很幸福。我很害怕破坏了那种幸福。我从来不愿意让你不开心,我太害怕了以至于我不敢告诉你我的故事。但是我知道,总有一天我要将这一切告诉你。"

他的妻子打断了他:"亨利,你可以放心,我对你的感情是不会随着你告诉我的事情的真相而有所改变的,何况我们一起走过了那么多年!"

"莱拉,你对我的感情意味着一切。一直都是这样的。在我们相遇之前,也有一个人,他是那么强大,就像我人生中的一盏指路灯。他给了我一种坚持人生道路和改变生活现状的愿望和力量。"

"你说的是杰里吗?"这时雨下得越来越大了。不过车内还是很暖和、很舒适——仿佛一个与世隔绝的天地,而这使亨利更容易开始讲述他的故事。

"多年以前,"他用一种低沉的语调说着,"我是一个放荡、狂暴的人。为什么呢,我也不知道,不过我确实是一个凶险的、内心邪恶的人。当然,这都是在遇到你之前的事了。我不诚实,很难让人信赖。那时我是天下第一号的吹牛大王。只要是我想要的就一定会据为己有,从不考虑其他人的权利和感情。

"而在我的这段令人唾弃的经历中出现的另一个人就是哈维·罗林斯医生,他是我的一个老同学,就住在离杰里坟墓不远的地方。

"杰里,就像我多次告诉你的那样,他是这个州最棒的猎犬之一。医生和他的妻子对他疯狂地着了迷。有一天,在一次跳跃中,杰里的腿部受了重伤。我带着他到了罗林斯医生那里,罗林斯医生顺利地将杰里的骨头固定好。没过多久,杰里就能像以前那样又跑又跳了。

"从那以后,我们就经常一起去打猎——医生、他的妻子海伦,还有我。医生带着他的狗,我带着杰里。但是杰里就是有某种神奇的嗅觉,经常能够找到小鹿的藏身之地。医生从不吝啬对杰里的赞赏之辞。

"但是，羞愧的是，当医生专注于我那只伶俐又聪明的猎狗时，我却被他的妻子——海伦那妩媚的娇姿迷倒了。在我们狩猎的途中，她和我很快就走到了一起，将医生单独留在那里狩猎。我是一个瞎了眼的白痴、自负而又令人讨厌的傻瓜。我根本就看不到我的所作所为是错误的，是不可宽恕的。

"海伦和我迫不及待地开始接吻。有一次，在一个空旷的树林中，当我们彼此拥抱的时候，我看到了杰里。他就坐在我们的前方，用他那棕色的眼睛悲伤地看着我们，一直看着我们。而他那双几乎同人一样的神情好像在说："不要那样做，主人！不要那样！"

"你的意思是，"亨利的妻子问道，"他一直跟着并看着你们吗？"

"是的，不管我和她走到哪里，无论什么时候我和她交谈，只要我一扭头就能看到杰里。有时他将头放在他的前爪上，有时就直直地坐在那里，而且他的眼睛从来没有从我的身上离开过，可以说看着我的一举一动。他的眼睛又总是流露出那种不赞成、悲哀的神情。上帝啊，现在回想起来，那只狗实际上是在和我交流，警告我……

"至于海伦，那个医生的妻子，嗯，她是那种很容易被甜言蜜语所迷住的轻浮的女人。在我的手中，她就像一滩柔软的烂泥。然而，她是有夫之妇……如果他发现了我们……但是这对于我内心的邪恶根本无济于事。我决定将那个女人据为己有。不管怎样，也要将医生推到一边，如果需要的话就将他永远推开。

"最后，我想出了将医生这个绊脚石除掉的计策。我总是对自己的枪法感到自豪。我从来没有，或是很少有打不中一只鹿或是飞翔的野鸭的时候。我告诉海伦，我想到解决问题的方法了，她不久就可以永远自由了。当然，我没有告诉她我的计划……

"我选了一个良机。一天，医生跑进了一片松树林，他紧跟着鹿的足印追赶着。他轻轻地举着手中的来复枪，小心地向那只鹿移动着脚步。我就跟在他的身后。我的计划马上就要实现了。

海伦在我的身后远远地跟着，而在我这边，就像平常一样，只有我的猎狗杰里。我的计划是与医生同时开枪。整件事情将会在一秒钟内解决。海伦会认为这只是一次狩猎中的意外事故。

"我已经准备好了，我的来复枪对准了罗斯林医生，他的后背正冲着我。

"前面传来一只鹿噼啪逃跑的声音。我一直盯着医生,他突然停了下来,静静地站在那里,现在他是个最好的靶子。

"我举起手中的枪,小心地观察着他。他开枪的那一刻,就是给我开枪的信号。时间到了,他举起了枪……一瞬间,一切都静得可怕……我轻轻地叩动扳机,然后慢慢地加力。我看到枪口冒着火花,听到那响亮的枪声……一阵低沉的呜咽声传来,大量的毛发飞舞起来,以及那最后砰的落地声……

"罗林斯医生立刻放下了手中的枪,转过身看着我。我的枪仍然冒着烟。"你也看见那只鹿了。"医生说,然后他注意到躺在我们中间松针上的是——杰里。那只狗就躺在那里,头放在爪子中间。他那血迹斑斑的眼睛始终盯着我。医生朝着杰里跑过去,并沉痛地看着他。"太可怕了!太可怕了!太可怕了!"他不停地呻吟着……"这漂亮的猎犬……噢,亨利,你一定感到很痛苦吧!现在,不要责备自己了……这只是个意外。"他走到我身边,脸上挂着温暖而又最痛苦的表情。我们紧挨着站在一起。我的眼前一片模糊,说不出话来,一动不动地站在那里。最后他说:"亨利,那只狗一定是做了一次不可思议的跳跃,正好跳在了那枚子弹的前面。"

亨利感觉妻子紧紧地抓着他的手臂。他们的车在潮湿的高速路上缓慢前行。天渐渐暗了下来,仍然下着雨。他们离杰里的墓地每远一分钟,就感觉杰里离他们越来越近。

Jerry

Harriet L. Nye

Henry Williams and his wife drove out to the Great Woods to visit Jerry's grave. He put some evergreens on the headstone and lowered his head and moved his lips in silent prayer.

The long silent moments at the graveside were extremely painful. They brought back the past in clear and sharp detail. In was a past that was fading, but, Henry refused to let it disappear from memory. He kept it as green as the ferns he placed on the small headstone of Jerry's grave. He came back for many years... too many to count...

In the gray, cold rain, Henry's wife watched him closely, as he moved around the burial ground. What she saw in his face made her miserable. Again and again she had asked him to tell her about Jerry. But he would tell her nothing—only that the grave was Jerry's, and that Jerry was the name of a dog, the finest, most intelligent dog he had ever known. Lila was not satisfied with this. She wanted to know what had happened to Jerry.

The trip to the burial ground got worse for her each time. The pain her husband suffered on these visits seemed too intense. He acted as if he had done some terrible wrong and had not yet paid the price for it... even after so many years...

As they drove back to the city, Henry's wife thought this would be a good time to try again to get some answers from him. She wanted to help him, to share his pain. She could no longer stand aside and watch him suffer so. He must, once and for all, get what was troubling him off his chest.

"Henry, "she said with a firmness in the tone of her voice that was new and strange to him, "I want to know what happened to Jerry... I want you to tell me everything, please... This time you must. I refuse to take 'no' for an answer."

He was silent for a time, taken by surprise. He seemed nervous, unsure of him-self, answering at first in a dry whisper. Finally, he spoke up in a clearer voice: "Lila... my dear Lila... I don't know how to begin. You and I have had a full life to-gether, a good life. I believe. We have raised fine children and watched them grow and get married. We have been happy together. I am afraid to destroy that. I never wanted to make you unhappy, and was too frightened to tell you my story. But I al-ways knew the day would come when I would have to."

His wife stopped him: "Henry, you can be sure that my feelings toward you will not be changed in any way by what you tell me... too many years are behind us..."

"Lila, what you feel for me means everything. It always has. Before you there was someone else who was also a great force, a guiding light. He gave me the desire. the strength to go on and change my life."

"You mean Jerry?" The rain had now become a steady downpour. But the car was warm and pleasant—a world removed from the outside. It made it easier for Hen-ry to begin his story.

"Years back," he said in a heavy voice, "I was a wild, vicious individual. Why, I don't know, but I was ugly, truly evil. This, of course, was before I met you. I was dishonest, could not be trusted. I was a braggart, if ever there was one. I took what I wanted and cared little for the rights or feelings of the other fellow.

"And the other fellow in this sickening story of mine was Doctor Harvey Rollins, an old school friend of mine. He lived not far from Jerry's grave.

"Jerry, as I have told you many times, was one of the best hunting dogs in the state. The doctor and his wife were crazy about him. Once, in a great leap, Jerry had badly hurt his leg. I took him to Doctor Rollins, who did a fine job fixing the dog's bone. Jerry was soon able to run and jump as well as ever.

"After that, we took hunting trips together—the doctor, his wife, Helen, and my-self. The doctor had his dogs and I had Jerry. But it was Jerry who by some magic sense always seemed to know just where the deer were hiding. The doctor never tired of praising him.

"But, to my shame, while the doctor was taken up with the intelligence and skills of my dog, I became occupied with the charms of his wife, Helen. She and I soon be—gan too walk off together on our hunting trips, leaving Doctor alone on the hunt. I was a blind fool, a vain, hateful fool. I could not see that what I was doing was wrong, was unpardonable.

"Helen and I lost no time and soon began kissing. One time, in a clearing in the woods, as we had our arms around each other. I noticed Jerry. He was sitting right before us, with his big brown eyes sadly upon us. He kept watching us. The expres—sion in those almost human eyes seemed to be saying—"Don't do that, master! Don't do that! "

"You mean," asked Henry's wife, "he followed you and watched you all the time?"

"Exactly. No matter where I walked with her, no matter when I talked to her , all I had to do was to turn my head and there was Jerry, either lying down with his head resting on his forepaws, or sitting up. And he never took his eyes off me, watching ev—ery move I made. And always with that disapproving. mournful expression in his eyes. God, when I think of it now, that dog was practically talking to me, warning me...

"As for Helen, the doctor's wife—well, she was one of those light—minded crea—tures easily influenced by words and promises. In my hands she was like soft clay. However, there was her husband... If he ever found out about us... But there seemed to be no limit to the evil in me. I decided that I had to have this woman for myself. Somehow, the doctor had to be pushed aside, permanently if need be.

"Finally, I worked out a plan for getting him out of my way. I had always been proud of my skill with a gun. I never—not often, anyway—missed hitting a deer, or a duck on the wing. I told Helen I had a solution and that she would soon have her freedom, at last. Of course, I did not tell her my plan...

"I chose my moment. One day, the doctor was pushing his way through a pine grove, hot on a deer's trail. He was holding his rifle, loosely, moving carefully toward the animal. I was straight behind him. My plan was taking shape right before my eyes. Helen was far enough behind me. And at my side, as usual, was my own hunt—

ing dog, Jerry. My plan was to fire my shot at the same time the doctor fired his. The whole thing would be over in a second. Helen would consider it a natural hunting ac–cident.

"I was ready, my rifle aimed toward Doctor Rollins, whose back was turned to me.

"There was a crackling noise of a deer moving up front. I kept my eye on the Doctor. He came to a sudden stop. He stood still, motionless. He was now a perfect target.

"I raised my gun, carefully watching him, The moment he fired would be my signal. It had now come. He raised his rifle—For a second, a fierce silence... I pressed the trigger gently, then harder, all the way. I saw the flame leap from the muzzle of my gun and heard the loud report... There was a low whimper. a mass of hurtling fur and a final thud...

"Doctor Rollins quickly lowered his gun, and turned around to look at me. My rifle was still smoking. "You saw that deer, too." said the doctor. Then he noticed what lay between us, on the pine needles—Jerry. The dog lay there with his head be–tween his paws. His eyes still kept staring at me, out of a red smear. The doctor ran toward Jerry and looked down at him with an intensely painful look. "How terrible! how terrible! how terrible! " he moaned... "This beautiful creature...Oh, Henry, you must be feeling awful! Now, don't go blaming yourself... Accidents will happen. " And he came gently toward me with the warmest and most sorrowful expression on his face. We stood close together for a time. in a fog, speechless, unable to move. At last he said, "Henry, that dog must have made, an impossible leap to get in front of that bullet. "

Henry felt his wife's tight grip on his arm. Their car moved slowly along the wet highway. It was getting dark. It was still raining. Every minute that took them farther and farther away from the grave brought Jerry closer and closer to both of them.

一只纳瓦霍狗

佚名

下午5点，夜幕降临，舞会也已经接近尾声。在独自回家的路上，我买了一只纳瓦霍狗。

我和那个瘦小而机警的卖狗人讨价还价了一番，最后以5美圆的价格成交。她是一只忠诚、善良且非常勇敢的小黄狗，那个人还给了我一截绳索，以便将她拉回家。

这只狗不大不小，是那种随处可见、并不引人注意的动物。她对我很排斥，然而，我能看出来，她也准备要回报我对她的那片深厚情谊。据我推测，她只是需要对她的生活方式作一些小小的调整，将她的激情转移到其他方面上，这样才能与我和谐相处。尽管一路上她几乎要被绳索勒死了，但她仍然欢快地摇着她那毛茸茸的尾巴。

那天晚上，我把狗拴在了车库里，并为她准备了一张既暖和又干净的铺垫、健康的食物和新鲜的水，然后把车库门锁上了。但是到了第二天的早晨，那只狗就不见了，虽然我的内心深处早就有了这种感觉，她一定会逃走的，对此我深信不疑。我从她的眼睛里已经看出来了。她将绳索咬成两段，从车库的通风口跑了出去。虽然我认为通风口对于她来说是那么小，但是，可以肯定的是，有志者事竟成，而纳瓦霍狗就具有这种不屈不挠的意志力。

当时，我虽然感到备受打击，但是又很奇怪地平静了下来，就像我已经透过这件事情悟出了一些真理似的。那只狗只是做了她不得不去做的事情，那是她必须完成的事，她只是对自己、太阳、月亮展现出了最真实的一面。她很清楚自己在万物中所处的位置。随着车辙印她知道怎么回到自己的家。我可以想象到当时的情景：几英里之外，她迈着沉重而缓慢的步子走在那个熟悉的影子里，在经历过那个痛苦的夜晚之后，她的尾巴有些下垂，但仍然摇摆着，她冥思苦想着人类那奇怪的行为。

A Navajo Dog

Anonymous

Dusk was falling at five o'clock, when the dancing came to an end, and on the way home alone I bought a Navajo dog.

I bargained for a while: with the thin, wary man whose dog it was, and we set-tled on a price of five dollars. It was a yellow, honest—to goodness, greathearted dog, and the man gave me a bit of rope with which to pull it home.

The dog was not large, but neither was it small. It was one of those unremark-able creatures that one sees in every corner of the world. It was full of resistance, and yet it was ready to return in full measure my deep, abiding love. I could see that. It needed only, I reasoned, to make a small adjustment in its style of life, to shift the fo-cus of its vitality from one flame of reference to another, in order to be perfectly at home with me. Even was nearly strangled on the way it wagged its bushy tail happily all the while.

That night I tied the dog up in the garage, where there was a warm, clean pallet, wholesome food, and fresh water, and I bolted the door. And the next morning the dog was gone, I had read such a future in its eyes. It had gnawed the rope in two and squeezed through a vent in the door, and opening much too small for it, as I had thought. But, sure enough, where there is a will there is a way, and the Navajo dog was possessed of one indomitable will.

I was crushed at the time, but strangely reconciled, too, as if I had perceived some truth beyond billboards. The dog had done what it had to do, had behaved ex-actly as it must, had been true to itself and to the sun and moon. It knew its place in the order of things, and its place was away out there in the tracks of a wagon, going home. In the mind's eye I could see it at that very moment, miles away, plodding in the familiar shadows, its tail drooping a little after the harrowing night, but wagging, its dog's mind contemplating the wonderful ways of mankind.

拨打 911 电话的小狗

珍妮·玛丽·拉斯卡斯

当莉娜·比斯利为她的新服务犬起名字的时候,她想到了《圣经》中她最喜欢的一句话:"信念是希望的物质载体,是未见之事的证据。"

"信念,"她抱着这只罗特韦尔小狗说道,"以后我就叫你信念吧。"

那是在 2001 年,莉娜已经 46 岁了,她离婚后和她 20 岁的儿子——迈克尔住在华盛顿州普吉特湾的一处居所。她承认,要适应一只新的服务犬是有些困难。莉娜与轮椅为伴,并患有癫痫病。近 10 年她一直依赖着她的第一只服务犬布朗森,他帮她处理一些日常琐碎的事情,严格说来,是在她癫痫病发的时候给予帮助。布朗森从服务线上退休了,成了莉娜和她儿子的普通宠物狗。

从内心来说,莉娜有些疑虑,不知她自己能否还像信赖布朗森那样再去信赖另一只狗。在她的心目中,布朗森就是她的守护天使。

"好吧,信念,"她对着她的新狗说,并流露出那种急切的眼神,"我们还有好多工作要做呢,那么让我们从现在开始吧。"

据科学家推测,有些狗有着极其敏锐的嗅觉,可以发觉到病人病发之前体内产生的极其微小的化学变化。不过只有少数的狗知道在危险来临的时候将嗅觉转换成相应的警报。

信念最终被训练成功,能够理解并回答 150 多种命令。但是直到 2004 年 9 月 6 日的那个晚上,莉娜才真正了解到信念能够做什么。当时,莉娜和她的儿子住在华盛顿州的里奇兰德。那是一个很普通的夜晚,迈克尔到当地的杂货店上晚班,莉娜在上床休息前,感到有些不舒服,像是感冒了。她看了看在起居室躺着的布朗森,然后回到自己的卧室。信念一直寸步不离跟着她,并没有去躺在挨着床边的篮子里,只是一直站着,看着莉娜……并说着话。听起来就像是人们在谈话,发出一种"噜噜噜噜"的声音。

"你在说什么呢?"莉娜问道。就在这时,信念以她那85磅重的身体跳到莉娜的床上——这是她的禁地——并转着圈。她不理会莉娜要她下床的要求,而这些完全不像平时那只温顺的小狗。

莉娜想起训狗师说过的话:"相信你的狗!"如果一只狗的行为有些异常的话,可能是因为她知道一些你不知道的事情——但是你需要知道的。

"好吧,信念,我相信你,"她说道,"我这就起床。"她坐到轮椅上,检查着房子,并没有发现与平常有什么不同,于是决定喝一杯热巧克力。

她来到炉子旁,试着去拿那个空水壶,就在这时,世界变得漆黑一片。她从轮椅上摔了下来,头撞到橱柜门上,倒在地上失去了知觉。这是疾病的突发状况,尽管不是由于她的癫痫病直接引发的。莉娜患有肝功能衰竭,事后医生告诉她,用药的副作用就是使得她几乎丧失了肝功能。

而摔倒时的碰撞又使得莉娜的癫痫病立刻发作起来。就在这个时候,信念的英雄气概表现了出来。这只狗将无绳电话衔在嘴里,用鼻子按着狗专用的911快速拨号键,她受过识别这个键的专业训练。当接线员珍妮·布坎南应答的时候,信念在电话里狂吠着。她一遍遍地叫着。大多数的911接线员是没有受到过翻译狗叫的这种培训,但是在本托县东南的交流中心,对所有的来电都必须作出反应。布坎南发现狗叫的规律——听起来好像是在她说完话之后才发出声音,就像是那只狗在回答她的问题。肯定这个声音不是背景音乐而是一个求救电话,布坎南派出了警察。当电话里的声音消失后,信念又回到莉娜的身边,为她做着癫痫病的复健工作,将她推到"恢复姿势",侧躺着,这样可以使病人的喉咙畅通。

斯科特·莫雷尔警官到达现场,打开了走廊上的移动探测灯。信念和布朗森透过窗户往外看,他们都受过识别警察、消防员以及医护人员制服的专业训练,可以辨认出他们不是闯入者,而是朋友。信念用鼻子将她的小狗专用门把手顶开,让莫雷尔进来,叫着向厨房跑去,让莫雷尔跟着她。

莉娜在医院住了三个星期,信念有时候会陪着她。但是莉娜对于自己是怎么获救的一直不是很清楚。直到她回到家里,联系上莫雷尔警官和布坎南之后,她才能够将信念救了自己的这个不可思议的壮举拼凑起来。

"这一定是爱与奉献,"莉娜说道,"从那晚起,我们的关系就发生了变化。我想信念一定是找到了自己的生活目标,同时我也发现她是一个真正的天使。"

The Dog Who Dialed 911

Jeanne Marie Laskas

When Leana Beasley wondered about a name for her new service dog, she thought about one of her favorite Bible quotes: "Faith is the substance of things hoped for, the evidence of things not seen."

"Faith, "she said, cradling the **rottweiler**[1] puppy. "I'll name you Faith. "

That was in 2001, and Leana, now 46, who is divorced and lives with her 20 — year—old son, Michael, in a house in Puget Sound, Washington, admits she found the transition to the new dog difficult. Leana is wheelchair—bound and suffers from **epilepsy**[2]; for nearly a decade she had come to depend on Bronson, her first service dog, to help her with chores and errands and, most critically, to assist her in the event of epileptic seizures. Bronson was retiring from service and evolving into a regular pet for Leana and her son.

Deep down, Leana doubted she'd ever trust another dog as deeply as she did Bronson, the creature she had come to regard as her guardian angel.

"Okay, Faith, " she said to her new dog, a **brindled**[3] bundle of energy with ea—ger eyes. "We have a lot of work to do, so let's get started. "

Scientists **speculate**[4] that some dogs, with their supremely sensitive noses, might be able to detect subtle changes in human body chemistry that occur just before a seizure. But only a select few know how to interpret that olfactory information as worthy of alarm.

Faith was eventually trained to understand and answer more than 150 com—mands, but it wasn't until the evening of September 6, 2004, that Leana would learn what, exactly, Faith was made of. Leana and her son were then living in Richland,

Washington. It was a typical evening: Michael had left for his night shift at the local grocery store, and Leana headed to bed, feeling a little sick, as if she were getting the flu. She checked on Bronson, asleep in the living room, and went into her bedroom. Faith wouldn't leave her side. She wouldn't lay down in her basket next to the bed, but instead stood there looking at Leana and. . . talking. That's how it sounded, like a kind of chatter "Roo roo rooo rooo. "

"What is it ?"Leana said. Soon enough Faith, all 85 pounds of her, jumped on Leona's bed—a forbidden **territory**[5]—and ran in circles. She would not answer Leanne's command to get down, which was completely out of character for the obe-dient dog.

In her mind Leana heard the voice of the trainer: "Trust your dog! "A dog be-having strangely probably knows something you don't know—and need to.

"Okay, Faith, I'm trusting you, "she said. "I'm getting out of bed. " She got in her wheelchair and investigated the house and, finding nothing unusual, decided to make herself hot chocolate.

She reached across the stove for the empty water kettle, and that's when the world went black. She fell out of her wheelchair, hitting her head on the kitchen cab-inet door, and lay unconscious on the floor. This was a medical emergency, though not directly caused by her epilepsy. Leana was experiencing liver failure; doctors later said that an adverse reaction to her medication made her liver nearly shut down.

The contusion suffered during the fall caused Leana to immediately go into a grand mal seizure, and at that point Faith's heroism kicked into overdrive. The dog retrieved the cordless phone with her mouth, and with her nose pushed the dog—friendly 911 speed—dial button she had been trained to identify. When the dispatcher, Jenny Buchanan, answered, Faith barked into the phone. She barked and barked. Most 911 operators are not trained to translate the woofing of dogs, but at the Benton County's Southeast Communications Center, all calls must be acted on. Buchanan de-tected a pattern to the barks—they seemed to come after she spoke, as if the dog were somehow answering her. Deciding that this was not just background noise but a plea for help, Buchanan dispatched police. When the voice stopped coming out of the phone, Faith went back to Leana and did her seizure–response work, pushing her into the "recovery position" on her side, which cleared throat.

When the police officer, Corporal Scott Morrell, arrived, tripping the motion–detector light on the porch. Faith and Bronson watched from the window. Both had been trained to recognize the uniforms of police, firefighters and medical personnel not as intruders but as friends. With her nose, faith unlatched the special doggie lock on the door and let Morrell inside, barking as she ran to the kitchen, urging him to follow.

Leana was in the hospital for three weeks, accompanied by Faith for part of the time. But Leana never had a clear idea of her rescue. It wasn't until she returned home and contacted Morrell and Buchanan that she was able to piece together the story of Faith's amazing feat.

"It must be love and devotion," Leana says. "After that night our relationship changed. I think Faith discovered her purpose. And I found out who she was: a true angel."

1. rottweiler [rɔtˌwailə(r)] *n.* (德国种) 罗特韦尔犬
2. epilepsy ['epilepsi] *n.* <医> 癫痫症
3. brindle ['brindl] *n.* 斑点;有斑纹的动物
4. speculate ['spekjuˌleit] *v.* 推测;思索;做投机买卖
5. territory ['teritəri] *n.* 领土;版图;地域

无辜的流浪者

洛里·S. 莫尔

一个年轻人绕着拉斯维加斯市中心繁忙的街角踱来踱去,他表情绝望,一只手举着皱巴巴的纸板,上面潦草地写着:身无分文——需要狗食,另一只手牵着一条狗链子。

狗链上拴着一只不满1岁的爱斯基摩小狗,离他们不远的灯柱上,系着一只大一些的相同品种的狗。严冬将至,他在凛冽的寒风中嚎叫着,那悲惨的叫声数里外都能听见,他似乎知道自己的命运。他的身旁立着一个牌子,写着"待售"的字样。

我暂时忘了自己的目的地,迅速掉转车头,径自驶向这3个无家可归者。我的车子的后备箱里一直都存有猫狗的粮食,多年来我一直有这种习惯。我以这种方式来帮助那些我不能收养的动物,这些猫狗粮也能帮助我引诱那些受惊吓的狗逃离马路上的危险。帮助那些在困境中的动物一直是我的自发行为。

我把车子停在最近的地方,拿出一包5磅重的狗食和一罐水,又从钱包里掏出20美圆。我小心翼翼地走近那个衣衫褴褛的年轻人和他的可怜的狗狗们。如果这个人伤害了这些动物,或者把他们当成博得怜悯的工具,我就会很气愤。大狗正可怜地仰天鸣嚎着。就在我走近他们之前,一辆卡车在他们旁边停下来,问大狗卖多少钱。

"50美圆,"角落里的年轻人答道,然后很快补充了一句,"但我确实不想卖。"

"他有执照吗?"

"没有。"

"他阉割过吗?"

"没有。"

"他多大了?"

"5岁。我真不愿把他卖掉,我只是需要一些钱给他买点吃的。"

"如果我有50美圆,就会把他买下。"绿灯亮了,卡车加速开走了。

年轻人摇了摇头，继续无精打采地在人行道上踱来踱去。注意到我向他走来，他便停下来看着我，小狗也开始摇晃尾巴。

"嗨。"我走近后，和他打了个招呼。年轻人文雅而友好，从他的眼神可以看出，他确实遇到了麻烦。

"我这里有一些食物可以给你的狗吃。"我说。他愣了愣，拿起袋子，我又把水放在他们面前。

"你还带来了水？"他惊讶地问。我们在大狗旁边蹲下，小狗欢喜地跟我打招呼。

"那个叫 TC，他叫狗狗，我叫韦恩。"那条悲伤的大狗早就停止吠叫，来看罐子里的东西了。

"发生了什么事，韦恩？"我随口问道，而后又感到有些冒失，但他却答得简单而干脆。"哦，我刚从亚利桑那搬到这里，还没找到工作。这个节骨眼儿上，我连狗都养不起。"

"那你现在住在哪里？"

"就住在那边的卡车里。"他指着停在附近的一辆破旧不堪的车子说。车身很长，还有个外壳，至少他们暂时有了避风港。

小狗爬到我的膝盖上，伏着不动了。我问韦恩做什么工作。"我做技工和焊工，"他说，"但这里找不到相关的工作，我找了好久。这两只狗是我唯一的亲人，我真的不想卖掉他们，可又实在没有办法养活他们。"

他一遍又一遍地说着：他不想卖掉他们，但又养不起他们。每当他重复这些话时，脸上都露出痛苦的表情，就像他不得已要卖掉自己的孩子一样。

这个时候，不经意地递给他一张 20 圆似乎最合适不过了，希望我不会进一步刺伤他已经颤抖着的自尊。"哦，拿这个给自己买些吃的。"

"噢，谢谢，"他缓缓答道，目光不敢直视我，"这都够我们找个房间过夜了。"

"你在这已经多久了？"

"整整一天了。"

"没人停下来帮你们吗？"

"没有，你是第一个。"当时已是傍晚，夜幕很快降临了。太阳落山时，这边沙漠地区的温度会降到华氏 30 多度。

我的脑子飞快地转着，心想今天他们可能没吃上一顿饭，或许很多天没吃了，只是长久地待在他们暂时勉强做栖息之所的破车内，冻得缩成一团。

在这个城市里看到乞丐是司空见惯的事，但这个人却与众不同，因为他不是为自己乞讨。他更关心的是他的狗，而把自己的温饱问题置之度外。作为一个养着9只狗，并且非常喜爱宠物狗的我，被他深深感动了。

我始终不明白当时是什么样的感情激励着我去采取下一步行动，我只是觉得，这是我必须做的事。我问他能否在那里等我回来，他点点头，露出一丝笑容。

我开车飞驰到最近的食品杂货店，像是被谁催促着一样，我疾步走进去，推了一辆手推车。我从第一个货架开始，一直走到另一头才停下来。我恨不得以更快的速度把那些东西拿下货架。我想，就只买些必需品，够他们吃几个星期，能维持他们生存的食物。花生油和果冻、面包、罐头、果汁、水果、蔬菜、狗粮、更多的狗粮（准确地说，是40磅），还有磨牙玩具，他们的生活需要乐趣。我还买了一些其他的必需品，终于大功告成了。

"一共是102.91美圆。"收银员说。我眼睛眨都不眨一下，几乎看都没看支票就签了字。不久就要缴分期房款了，我并不在意这计划之外的100多美圆的花销。没有什么能比解决这个家庭的温饱问题更重要的事情了。我惊异于自己这种不可遏制的动机，驱使自己在一个素不相识的人身上花掉100多美圆。然而，与此同时，我又觉得自己是世界上最幸运的人。感谢上苍，能让我有机会给这个人和他所爱的伴侣一点点东西，而我却有许多这样的东西。

当我拿着这些东西回来时，韦恩喜出望外。"这点东西……"我说。这时那两只狗眼巴巴地望着我，我急忙去抚摩他们，以避免尴尬。

"祝你好运。"我把手伸向他说道。

"谢谢你，愿上帝保佑你，现在我不用卖狗了。"他的笑容在渐浓的夜色中更加灿烂了。

有时，人确实比动物复杂得多，但有时他们却又很容易读懂。韦恩是个好孩子，他把狗看成是家庭成员。在我的信仰字典里，这样的人理应获得快乐。

之后，在回家的路上，我又特意从那个街角驶过。韦恩和那两只狗已经走了，但是他们却会长久地驻留在我的心间。也许有朝一日我会再次邂逅他们，那时他们会一切如意的。

Innocent Homeless

Lori S. Mohr

The hastily scrawled sign on the crumpled cardboard read: BROKE—NEED DOG FOOD. The desperate young man held the sign in one hand and a leash in the other as he paced back and forth on the busy corner in downtown Las Vegas.

Attached to the leash was a husky pup no more than a year old. Not far from them was an older dog of the same breed, chained to a lamppost. He was howling in-to the brisk chill of the approaching winter evening, with a wail that could be heard for blocks. It was as though he knew his own fate, for the sign that was propped next to him read: FOR SALE.

Forgetting about my own destination, I quickly turned the car around and made a beeline back toward the homeless trio. For years, I've kept dog and cat food in the trunk of my car for stray or hungry animals I often find. It's been a way of helping those I couldn't take in. It's also what I've used to coax many a scared dog off the road to safety. Helping needy animals has always been an automatic decision for me.

I pulled into the nearest parking lot and grabbed a five pound bag of dog food, a container of water and a twenty—dollar bill from my purse. I approached the ragged-looking man and his unhappy dogs warily. If this man had somehow hurt these crea-tures or was using them as come—ons, I knew my anger would quickly take over. The older dog was staring up at the sky, whining pitifully. Just before I reached them, a truck pulled up alongside of them and asked how much the man wanted for the older dog.

"Fifty bucks," the man on the corner replied, then added quickly, "but I really don't want to sell him."

"Is he papered?"

"No."

"Is he fixed?"

"No."

"How old is he?"

"Five. But I really don't want to sell him. I just need some money to feed him."

"If I had fifty bucks, I'd buy him." The light turned green, and the truck sped off.

The man shook his head and continued dejectedly pacing the sidewalk. When he noticed me coming in his direction, he stopped walking and watched me approach. The pup began wagging his tail.

"Hi," I offered, as I drew nearer. The young man's face was gentle and friendly, and I could sense just by looking in his eyes that he was someone in real crisis.

"I have some food here for your dogs," I said. Dumbfounded, he took the bag as I set down the water in front of them.

"You brought water, too?" he asked incredulously. We both knelt down next to the older dog, and the puppy greeted me enthusiastically

"That one there is T.C., and this one's Dog. I'm Wayne." The sad, older dog stopped crying long enough to see what was in the container.

"What happened, Wayne?" I asked. I felt a bit intrusive, but he answered me directly and simply." Well, I just moved out here from Arizona and haven't been able to find work. I'm at the point where I can't even feed the dogs."

"Where are you living?"

"In that truck right there." He pointed to a dilapidated old vehicle that was parked close by. It had an extra long bed with a shell, so at least they had shelter from the elements.

The pup had climbed onto my lap and settled in. I asked Wayne what type of work he did. " I'm a mechanic and a welder," he said,"But there's nothing out here for either. I've looked and looked. These dogs are my family; I hate to have to sell them, but I just can't afford to feed them."

He kept saying it over and over. He didn't want to sell them, but he couldn't

feed them. An awful look came over his face every time he repeated it. It was as if he might have to give up a child.

The time seemed right to casually pass over the twenty–dollar bill, hoping I wouldn't further damage his already shaky pride. "Here. Use this to buy yourself something to eat."

"Well, thanks," he slowly replied, unable to look me in the face. "This could get us a room for the night, too."

"How long have you been out here?"

"All day."

"Hasn't anyone else stopped?"

"No, you're the first." It was late afternoon and quickly getting dark. Here in the desert, when the sun dropped, the temperature would dip into the thirties.

My mind went into fast–forward as I pictured the three of them going without even a single meal today, perhaps for several days, and spending many long, cold hours cooped up in their inadequate , makeshift shelter.

Seeing people beg for food isn't anything new in this city. But this man stood out because he wasn't asking for food for himself. He was more concerned with keeping his dogs fed than with his own welfare. As a pet–parent of nine well–fed and passionately loved dogs of my own, it hit a deep chord in me.

I don't think I'll ever really know what came over me at that moment, inspiring me to do what I did next, but I just knew it was something I had to do. I asked him if he'd wait there for a few minutes until I returned. He nodded his head and smiled.

My car flew to the nearest grocery store. Bursting with urgency, I raced in and took hold of a cart. I started on the first aisle and didn't quit until I reached the other side of the store. The items couldn't be pulled off the shelves fast enough. Just the es–sentials, I thought. Just food that will last a couple of weeks and sustain their meager existence. Peanut butter and jelly. Bread. Canned food. Juice. Fruit. Vegetables. Dog food. More dog food (forty pounds, to be exact). And chew toys. They should have some treats, too. A few other necessities and the job was done.

"The total comes to $102.91. " said the checker. I didn't bat an eye. The pen ran over that blank check faster than I could legibly write. It didn't matter that the mortgage was due soon or that I really didn't have the extra hundred dollars to spend. Nothing mattered besides seeing that this family had some food. I was amazed at my own intensity and the overwhelming motivation that compelled me to spend a hundred dollars on a total stranger. Yet, at the same time, I felt like the luckiest person in the world. To be able to give this man and his beloved companions a tiny bit of something of which I had so much opened the floodgates of gratitude in my own heart.

The icing on the cake was the look on Wayne's face when I returned with all the groceries."Here are just a few things... " I said as the dogs looked on with great anticipation. I wanted to avoid any awkwardness, so I hastily petted the dogs.

"Good luck to you," I said and held out my hand.

"Thank you and God bless you. Now I won't have to sell my dogs." His smile shone brightly in the deepening darkness.

It's true that people are more complicated than animals, but sometimes they can be as easy to read. Wayne was a good person, someone who looked at a dog and saw family. In my book, a man like that deserves to be happy.

Later, on my way home, I purposely drove past that same corner. Wayne and the dogs were gone. But they have stayed for a long time in my heart and mind. Perhaps I will run into them again someday. I like to think that it all turned out well for them.

没有给您的留言

阿诺特

> 它跟主人的关系，像是传统而古板的婚姻关系，没有一丝一毫分手、离婚的念头，从一而终，狗不懂背叛、欺骗与怀疑。

——杜白

当我们收留塔德——一只波士顿狗的时候，正好在女儿家。那是一只很可爱的小狗，只有 3 个月大，他成了整个家庭关注的焦点。每天早晨，他一听到我的女儿凯拉在楼下踱步的声音，就会一直跟着她，因为他知道她要上班去了。当凯拉下班回家的时候，我们就会让他在门口等着。

3 个星期之后，我们离开了女儿的家。在旅途中，我们每晚都会让塔德和凯拉通话。在家的时候，每一次我们给凯拉打电话或是她打给我们，我们总会让塔德接电话的。他抓着话筒，专心地听着电话，试图通过电话看到凯拉。

在一个星期六，我们出去散步，凯拉打来电话，并留下一条信息。当我按键听留言的时候，塔德就站在我的身边。他竖起脑袋听着她的留言，咧着嘴朝我笑。我又给他播放了一遍。

几天之后，我在淋浴，听到答录机响了，并传来凯拉的声音。我听着她的留言一遍遍地重复，答录机又传来"留言结束"时，我感到有些奇怪。几秒钟后，凯拉的留言又开始了。

我很好奇发生了什么，于是裹着一条浴巾走出浴室，朝起居室看过去。塔德站在那里，听答录机。我停下来看着他。当留言结束的时候，他用两条后腿支撑起身子站在矮桌的边缘，伸着一只爪子拍打着答录机，留言又开始了。他蹦到地板上，开心地听着。

我告诉他"不可以"，于是把他从答录机旁边赶走，并将留言抹掉了。几天之后，我在厨房听到"没有给您的留言"。我往起居室探了探头。塔德又在玩答录机了。我看着他竖着脑袋盯着答录机看。然后他倚着桌子边站立着，并拍打着按钮："没有给您的留言"。他又转到桌子的另一端，重复着先前的动作，还是同样的结果。这使他很生气。他转身来到先前站的地方，伸着两只爪子连拍带抓地玩着答录机。"没有给您的留言"又重复起来。

我说："塔德，离开答录机。"他看了看我，然后转过身去看答录机，疯狂地拍着它。当答录机又传来同样的信息时，他跑到我的身边，然后又跑回去，等着我做些动作。我意识到他是想听听凯拉的声音，可是我已经将留言抹掉了。

晚上，我给凯拉打了电话，让她跟塔德说话，并给他留一条信息。我解释说塔德要听她的留言，但是被我抹掉了。于是当他试着再去听的时候，却听不到她的声音，感到很不高兴。

凯拉给塔德讲话，并给他留了一条特殊的留言，这样无论在什么时候，只要他想听凯拉的声音按播放就可以了。我们称之为小狗的爱，这是 21 世纪的时尚！

You Have No Messages

Zardrelle

We were visiting our daughter when we adopted our Boston terrier, Tad. An **adorable**[1] puppy, just three months old, he became the family's center of attention. Each morning, as soon as he heard my daughter Kayla moving around downstairs, he followed her all the time, because he knew she would go to work. When she came home from work, we had him waiting for her at the door.

After three weeks we left for daughter's home. On the drive, we let Tad talk to Kayla on the phone each night. Once home, every time we called Kayla or she called us, we always put Tad on. He scratched the phone and listened intently and tried to look into the phone to see her.

One Saturday, Kayla called while we were out. She left a message. Tad was standing beside me when I pressed the button to listen to the message. He listened to her talking and cocked his head, **grinning**[2] at me. I played it again for him.

A few days later, I was taking my shower when I heard the answering machine come on and Kayla leave a message. I thought it was strange when I heard her message repeat and the machine announce, "End of messages." A few seconds later Kayla's message began yet again.

Wondering what was going on, I climbed out of the shower, wrapped a towel around myself and headed into the living room. There stood Tad, listening to the answering machine. I stopped and watched. When the message finished, he stood up with his feet against the edge of the low table, reached over with one paw and slapped the answering machine. The message came on again. He dropped back on the floor and listened happily.

I told him "no," and distracted him from the answering machine while I erased the message. A few days later I was in the kitchen when I heard, "You have no messages." I headed for the living room. Tad had started the machine again. I watched as he cocked his head and looked at the answering machine. Then he stood with his feet on the edge of the table and tapped the button again: "You have no messages." He walked around to the other side of the table and repeated the process with the same results. This really **irritated**³ him. He returned to his first position, took both paws and began slapping and clawing the answering machine. It repeated: " You have no messages."

I said, "Tad, leave the answering machine alone." He looked at me and then turned back to the answering machine, digging at it furiously. When it repeated the same message, he ran to me and then ran back to the answering machine, waiting for me to do something. I realized he wanted to hear Kayla talking, but I had erased the message.

I called Kayla that night and asked her to call Tad and leave him a message. I explained that Tad had listened to her message, but I had erased it. When he tried to listen to it again and didn't hear her message, he had been unhappy.

Kayla called Tad and left a special message for him that he can play and listen to whenever he wants to hear Kayla's voice. We call it puppy love, twenty–first–century style!

1. adorable [əˈdɔːrəbl] *adj.* 可崇拜的;可爱的
2. grin [grin] *v.* 露齿而笑
3. irritate [ˈiriteit] *v.* 激怒;使急躁

思 念

纳米特·库马尔

外面下起了雨,他正在想念她——那些他们一起走过的日子,只有在那段时光中,他才有被爱的感觉。

今天傍晚的时候,他提前下班回家了,他又想起了她。实际上,她一直都在他的脑海中,即使此时他并不想念她,但是她依然在他心灵的某一个角落。然而今天,他无法将她从自己的脑海中抹去。他仍然能感受到她最后的爱抚,回忆着和她在一起时的温馨时刻。他还记得,她离开的那天,也下着雨!

他们初次相遇的那天同样下着雨,很冷,她就像一只"落汤鸡",浑身发抖地站在他的屋子外面躲雨。他将她带进了屋里,一起度过了那个夜晚。他为她准备好食物,一起共进晚餐。那个宁静的夜晚,就像她一样,他喜欢上了她。对于他的好,她也有了回应。天色已晚,外面还在下雨,于是,他给她准备了一张温暖而舒适的床。那天晚上,她住下了。他们决定,生死不离。

在以后的几个月中,他们的友情日渐浓厚。每天早上,她都会用她娇柔的声音把他唤醒,如今,这已经成了她的习惯。他们都很害羞腼腆,各自保留着一份温情。他们经常在他下班回家后出去散步。她是他唯一的朋友,她欣喜地享受着他给予的爱。每当他呼唤她时,她那绿色的双眸就会闪烁着光芒。她整天待在他的家里,期待着他在傍晚的时候回来。

有一天,他下班回到家时,他呼唤着她的名字,因为他们该去散步了,可是她没有回应。他开始到处找她,她躺在睡椅上睡着了。他爱抚着她的额头,很烫。她病了,他把她送进了医院,她被诊断出患了恶疾。当他知道她已不久于人世时,他痛苦极了。他非常爱她,用更多的时间陪伴着她,给她准备了最喜欢的饭菜,可是她日渐消瘦,几乎无法进食。

那是星期日,他正准备去教堂,却听到了她的呻吟声。他急忙冲过去看她,可是她……她已经不省人事了。他叫来了当地的医生,然而她已经走了。当天她就被下葬了。他哭了,他想念着她。那天,他甚至没有吃饭。

今天,他要去她安息的地方看望她,那个狗狗公墓,离他家并不远……

Miss Her

Namit Kumar

It was raining, he was missing her, missing the time they had spent together, the only time of his life when he felt loved.

It was afternoon, nearly twilight. He had come from his office a bit early today. She was coming to his thoughts. Actually, she was never out of his mind, he didn't miss her now, but she was somewhere at the back of his thoughts. But today he was unable to get her out of his mind. He could still feel her last touch, remember the good time they had spent together. He still remembered, the day she left him, it was raining.

It was also a rainy day when they first met. It was cold and she was all wet and shivering, standing beside his **flat**[1] for shelter. He had welcomed her in, they shared that evening. He cooked dinner for her. They had it together. It was a quiet evening, as she was, he liked her. She also had developed a liking for him as he was very nice to her. It was late and raining outside, so he made a warm and **cozy**[2] bed for her. She slept at his place that night. They had made a decision that they will he staying together.

They got closer to each other all those months of their friendship. Every morning she used to wake him up with her soft voice. By now he had developed her habit. Both of them were shy and reserved of kind. They used to go for long **stroll**[3] in the evening after he came from work. She was his only friend and enjoyed all the attention that he gave her. Her green eyes also used to twinkle even as he used to call her name. She stayed at his home all day and waited for him to return in the evening.

One day when returned from his office after work, he called her name, it was time for that walk. She didn't reply. He started looking for her all over. She was there on the couch, asleep. He touched her head, she was hot. She was ill. He took her to the hospital. She was **diagnosed**⁴ with some serious ailment. He was sad as he knew that she wasn't going to live any longer. He grew more affectionate, spent more time with her, made her favorite food but she was growing leaner and started eating less.

It was Sunday, he was about to leave for the church. He heard her moan, he rushed to see her but she was unconscious. He called the local doctor but she was dead by then. She was **buried**⁵ the same day. He cried for her as he was already missing her. He even skipped dinner that day.

Today he will go to visit her, where she is resting in peace, dogs' cemetery is not really far from his house...

1. flat [flæt] *n.* 公寓
2. cozy ['kəuzi] *adj.* 舒适的；安逸的；惬意的
3. stroll [strəul] *n.* 漫步；闲逛
4. diagnose ['daiəgnəuz] *v.* 诊断
5. bury ['beri] *v.* 埋葬；掩埋

你是我的命定天使

You Are My Fated Angel

我已经享受到了充裕的爱，谢谢你们曾经将我拥入怀中，曾经亲吻我湿湿的鼻尖，这里，将是我最完美的归宿。

寻物狗罗尔夫

佚名

狗若爱你,就会永远爱你,不论你做了什么事,发生什么事,经历了多少时光。

——杰佛瑞·麦森

在丹麦的富南岛上,每天都能看见一辆小巧的蓝色敞篷车沿着小路奔驰着。一条黑色的大狗坐在司机的旁边,仿佛在听司机的指令似的。无论何时,只要这辆敞篷车开过来,富南岛上的居民都会转过身盯着看,有一些好奇,也有一些羡慕。因为车上写着:"寻物狗罗尔夫"和一个电话号码。

是的,那辆蓝色敞篷车里的乘客就是罗尔夫,他是一只帮人们寻找失物的狗。7年间,罗尔夫和他的主人已经寻找到价值 400 000 美圆的失物了,包括手表、珠宝、工具、钱、母牛、白鹅、猪和其他的狗。那么罗尔夫的秘密武器是什么呢? 就是他那个灵敏的鼻子!

拥有这样鼻子的主人是一只 10 岁大的德国牧羊犬。这只德国牧羊犬的主人是斯文·安德森。他们每年都会接到六百到七百个这样的求援电话。他们平均 5 次中有 4 次能够顺利地按照失主的要求找到失物。

每当安德森家的电话一响,罗尔夫就立刻提高警惕,猛冲到车上,迫切地要出发去寻找失物。

一路上,斯文一遍又一遍地重复着他们即将寻找的失物的名字。因此,当他们到达事发地的时候,罗尔夫就可以马上进入工作状态。他围着事发地点打着转,又原路返回,再不停地转着。直到他在现场嗅出失物微弱的气味为止。

一年春天,我去了富南岛,打算去证实罗夫尔的侦探工作并不是某种神话。喝过咖啡,吃了些点心之后,斯文和我一边交谈一边注视着罗尔夫。那只狗看起来有些神秘,既机警又不失平静。电话铃响了,然后我就听到斯文说道:"一个钱包? 我不能保证,但是我们会尽全力帮您的。"

一个小时之后我们到达了公园,与阿克塞尔·詹森一起在树下踱步。电话就是他打的,他的钱包丢了。

大约半个小时,罗尔夫一直在漫无目的地走着"之"字路。斯文偶尔会将他叫回来或是再告诉他一些事情让他继续寻找。钱包还是没有找到。

我们来到森林的另一处。罗尔夫再一次漫步在湿软的地上用鼻子嗅来嗅去。斯文一次又一次地鼓励他。不知道过了多长时间,我注意到罗尔夫绕的圈子在变小。斯文现在站在沟渠的边上,神情紧张,好像是在下达命令,而这只有罗尔夫能够听到。

突然,罗尔夫开始在松软的地上刨着。他停了下来,四处看看,又在几步远的地方刨起来。然后他又改变主意,向右边挖去。突然,他高昂着头跑出那片沼泽地。他的嘴里叼着一个黑色的东西。那是一个钱包! 詹森惊奇而又快乐地大声叫着。

"告诉我吧,斯文,"过了一会儿,我说道,"一只狗是怎样在一个灌木丛生的大森林里,找到那个只有 5 英寸宽 7 英寸长的钱包呢? "

斯文笑着回答道:"我知道在最初的那 75 英亩地中什么也没有,因为罗尔夫对那里一点兴趣都没有。但是在沼泽地中我可以从罗尔夫的表现中看出他已经寻找到一些蛛丝马迹了。罗尔夫在 10 天前钱包丢失的地方的空气中嗅出了它的气味。"

斯文是怎样得到这样一只有着侦探般鼻子的狗呢? 他是从一窝小狗中挑出罗尔夫的,因为罗尔夫的脑袋最大,而且急切地在地上嗅来嗅去。

当罗尔夫只有 5 个月大的时候,第一次找到了一件失物。那是邻居家的手表。经过一年的细心培训,罗尔夫成为了一条职业寻物狗,时刻准备工作。

有一次,斯文接到了一个不同寻常的电话。有人在一场家畜展览上打了一个很大的喷嚏,以至于掉了一个金币。罗尔夫能够找得到吗? 当然可以了! 那枚金币离他打喷嚏的地方只有几尺远。

还有一次就是罗尔夫救了一个 11 岁的小女孩,使她免遭苛责。那个小女孩拿着祖母的手表玩,但是不小心手表掉到了一个干草堆中。大约有 50 个孩子加入到寻表的活动中,却没有找到;第二天,警察带着两只警犬过来,也以失败告终。

9天之后,罗尔夫被派去寻找。不过他对干草堆没有兴趣,却在旁边的小坑里嗅了起来。几分钟后,他就找到了那只手表。原来是有人将一叉干草堆到那个坑里了。

罗尔夫也并非一直很成功,但是每次他都很尽力,有的时候又太尽力了。斯文曾经因为罗尔夫没有找到一只手表而训斥了他。罗尔夫走了,不一会儿他就衔着那只丢失的手表凯旋而归。而在他的后面跟着一个怒气冲冲、半裸着身体的男人。那个人嚷嚷道:"我正在穿衣服,这只狗就用他的脑袋戳门,从桌子上衔起我的手表就跑,他是个贼!"

安德森的房间里从未丢失过任何东西。罗尔夫会从地上捡起硬币、钉子、扣子。斯文将一个勺子放在地板上,然后将在隔壁的罗尔夫叫过来。他命令罗尔夫躺下。我们继续交谈。罗尔夫不理解我们在说什么。几分钟之后他站了起来,将勺子衔在嘴里拿到主人的身边。

安德森与罗尔夫毋庸置疑是一对很好的搭档,并且互相理解。当罗尔夫在一次工作中失败了,斯文就会整晚不眠,脑子里反复思考着他们在事发现场的搜寻工作。经常是他起床带着罗尔夫再次回到失败地,凭借手电筒的微光在那里寻找。

"夜晚很安静,"他说道,"那是寻找东西的最佳时刻。"而且通常很成功。"当我们找到失物的时候,"他说,"再也没有比这更开心的事情了。我不知道罗尔夫和我谁更高兴。于是我会放松自己,直到电话再一次响起!"

Rolf, the Dog Who Finds Things

Anonymous

Day after day, a small blue truck speeds along the roads of Denmark's island of Funen. A big dark dog sits beside the driver, looking at him as if listening to his instructions. Whenever the truck goes by, the people of Funen turn and stare, some in wonder, others in recognition. For on its side are printed the words Sporhunden Rolf (Rolf, the Tracking Dog) and a telephone number.

Yes, the passenger in the blue truck is Rolf, a dog that is hired to find things people have lost. Within seven years, Rolf and his owner have found close to $400, 000 worth of missing items. Among them are watches, Jewelry, tools, money, cows, geese, pigs and other dogs. And what is Rolf's secret? His sensitive nose!

The owner of that nose is a ten-year-old German Shepherd. And the owner of the German Shepherd is Svend Anderson. Together they answer the 600 to 700 calls for help that they get each year. Four out of five times they find what they are asked to look for.

Whenever the telephone rings in Anderson's house, Rolf is instantly alert. He dashes to the truck, eager to be off.

On the way, Svend repeats again and again the name of what they are going to look for. So, by the time they arrive, Rolf is ready to get to work. He circles, backtracks and circles again. This he continues until he picks up the faint scent of an object lying in a spot where it doesn't belong.

One spring I went to Funen to make sure that Rolf's detective work was not some kind of fairy story. Over coffee and cakes Svend and I talked and watched Rolf.

The dog's stare was mysterious. He seemed alert yet calm. The telephone rang, and then I heard Svend saying, "A wallet? I can't promise, but we'll do our best. "

An hour later we were in a park, tramping among the trees with Axel Jensen, the man who had phoned. Jensen had lost his Wallet.

For half an hour Rolf roamed in wide, broken zigzags. Occasionally, Svend would call him back or tell him to keep looking. No wallet was found.

We drove to another part of the forest. Again Rolf roamed with his nose to the boggy earth. Svend encourage him from time to time. I don't know at what moment we began to notice that Rolf was padding about in small circles. Svend was now standing at the edge of a ditch. He was tense, as if giving orders that only Rolf could hear.

Suddenly, Rolf began to paw the soft earth. He stopped, looked about and scratched again a few feet away. Then he changed his mind and began to dig further to the right. All at once he trotted out of the bog, head high. He was holding some-thing dark in his mouth. It was the wallet! Jensen roared with surprise and joy.

"Tell me, Svend," I said later, "how on earth does a dog go about finding a wal-let five by seven inches in a huge forest covered with undergrowth?"

Svend smiled as he replied, "I knew there was nothing in the first 75 acres be-cause of Rolf's lack of interest. But in the swamp I could tell from the way Rolf act-ed that he had picked up a trail. The scent had reached him through the air from the spot where the wallet was dropped ten days ago. "

How did Svend come to own this dog with a detective's nose? He picked Rolf from a litter of seven pups because Rolf had the biggest head and snuffled more ea-gerly along the ground.

When he was only five months old, Rolf found his first missing object. It was a neighbor's watch. After a year's careful training, Rolf became a professional, ready for work.

One time Svend had an unusual call. A visitor to a cattle show sneezed so hard that he lost a gold falling. Did Rolf find it? Of course! And the speck of gold lay several yards from the place of the sneeze, in ground that had been trampled by hundreds of feet.

Another time Rolf saved an 11-year-old girl from a stern scolding. She was playing with her grandmother's fine watch when she lost it in a haystack. About 50 children were turned loose to look for it. No luck. Next day the police came with two dogs; both failed.

Nine days later, Rolf was sent for. Paying no attention to the haystack, Rolf began to nose about in a pit some distance away. He found the watch in a matter of minutes. Someone had dumped a forkful of hay from the stack into the pit.

Rolf does not always meet with success, but he tries very hard. Sometimes he tries too hard. Once when Svend scolded him sharply for failing to find a lost watch, Rolf crept away. He returned a little later in triumph with a watch in his mouth. Close behind him was an angry, half naked man. He shouted: "I was getting dressed when this dog poked his head in the door and lifed my watch from the table. He's a thief! "

Nothing ever gets lost in the Andersen house. Rolf picks up coins, nails, buttons, all without being told. To show me this, Svend put a spoon on the floor and then called Rolf in from the next room. The dog was ordered to lie down. We went on talking. Rolf couldn't stand it. In a few minutes he got up, seized the spoon in his mouth and brought it to his master.

Andersen and Rolf definitely are partners. Between them there is a deep understanding. When Rolf fails on a job, Svend lies awake that night. In his mind he goes over and over the ground they searched. Often he gets out of bed and drivers with Rolf to the scene of their failure. There they go hunting again by flashlight.

"The night is quiet, " he says, "It's a good time to hunt a thing that is lost." Often they find it. "When we find something," says Andersen, "there's no feeling like it. I don't know who is happier, Rolf or me. Then I can just relax—until the telephone rings again! "

系红蝴蝶结的小狗

佚名

不管我睡得有多沉,依旧能听到你们的呼唤,所有的死神都无力阻止我兴奋快乐地对你们摇尾巴的心意。

——尤金·奥尼尔

在我8岁那年,她走进了我的生活。父亲是在工作时发现她的。她迷路了,还很饿。父亲看了看她说:"你似乎可以拥有一个温馨的家了。"父亲打开车门,她一下子跳了进去,尾巴一路上都摇个不停。

当父亲和小狗到家时,我还在学校。父母亲已经喂过了她,还给她洗了澡。她是我的第一个宠物。

我一直都想要一只狗。父母告诉我,等我长大之后,有了责任感,就可以拥有一只小狗了,哦,我猜他们认为时间已经到了。

我从公交车上跳了下来,并不知道家里有什么在等待着我。走进家门,令我感到惊奇的是,一只黑白相间的小狗,头上还扎着蝴蝶结,朝我跑了过来,还舔了我好几下。一种十分特殊的友谊就此产生。如今,她需要一个称呼。哥哥嘲笑她,说她的尾巴很丑,不能前后摇摆,只能转圈摇摆。他用一只手指绕着他的耳朵说:"她很古怪。"因此,"古怪精灵"成了她的名字。她很聪明,我教她玩捉迷藏,一玩就是几个小时,我们每天一起学习,一起成长。

11年来,我们一直在一起,成了挚友。后来她患上了关节炎,年龄也大了。父母知道应该怎么做,可是他们让我来裁决,让我做决定。

她承受着巨大的痛楚,药物似乎也帮不上忙。她几乎不能走路了。我看着她深褐色的眼睛,明白是时候让她离开这里了。

我抱着她来到了兽医站,将她放在了桌子上。"古怪精灵"向前歪着头,舔了一下我的手,似乎在说,她明白,要坚强一些。她的尾巴依旧像往常那样转着圈摇摆着。兽医先给她打了一针镇静剂,因为最后要在她的前爪上打一针,会很痛。她先睡着了,可是尾巴还在不停地摇摆。随后,兽医在打针之前问我:"你确定吗?"我的心情十分沉重,满眼泪水,点了点头。

最后一针扎了下去。我盯着她摇摆的尾巴,几秒钟之后,尾巴不动了。兽医听了听她的心跳,说:"她走了。"我用她最喜爱的毯子将她裹住,抱了出来。

我将她带回家,埋葬在草地里,她喜欢在这里玩耍、追兔子。这是迄今为止我做过的最痛苦的事。

我有很多年没有去她的墓地了,不过最近我去了。她的墓地上长了一枝野花。我坐下来,看着在风中摇曳的鲜花,明白这就像"古怪精灵"的尾巴一样,绕着圈摇摆。现在我明白了,这位特别的朋友将会一直陪伴着我。

The Puppy with a Red Bow

Anonymous

She came into my life when I was eight years old. My dad found her at work. She was stray and starving. He took one look at her, and said, "Seems like you could use a good home." He opened up the door to his pickup and she jumped in. Her tail **wagged**[1] all the way.

I was still at school when dad arrived home with the puppy. Mom and dad fed her and gave her a bath. This would be my first pet.

I had always wanted a dog. My parents told me when I was old enough and re-sponsible, I could have one, well, I guess they figured the time was right.

I hopped off the bus, not knowing what waited inside for me. I walked through the door, and to my surprise, a white and black puppy with a red bow stuck to her head **greeted**[2] me with many puppy kisses. A very special friendship was born that day.

Now she needed a name. My older brother laughed at her and said her tail was deformed. She didn't wag her tail back and forth. but went in a circle. He motioned his finger around his ear, and said, "She's squirrelly." Thus my puppy, Squirrelly, got her name.

She was a smart dog. I taught her to play hide and seek. We would play for hours, spending our days learning and growing together.

Eleven years we were together, best of friends. Arthritis and old age set in on her. My parents knew what had to be done, but they stood back and let me find and make the decision myself.

She was suffering so much and the medicine didn't seem to help anymore. She could barely walk. I looked into those deep brown eyes and realized it was time to let her go.

I carried her into the vet's office, placed her on the table. Squirrelly leaned her head forward, gave a lick to my hand. As if to say she understood and stayed strong. Her tail was wagging in that circle as it always did.

The vet gave her a **sedative**[3] first, for the final shot was given on her front paw, and that was painful. She first went to sleep, but her tail still wagged. Then the vet asked before giving the final shot, "Are you sure?" With a heavy heart and tear filled eyes, I nodded yes.

The final shot was given. My eyes fixed upon her wagging tail. A matter of seconds and it stopped. The vet listened for a heart beat, and said, "It's over." I wrapped her up in her favorite blanket, and carried her out.

I took her home and buried her in the pasture, where she loved playing, and chasing rabbits. It was the hardest thing I had ever done.

I didn't go back to her grave for many years, but recently I went. Growing on her grave was a single wild flower. I sat and watched it swaying in the wind, and realized that it was swaying in a circle, just like Squirrelly. I know now that,that special friend will be always with me.

1. wag [wæg] v. 摇摆；摇动
2. greet [griːt] v. 问候；向……致意
3. sedative ['sedətiv] n. 镇静剂；止痛药

小 狗

佚名

> 只有狗的忠诚是坚不可破的。
>
> ——康拉得·洛沧兹

一天，一只小狗对他的妈妈说："我该怎么做，才能向我们仁慈的主人表示感谢，让自己对他有价值呢？我不能像马那样背负重物；不能像奶牛一样给他提供牛奶；不能像羊那样用自己的毛皮为他做衣服；不能像鸡鸭那样为他产蛋；不能像猫那样抓老鼠；不能像金丝雀一样为他歌唱；也不能像我们的亲戚——大黄狗一样为他赶走强盗。我就是死了，对我的主人也毫无用处，还不如大肥猪呢！我一无是处，没有存在的价值。我不知道怎样做才能引起他的关注。"可怜的小狗说着，失落地垂下头。"好孩子，"他的妈妈说，"虽然你的本领不大，但你的好心足以弥补所有的不足。深深地爱主人，并在你力所能及的范围内用各种方式向他表现你对他的爱，就会使他快乐。"

妈妈的话使小狗得到了安慰。主人过来了，小狗跑过去，舔他的脚，在他面前嬉戏，时不时地停下来，摇摇尾巴，非常恭敬而深情地看着主人。主人注意到了他，说道："哦，小费多！你真是个诚实而又可爱的小家伙。"主人边说边停下来拍拍他的头。可怜的费多高兴得几乎要发狂了。

现在，费多成了主人散步时必不可少的伙伴。他在主人身边玩耍、跳跃，用各种方式嬉闹着逗主人开心。并且，他还十分小心，以免自己的脏爪子让主人不快。他也不跟着主人走进客厅，除非受到主人的邀请。他还试着做些小事来体现自己的价值：当麻雀偷食小鸡的食物时，他会把它们赶走；当有陌生的猪或者其他动物企图进入院子时，他就跑过去对着它狂吠。他还看管鸡、鸭、鹅和猪，以免它们乱跑，尤其不准它们在花园里捣乱。不管是白天还是晚上,只要房子周围有可疑的动静,他就会提醒大黄狗。有时,他的主人会脱掉外套去田里帮工人干活,费多就会在旁边守着,不让其他人或者动物碰它。通过这种方式,他开始被认为是主人忠实的财产守护者。

有一次,他的主人生了一场大病。费多一直守候在门口,没有人可以说服他离开,甚至是进食物;当他的主人恢复,可以站起来时,费多便得到允许进入房间,他极为开心地奔向主人,那种狂喜让所有人感动不已。这使他得到了主人的钟爱。不久,他便得到了一个为主人效劳的大好机会。

那天,天气炎热,主人吃完晚饭后就在凉亭下睡觉,费多守在他旁边。凉亭破旧不堪。这只小狗非常忠实地注视着他的主人,他觉察到墙在摇晃,天花板上有些水泥掉了下来。他意识到发生了危险,便开始朝他的主人叫喊,试图叫醒他,但是没有用。于是他跳起来,轻轻地咬主人的手指。主人被叫醒了,刚跑出凉亭,凉亭便倒塌了。费多跟在主人的身后,被一些碎片砸伤了。从此以后,主人无微不至地照顾他,把他当成自己的救命恩人。就这样,小狗对主人的忠诚和爱得到了最大的回报。

The Little Dog

Anonymous

"What shall I do," said a very little dog one day to his mother, "to show my gratitude to our good master, and make myself of some value to him? I cannot draw or carry burdens like the horse; nor give him milk like the cow; nor lend him my covering for his clothing like the sheep; nor produce him eggs like the poultry; nor catch mice and rats so well as the cat. I cannot divert him with singing like the **canaries**[1] and linnets; nor can I defend him against robbers like our relation, Towzer, I should not be of use to him even if I were dead, as the hogs are. I am a poor insignificant creature, not worth the cost of keeping; and I don't see that I can do a single thing to entitle me to his regard." So saying, the poor little dog hung down his head in silent despondency.

"My dear child," replied his mother, "though your abilities are but small, yet a hearty good−will is sufficient to supply all **defects**[2]. Do but love him dearly, and prove your love by all the means in your power, and you will not fail to please him."

The little dog was comforted by this assurance; and, on his master's approach, ran to him, licked his feet, gambolled before him, and every now and then stopped, **wagging**[3] his tail, and looking up to his master with expressions of the most humble and affectionate attachment. The master observed him. "Ah! little Fido," said he, "you are an honest, good−natured little fellow! "and stooped down to pat his head. Poor

Fido was ready to go out of his wits for joy.

Fido was now his master's constant companion in his walks, playing and skipping round him, and amusing him by a thousand sportive tricks. He took care, however, not to be troublesome by leaping on him with dirty paws, nor would he follow him into the parlour, unless invited. He also attempted to make himself useful by a number of little services. He would drive away the sparrows as they were stealing the chickens' meat; and would run and bark with the utmost fury at any strange pigs or other animals that offered to come into the yard. He kept the poultry, geese, and pigs from straying beyond their bounds and particularly from doing mischief in the garden. He was always ready to alarm Towzer if there was any suspicious noise about the house, day or night. If his master pulled off his coat in the field to help his workman, as he would sometimes do, Fido always sat by it, and would not suffer either man or beast to touch it. By this means he came to be considered as a very trusty protector of his master's property.

His master was once confined to his bed with a dangerous illness. Fido planted himself at the chamber–door, and could not be persuaded to leave it even to take food; and as soon as his master was so far recovered as to sit up, Fido, being admitted into the room, ran up to him with such marks of excessive joy and affection, as would have melted any heart to behold. This circumstance wonderfully endeared him to his master, and some time after, he had an opportunity of doing him a very important service.

One hot day, after dinner, his master was sleeping in a summer–house, with Fido be his side. The building was old and crazy; and the dog, who was faithfully watching his master, perceived the walls shake, and pieces of mortar fall from the ceiling. He comprehended the danger, and began barking to awaken his master; and this not sufficing, he jumped up, and gently bit his finger. The master upon this started up, and had just time to get out of the door before the whole building fell down. Fido who was behind, got hurt by some rubbish which fell upon him: on which his master had him taken care of with the utmost tenderness, and ever afterwards acknowledged his obligation to this little animal as the preserver of his life. Thus his love and fidelity had their full reward.

1. canary [kə'nɛəri] *n.* 金丝雀
2. defect [defect] *n.* 缺点；过失；瑕疵
3. wag [wæg] *n.* (使)摇动；摇摆

宠物情缘

佚名

领养狗，也许是人类唯一可以选择亲人的机会。

——莫德凯·席格

我养了一辈子的狗。记得很久以前，我家就一直养狗。因此，我对狗的喜爱也与日俱增。那些总带给我感动的狗，有的是别人送的，有的是自己跑来的。我觉得那些自己跑来的狗很特别，他们总是让我惊喜万分，而且从他们身上我也学到了很多珍贵的东西。

当我对未来充满迷茫时，奥齐走进了我的生活。那时，不到 30 岁的我还不愿为自己的行为负起责任，内心充满了消极想法，也不愿相信任何人。

后来，在发生的一连串事情中，我认识了两个盲童。他们拥有两只漂亮的导盲犬以及，你猜得到的，奥齐！

他们告诉我他叫奥齐，大约两岁，是被从前的租户抛弃的。尽管他们一直尽力照顾他，但依然觉得那里的环境对奥齐来说不够舒适。长久以来，奥齐已经和他们形影不离，但他们真的希望他能有一个好去处。

我当时并不想养宠物，因此这是我最不愿做的事情。但为了哄这两个男孩，我走进了奥齐的房间。我叫了他，但并没有得到回应。于是，我试探说："奥齐，你愿意跟我回家吗？"一只漂亮的黑狗从床底钻了出来，他有着一双我所见过的最大的眼睛。

他走到我身边，汪汪地叫了几声。我理解他所说的意思："还等什么呢？我们走吧！"他抓住了我的心，完全打动了我。我们持久的关系从此开始了。我们安定了下来。可以说，时至今日，每当想起我们在一起的那些时光，我都会惊异于自己学到了那么多东西。

居于首位的就是无条件的爱。无论我心情如何,奥齐总会像读一本书一样来理解我。

我觉得这实在令人惊奇。

他会用自己的方式让我知道他理解我,并安慰我,以便很快治疗我受伤的心!

当我悲伤时,他会待在我的身边,凝视着我。如今,想起那种姿态,我依然会感动地落泪。他会伸出爪子,温柔地抚摸着我的脸。无论之前多么烦恼,但你可以想象得到那一刻世界会变得多么美好。

我们第一次共同经历了地震。多么难忘的回忆啊!我们被地震弄得东倒西歪,于是我抓紧奥齐躲在了门框里。我对他说,大自然母亲在打嗝。和我一样恐惧的他似乎明白我在尽力安慰他。

地震过后,我将一些行李装进袋子,放到车里。看我忙着,奥齐似乎知道我要做什么。当我准备离开时,他跳进袋子,汪汪地叫着。我明白他的意思:"嘿,不要丢下我。"

当你经历了这些时刻,就会明白那是多么特别。因为他象征着包含肢体语言在内的特殊感情纽带的形成,而且更令人无法忘怀的是这一切居然发生在一只狗的身上。

我一直认为奥齐有理解某些话的特异功能。早晨起来,我会大叫:"吃早饭了。"奥齐会马上跳下床冲向厨房。而我会假装回去睡觉。我会这样逗他两次,第三次才会说:"吃早饭了。"这时,奥齐会停下来,看着我,仿佛在说:"不!我知道你在骗人!"

一直以来,奥齐都很健康,也从不挑食。如果我喂的饭不合他的胃口,我就会说:"吃点吧,我下次再也不会买了。"惊奇的是,他真的吃了!我给他洗澡,他很乐意。

奥齐15岁时,也就相当于人类的105岁,他确实老了。他得了西特斯综合征。对公狗来说,这是一种致命的疾病。如果得不到治疗,他就无法排泄。于是当他发病时,我就必须马上带他去看兽医。就这样过了几个月,兽医才给了我有效的药,治好了他。我要确保他吃了药,并好好地照看着他。兽医说,像奥齐这样的年纪,就不要抱什么希望了。但他康复得很好。

我们居住的地方只有奥齐一只狗。说实在的,他也是唯一的宠物,因此就成了吉祥物,在邻里间很受欢迎。每当他去串门,邻居们都会很高兴地用他最爱吃的肉来招待他。

奥齐生病大约一年后,渐渐丧失了视力和听力,肠道功能也失调了。我不得不跟在他的身后清理卫生,用点滴器喂他。我明白他已经时日不多,我想让他在熟悉的环境中离去。

我们一起走过的路是那么长!生命中能够拥有奥齐,我深感荣幸。

毋庸置疑,我的确认为我们能从宠物身上学到一些东西。我从奥齐身上学到了耐心、信任和爱。当事情万分严重,你处于崩溃边缘时,帮助更艰难的人会让你忘记自己的困难。奥齐生病时,我就是这样做的。当时真是祸不单行,但我全身心地照顾奥齐,便不再老想着自己,我的压力和担忧也随之减轻了。

为了能让奥齐过得更加舒适些,我休息了一段时间。我们在一起经历了那么多风风雨雨,我理应为他做些事情。

1991年2月1日,奥齐去世了,当时他16岁。

我将他抱起,轻声地对他说,他是一个勇敢的好伴侣,但如果他必须离开我,也没有关系。我答应他,我会好好的。伴着我的许诺,他汪汪地叫着,虚弱地向我道别。

我将他火化了,然后把骨灰埋在了宠物公墓里一棵漂亮的树下。

那时,老板看到,失去一只宠物对我来说就像失去了一位亲人,于是便给我放了几天假。

我的心碎了。但我说过我会好好的,也做过承诺,因此我会继续好好生活。一转眼,10年过去了,我依然想念着奥齐。他给我的生活带来了深刻而持久的影响,因此我花了这么久的时间写下了这一切。

我感觉他从未离开过我,而且会永远活在我的心中。自从他去世后,我不得不花时间来疗养心伤。

奥齐去世几个月后,我在睡梦中听到奥齐在我的耳边汪汪地大叫。我醒来便马上闻到了烟味。炉子上的锅着火了,是奥齐将我叫醒的。

因此,所有爱动物的朋友们请记住,能与你们的宠物相伴正是因为某种机缘所在。也许,与他们相处时你就会领悟到这一点,但有时只有在失去他们时你才会明白。尽情享受与宠物们在一起的美好时光吧,你会惊奇地发现,从他们身上你可以学到许多生命的真谛。

生命中能拥有奥齐,我感到万分荣幸,万分感激。

一个下雨天,我坐在餐桌旁,整理着资料,这时奥齐已经去世一年了。

我听到了很大的"汪汪"声从后门传来。

噢!那是另一段故事了……

Ozzie

Anonymous

I have been a dog person all of my life. For as far back as I can remember as a family we always had dogs. So, overtime I have developed a great deal of respect and admiration for our animal community. Some of the dogs that have touched my life have either been given to me or have come to me on their own. For the ones that come to me out of no where I find to be a big surprise and consider these very special indeed. As I have learned some very valuable lessons from them.

Ozzie came into my life at a time when I was uncertain about my future. I was in my late 20's and going through a period where I didn't want to accept any responsibility for any of my actions. My heart was heavy with negativity and distrust.

Then through a series of events I was introduced to two blind boys who had two beautiful guide dogs and, you guessed it Ozzie!

They told me his name was Ozzie and he was about 2 years old. He had been left behind by the previous tenant. They had tried their best to care for him but felt the environment for Ozzie was not very comfortable. Over time they had become attached but really wanted to see him go to a good home.

This was the last thing I wanted as I was not ready to care for a pet. To appease the boys I went into the room where they kept him. Calling for him I didn't get any type of response. So, I started to talk to him and asked, "Ozzie, do you want to come home with me?" Out from under the bed came this beautiful black dog with the biggest eyes I had ever seen!

He came right to me and barked. I understood that to mean, "What are we waiting for? Let's go!" He had totally won me over and had wrapped his paw around my heart. It was the beginning of a very long partnership! We settled in and I must say to this day when I think back on our time together I am amazed at how much I learned about myself.

Unconditional love was at this top of the list. No matter what kind of mood I was in, Ozzie had a way of being able to read me like a book!

This was something I marveled at.

He had his way of conveying to me that he understood and would offer comfort that would heal my spirits immediately!

If I was sad he would stay next to me and look into my eyes and in a gesture that brings tears to my eyes even today. He would reach out and gently touch my face with his paw. As you can well imagine things would then be okay with the world no matter what it was that was bothering me.

We experienced our first earthquake together. What a memory that was! I grabbed Ozzie and stood inside of the door frame as we were being jostled around, I told him it was Mother Nature hiccupping and as scared as he was he seemed to know I was trying to comfort him.

After the ground stopped shaking I began to put some supplies in a duffel bag to take to my car. Ozzie seemed to watch me and what I was doing. As I was preparing to leave he got in the bag and just barked and barked. I took that to mean "Hey, you are not leaving me behind! "

It's so very special when you have these moments as it is a sure sign of a very special bond that starts to grow to include body language and when it happens with a dog it is never forgotten.

I always felt that Ozzie had an uncanny ability to know what certain words meant. Mornings I would stir and call out "Breakfast". Oz would leap off the bed and run to the kitchen. I would pretend to go back to sleep. We would play this game about two times when finally for the third time I would say "Breakfast", Oz would start to leap pause and turn to me with a look that said "Oh No! I am wise to that! "

Ozzie was very healthy all his life and not a fussy eater. If there was a type of food that I would serve him that he didn't like I would ask him to "please eat it and I would not buy it again." I was very surprised when he would eat it! I would give him a bath which was something he enjoyed.

When Oz reached the age of 15 that is seven times a human's age so he indeed was a senior! He developed a condition known as Citistus. This is fatal for a male dog if not treated as they are not able to urinate. So he would have "attacks" and I would have to rush him to the vet. It went this way for a few months until the vet was able to give me medicine that stopped the problem. I had to be sure he took the medicine and watch him very carefully. At this age the vet said to expect anything and everything but he recovered nicely.

Where we lived Oz was the only dog. In fact he was the only pet. So, he became the "mascot" and was popular with all the neighbors. He would visit and keep company with some of the tenants and they were always delighted and would give him treats his favorite being any kind of meat.

About a year after his bout with the cititstus Ozzie's sight and hearing began to go, along with losing control of his bowels. I would have to clean up after him and feed him with an eye dropper. I knew he was going and 1 wanted him to be in familiar surroundings.

It had been such a long road we had traveled! I felt so honored and privileged to have been chosen to have Ozzie become part of my life.

There is no doubt that I truly feel that we learn some of our life's lessons from our pets. From Ozzie I learned Patience, Trust and Love. The biggest lesson to me was when things get out of control and you are nearing the end of your rope, help someone who is in worse shape, then you can take your mind off yourself. This was what happened to me when Ozzie was sick. I had many problems at that time, but I focused on caring for Ozzie, and it helped me release a lot of stress and worry when I was not thinking about myself.

I took some vacation time from my job and made Ozzie as comfortable as I could. After all we had been through a lot together and he deserved it.

On February 1, 1991 Ozzie died. He was 16 years old.

I had picked him up and was whispering to him what a brave and wonderful companion he had been, but it was okay if he had to leave me. I promised him I would be okay. With that he weakly barked his goodbye.

I had him cremated and his ashes scattered under a beautiful tree on the Pet Cemetery grounds.

At the time my boss viewed a loss of a pet the same as the loss of a family member and gave me some time off.

My heart was broken in a million pieces. I said I would be okay and I had made a promise so life went on. I still miss Ozzie and it's been 10 years! He made a lasting impression and impact on my life so deep that it has taken me this long to write about it.

I feel he is always with me, and will always hold a special place in my heart that has had time to heal since his passing.

A few months after Ozzie's death I had fallen asleep and had a dream about Ozzie barking very loud in my ear. I woke with a start to the smell of smoke. I had left a pan on the stove, and Ozzie woke me up!

So, for all you animal lovers remember your pets are with you for a reason. Sometimes you discover it while they are with you and sometimes not until they are gone. Enjoy your time with your pets you will be surprised what life lessons you can learn.

I am very honored and grateful for having Oz in my life.

About a year after Ozzie's death, I was sitting at the kitchen table. It was a rainy day and I was sorting through papers.

I heard a very loud "bark" at the back door.

Ah! That's another story...

狗医生

佚名

它虽不是最好的，却是我拥有过的最好的。

——狗墓园

　　麦克法兰医生是一位兽医，在我们家乡开了一家诊所，他被当地人称为"狗医生"。我们家的狗——拉加马芬，就在他的诊所就诊。有一段时间，我们不得不严格地按照处方控制拉加马芬的饮食，而这个处方中的食物只有这个兽医院出售。有一次，我去诊所取处方食物的时候，看到我所见过的最令人难过的一幕—— 一只狗拖着他已经瘫痪的后腿向前挪动着。

　　我向接待员询问有关那只狗的情况，她告诉我他叫斯里克。两年前，人们在路边发现了他，并将他带了进来。这个可怜的小家伙在中弹之后，只能等死了。可是，"狗医生"救治了他。当他恢复后，他们决定将他留在诊所里，作为吉祥物。

　　一开始，看着他只能用前面的两条腿拖着身体在办公室里走来走去，我感到很伤心。但是斯里克的那种精神，使我每见他一次，都会觉得他的痛苦越来越少。

　　没过多长时间，拉加马芬病了，我不得不带着他去诊所。他恐惧得要死，不愿意离开家。尽管他的病使他很痛苦，但是他仍然做着殊死挣扎。在我将他关进笼子之前，他已经逃脱三次了。

　　最后，我把拉加马芬装进车里，带着他去看了"狗医生"。拉加马芬哭嚎了一路。甚至在我将笼子放到办公室的时候，他还在挣扎。在这充满了陌生的狗味和人类的气味的奇怪地方，他感到很害怕。

　　当我在屋内环视一周后，注意到斯里克坐在房间另一端的一张小狗床上。显然,他对于我给他的王国所带来的一切骚乱无动于衷,继续舔着自己的腿。

我将笼子放在地板上,填写着有关狗的病情的单子,并试着不去听拉加马芬那刺耳的求救声。

突然之间,一切都静了下来,真的很安静。不再有尖叫声,不再有嚎叫声,我一边继续心算着拉加马芬的体重,一边歪着脑袋去听,仍然是静悄悄的。

当我意识到麦克法兰医生的办公室前门仍然开着的时候,我的心里一阵恐惧。糟了,我想,拉加马芬一定是逃出他的笼子,跑到外面去了!我丢下笔,转过身朝门口跑去。还没有跑两步,我就停了下来,被眼前的一幕迷住了。

拉加马芬仍然在他的笼子里,他那粉红色的鼻子挤在笼子栏杆上。他正在平静地和斯利克相互打着狗狗们才知道的招呼。斯利克从房间的另一端走过来安抚激动不安的小家伙。斯利克,伸着那条瘫痪的后腿,鼻子也挤压着栏杆,两只狗就这样静静地坐在那里。斯利克继续以只有狗狗们才知道的方式安抚着拉加马芬。

我笑了起来,意识到在这里还有一位"狗医生"呢!

The Dog Doctor

Anonymous

Dr. McFarland, a **veterinarian**[1] who goes by the name The Dog Doctor, has a practice in my hometown, where we bring our dog, Ragamuffin. At one point, we had to put Ragamuffin on a strict diet of **prescription**[2] food, sold only at the vet's office. One time, when I went there to get a refill, I saw one of the saddest sights I have ever seen—a dog whose hindquarters were paralyzed and could get around only by dragging his back legs behind him.

I asked the receptionist about the dog. She told me his name was Slick, and that some people had found him by the side of the road a couple of years earlier and brought him in. The poor little guy had been shot and left for dead. The Dog Doctor treated him and when he recovered, they decided to keep Slick as the office mascot.

At first, it just broke my heart to see him pull himself around the office, using just his front legs. But Slick has such spirit, that each time I saw him, I seemed to notice his difficulties less and less.

Not too long ago, Ragamuffin became ill and I had to take him to the vet. The dog was scared to death to leave our house. Although he was in horrible pain from his illness, he put up a terrific fight. He fought his way out of the dog carrier three times before I could secure it.

I finally got Ragamuffin into the car and headed over to see The Dog Doctor. Ragamuffin howled and cried the whole way. Even as I carried the carrier into the office, my dog was putting up a fight. He was terrified of being in this strange place filled with new dog and people smells.

As I looked around, I noticed Slick sitting on a little dog bed across the room, **oblivious**[3] to all the commotion I'd brought into his kingdom. He ignored us, continuing to groom himself.

Setting the carrier down on the floor, I tried not to listen to Ragamuffin's strident pleas for help as I filled out the proper paperwork.

Then suddenly it got quiet. Really quiet. No more screaming. No more howls, I cocked my head to listen as I continued to calculate Ragamuffin's weight in my head. Still, silence.

A sudden fear rushed over me as I realized that the front door to Dr. McFarland's office was still open. Omigosh, I thought, Ragamuffin must have gotten out of the carrier and run outside! I dropped my pen and turned to bolt out the door. I hadn't taken more than two steps when I stopped short—captivated by the scene before me. Ragamuffin, still in his cage, had his pink nose pressed up against the bars. He was exchanging a calm little dog greeting with Slick, who had managed to crawl all the way across the room to comfort the agitated Rags. Slick, with his paralyzed hindquarters splayed behind him, pressed his nose to the bars as well. The two dogs sat quietly, Slick continuing to soothe Ragamuffin's fears in a way only another dog would know how to do.

Smiling, I realized that there was more than one Dog Doctor around this place.

1. veterinarian [ˌvetəri'nɛəriən] *n.* 兽医
2. prescription [pri'skripʃən] n. 指示；规定；命令
3. oblivious [ə'bliviəs] adj. 遗忘的；忘却的；健忘的

我的蓝眼睛男孩

亚历山德拉·曼迪斯

我的小狗名叫哈里，我们是一对亲密无间的朋友。哈里是一只重达80磅的达尔马提亚狗，当我不安的时候，他会倾听我的诉说；当我忧郁的时候，他会抚慰我，陪着我走遍各地。他对于其他的人与物从来没有像对我那样尽心尽责，因为我是他最爱的妈妈。我收养他的时候，他才8个星期左右。对他我也有同样的感情，因为他是我的蓝眼睛男孩。

在一个阳光明媚的星期日早晨，我带着哈里去了中心公园。哈里很快就挣脱了绳索的束缚，跑上了狗山，跑去和其他的城市小狗一起玩了。与此同时，他们的主人们也享受着公园里的春日。

最近，我的心情很低落，因为我失业了。那份工作我已经做了10年。和哈里在公园里玩耍，可以让我在短时间内忘记失业的不愉快，还有我那拮据的经济前景。

我站在狗山下，与其他狗主人聊天。突然，我们听到有人在喊："他在我的腿上撒尿！"我转过身一看，山顶上有一位女士正指着我的那只可爱的小狗，很显然，他就是罪魁祸首了。我有些害怕，迅速跑到山上。哈里以前从未做过这样荒谬的事情。

当我来到那位女士旁边，我马上蹲下来，抓住哈里的项圈，这样他就不可能再做出一些奇怪的事情了。那位女士弯着腰，擦着她的腿。她脱掉了鞋子，因为小狗的尿顺着她的腿流到了鞋子里。

我们同时站直了身子，很惊奇地看着对方。

"亚历山德拉！"她说道。

"瓦莱丽！"她是我的前任老板——3个月之前就是她将我从公司开除了。

我为哈里的所作所为向她道歉，不过在回家的路上，我一直笑个不停，热切地拥抱了哈里，并送给他许多香吻。哈里，当然，也摇头摆尾，因为他做了一个惊人的表演——不过，幸运的是，他再也没有那样做过了。这一天，当我一想起哈里那令人惊奇的才华——为母亲报仇，就会开怀大笑。

My Blue-Eyed Boy

Alexandra Mandis

My dog, Harry, and I are very close. Harry, an eighty–pound Dalmatian, listens to me when I am upset, comforts me when I am blue and goes everywhere with me. He cares for no other person like he does for me, his beloved mama. Having raised him since he was an eight–week–old pup, I feel the same way about him—he is my blue–eyed boy.

One beautiful Sunday morning, Harry and I went to Central Park. Harry was running off **leash**[1] on Dog Hill, along with all the other city dogs, while their owners enjoyed a spring day in the park.

I was feeling down because I had been recently laid off from the job I'd held for ten years. Being in the park with Harry was one of the ways I forgot for a while that I was out of work—and that my **prospects**[2] were not looking good in a tough economy.

I was standing at the bottom of Dog Hill talking to another dog owner when all of a sudden, we heard someone shout, "He peed on my leg!" I turned to look, and lo and behold, at the top of the hill I saw a lady **gesticulating**[3] at my beloved boy, who apparently was the culprit. Horrified, I rushed up the hill. Harry had never done anything remotely like this before.

When I got to where the woman was standing, I reached down quickly and grabbed hold of Harry's collar in case he decided to do anything else **untoward**[4]. The woman was bent over, trying to clean up her leg. She was pulling off her shoe because the pee had dribbled down her leg all the way into her shoe.

We straightened up at the same moment, and for a shocked instant, we looked at each other.

"Alexandra!" she said.

"Valerie!" It was my former boss—the one who laid me off three months before.

I apologized to Valerie for Harry's behavior, but all the way home, I laughed and laughed, and gave Harry lots of kisses and hugs. Harry, of course, was **thrilled**[5] that he clearly had pulled off a winning stunt—though, fortunately, he has never re-peated his performance. To this day, when I think about all of Harry's wonderful qualities, his "revenge for mama" still makes me laugh the hardest.

1. leash [li:ʃ] v. 以皮带束缚；束缚
2. prospect ['prɔspekt] n.景色；前景；前途
3. gesticulate [dʒes'tikjuleit] v. 做姿势表达；用手势谈话
4. untoward [ʌn'təuəd] adj. 倔强的；麻烦的
5. thrill [θril] v. 发抖

自然送来的"礼物"

C. 埃德加·霍尔

当财富消失，声誉扫地，它对你的爱依然如天空中运行不息的太阳一样永恒不变。

——《狗的礼赞》

1925 年 3 月 18 日，尽管当时的我只有 5 岁，但我仍然清楚地记得那一天席卷伊利诺伊州南部地区、被称作"小埃及"的龙卷风，而我们所居住的小煤城正巧就在龙卷风的必经之路上。狂风大作，那声音听起来像是十几辆机车呼啸而过。我们在厨房里挤成一团，声响震耳欲聋，好像要摇散我们的骨头似的。

突然，一切都结束了。那种寂静令人感到很不自然，心里充满了恐惧和不安。打开房门，母亲凝视着眼前那令人惊恐的景象，束手无措。瓦砾残骸遍地都是，道路被堵塞。受到惊吓的人们就像牛似的漫无目的地在街道上走着，不知道还能做什么。突然，一声低沉的、痛苦的呜呜声从母亲的脚下传来，打破了这陌生的寂静。

一只浑身湿漉漉的、惊恐万分的、剧烈颤抖的髦毛狗躺在门与屏风中间。

"哎呀，"母亲说着便弯下身去，"你从哪里来啊？"

那只湿漉漉的小狗胆怯地摇着他的尾巴，伸着舌头舔着母亲的手。

杰基，是我们给他起的名字。他毫无保留地接受了我们这个大家庭，而我们也慷慨地将爱施予给这只无家可归、又很幸运的小狮子狗。

几乎是立刻，我们意识到杰基是一只很独特的狗—— 一只非常聪明的狗。他那被浓密卷毛包围的、充满好奇的黑眼睛闪烁着生命的活力。

在小狗成为我们家中一员的两年后，一个流浪汉敲我们家的后门，乞讨一些食物，这种请求并没有什么特别的。因为在那些日子里，有好多流浪汉停在我们家的门前。他在门廊处等着,母亲给他拿出一碟子食物。当他坐下来吃饭的时候,我们几个男孩子就围着他,于是他开始给我们讲他所到过的地方以及见过的东西。我们都被他的故事深深地迷住了。

突然他停了下来。我们朝他凝视的地方看过去,杰基站在那里。他们互相看了很长时间,接着,那个流浪汉的脸上露出了笑意。"你这个小淘气鬼,"他说着,并用一个听上去怪怪的名字叫着杰基。"你在这里做什么呢?"

这只小狗也异常兴奋,围着那个流浪汉又叫又跳,似乎没有停下来的意思。毫无疑问,他一定认识那个流浪汉,而且很熟悉。经过一番爱抚和交谈,那个老流浪汉发出一声简短的命令。马上,杰基就控制住了自己的情绪,然后温顺地躺在那个老人的脚边。

"孩子们,你们是从哪里捡到这只狗的?"那个流浪汉问道。

"1925年的那场大飓风过后,我们发现他就夹在门与屏风之间。"我的哥哥说道。

"是啊,这样就说得通了,"那个流浪汉说,"1925年,我正和一个马戏团在密苏里州。那场飓风的威力很大,整个大帐篷都被扯成了碎条,一切东西都被毁了。

"当时,这只小狮子狗是一只一流的表演狗。他非常值钱,保险金就高达几百美圆。他真是一只幸运的小狗啊。被刮了这么远,还没有受伤。"

突然,那个流浪汉问道:"孩子们,你们有没有一个铁环?"

"当然有了,我给你拿一个。"我的哥哥说着便很快跑回家拿了一个铁桶,将其中的一个铁圈摘下来,又迅速跑了回来,递给那个流浪汉。

流浪汉的那双被破旧帽子遮掩的蓝色眼睛闪烁着光芒。他那长满浓密灰色胡须的脸上露出了微笑。

"看好了,"他说着,"除非你们这些孩子去过马戏团,否则你们肯定没有看过这些。"

他走到院子里,举着那个铁环,离地大概有2英尺高。

"准备好,"他冲着杰基说道,仍然用着那个听起来很怪的名字。杰基兴奋地颤抖着。随着命令,他一跃而起,穿过了那个铁环——向前,然后向后。流浪汉继续发出命令,他猛地穿过那个铁环,来回跑着。他先是用后面的两条腿跳着舞,然后是前腿。那个见多识广的老流浪汉让杰基表演马戏团中的绝技,我和哥哥们看得都发愣了。

"他的反应在一些表演上有些迟钝了,但是他肯定还没有忘记。"那个流浪汉说着。"又能够在一起了,这真是太棒了。又回想起了以前,是不是啊,小朋友?"他一边深情地说着一边拍着杰基的头。

于是流浪汉站了以来,脸上露出一种被遗弃的表情。"我想我最好还是离开吧。"他喃喃自语道,头慢慢地转向大门。杰基毫不犹豫地跟在他的脚后。

"杰基,回来!"我们三个齐声喊道,然而我们的话没起一点作用,眼泪滑下脸颊。我们知道,我们已经失去了他。

那个流浪汉停下来,低着头看着杰基说道:"我们在马戏团的日子结束了,朋友,再也不会回来了,而且这种居无定所的生活不适合你,你最好还是留在这里。"杰基站在那里,看着那个流浪汉离开,但仍准备随他而去。

到了门口,那个人静静地站了几秒钟,然后慢慢地转过身。"孩子们,马戏团的狗是永远不会忘记那顶大帐篷的,"他说着,"你们最好把他锁在屋子里直至明天早晨,我不希望看到你们失去他。"

我们依照他的话做了。杰基和我们在一起生活了很多年,尽管他是我们曾经养过的小狗中最聪明的一只,但我们再也没有劝说他表演马戏团的绝技了。我们认为最好还是将那个流浪汉的话记在心里,让他永远忘却在马戏团的日子。

Natural Gift

C. Edgar Hall

March 18, 1925. Though only five years of age, I well remember the day the great tornado swept over "Little Egypt", as the southern tip of Illinois is called. The little coal—mining town in which we lived lay directly in its path. The howling wind sounded as if a dozen locomotives were roaring past. We huddled in the kitchen as the roaring filled our ears and seemed to shake our very bones.

Suddenly it was over. The quietness felt unnatural and an eerie, uneasy feeling gripped us. Opening the door, my mother stood transfixed as she gazed upon the aw—ful scene. Debris lay everywhere. The street was impassable. People, some obviously in shock, milled around like cattle, unsure of what to do. The strange silence was suddenly broken by a subdued, pitiful whining at Mother's feet.

Trembling violently, a wet and frightened little poodle lay wedged between the door and the screen.

"My stars," my mother said, bending over, "Wherever did you come from?"

The bedraggled little dog timidly wagged his tail and began licking Mother's hand.

Jacky, as we named him, accepted our large family without reservation. We in turn lavished our love upon the displaced but lucky little poodle.

Almost immediately we realized Jacky was an exceptional dog—a very smart one. Surrounded by masses of curly hair, his dark inquisitive eyes sparkled with life.

The little dog had been a part of our family for about two years when a hobo knocked at the back door and asked if we could give him something to eat. The re—quest wasn't at all unusual. In those days, many hobos stopped at our corner. Mother brought a plate of food to the porch where he waited. As he sat down to eat, we boys gathered around him. He began telling us all the places he'd been and the many things he'd seen. We were spellbound by his tales.

All of a sudden he stopped. We looked in the direction he was staring, and there stood Jacky. For several moments they looked at one another. Then a huge smile came across the old hobo's face.

"You little rascal," he said, calling him by some strange–sounding name. "What are you doing here?"

The little dog became hysterical with joy. He was all over the hobo, barking and jumping as if he would never stop. There was no doubt he knew the hobo and knew him well. After caressing and talking to Jacky, the old hobo uttered a brief command. Immediately, Jacky controlled his enthusiasm and lay down obediently at he old man's feet.

"Boys, where did you get this dog?" asked the hobo.

"We found him lodged between the door and the screen during the big tornado of '25," said my brother.

"Yes, sir. It adds up," said the hobo."I was with a circus in Missouri in March of '25. That was sure some blow. The big tent was ripped to shreds. Everything was demolished.

"This poodle was the number–one top show dog. He's so valuable he was in–sured for hundreds of dollars. Lucky dog, he is. Blowed all that distance and not get–ting hurt.

Suddenly the hobo asked, "Do you have a barrel hoop, boy?"

"Sure, I'll get you one," said my brother. Running quickly to an old barrel, he lifted off one of the steel bands. He dashed back and handed it to the hobo.

From beneath his old battered hat the hobo's blue eyes sparkled. A smile broke through his heavy gray beard.

"Watch this," he said."Less you boys been to a circus you ain't never seen any–thing like this."

He walked out into the yard and held the loop a couple of feet above the ground.

"Get ready," he said to Jacky, again using that strange-sounding name. Jacky trembled with excitement. On command he sprang forward and leaped through the loop—forward, then backward. As commands continued, he hurled through the hoop, turning end over end. He danced on his hind legs, then on his front legs. My brothers and I stared in awe as the knowledgeable old hobo put Jacky through his circus tricks.

"He's a little rusty on some of 'em, but he sure ain't forgettin' any of it." said the hobo. "Sure is great bein' together again. Brings back memories, don't it little friend?" he said fondly as he patted Jack's head.

Then with a forlorn look about him, he straightened up. "I guess I best be goin'. " he mumbled and headed slowly towards the gate. Without hesitation, Jacky followed at his heels.

"Jacky, come back! "all three of us called. But it did no good. Tears trickled'down our cheeks. We knew we had lost him.

Then the hobo paused. Looking down at Jacky, he said, "Our circus days is over, friend. Over and done. And the tramping life's no life for you. You best stay here." Jacky stood, watching the hobo walk away, still poised to follow.

Reaching the gate the man stood motionless for several seconds, then slowly turned around. "Boys, a circus dog never forgets the big top," he said. "You'd better lock him in the house till morning. I'd hate to see you lose him. "

So we did. Jacky lived with us for many years, and although he was the smartest dog we ever had, we could never persuade him to perform circus tricks again. We figured he'd taken the hobo's words to heart and put his circus days behind him once and for all.

查理

佚名

> 我很高兴当时我决定和这只卷毛狗共度晚年，因为它不仅与我分享了它的生命，而且确实也做到了使我健康地活着，与它分享我的生命。
>
> ——狗迷

我不想写有关查理的故事，因为我知道我会哭。他离开我们已经很长时间了，但是他依然在我的心里。读过其他一些有关狗的优美的故事，于是我决定把查理的故事写下来，他也需要被人们记住。

我该从哪里开始讲述有关查理的故事呢？从他那小哈巴狗的鼻尖到他那来回摇摆的尾巴稍看来，他并没有什么独特之处，只是一只狗而已。漂亮，是我对他唯一的描述了，尽管他是一只流浪狗，却有着皇室般的仪态。他有着银灰色的长毛，脖子下面还点缀着一团白色的斑纹，犹如一颗璀璨的星星。因此我几乎能够想象得出来，他的一个祖先具有"波斯公主"的血统。

查理非常爱我们，不过他大部分时间是在宽容我们。我和女儿想抱他、依偎他时，查理就一直忍耐着直到我们放开他，他才跑走。另一方面是因为我的丈夫查尔斯，很明显，他对查理没有一点兴趣，而且还经常发表评论说狗没有任何价值。我通常会想他对查理的愤恨，是否因为查理以他的名字命名却没有征求他的意见呢。

我曾经听说，在一个家庭中狗只会选择依恋一个人，而令大家吃惊的是，查理选择的是查尔斯。每天晚上查理在吃完饭之后，都会花大约一个小时的时间来舔舐自己，然后跳到我丈夫的腿上，打起了小盹。他们谁也不理睬谁，只是彼此忍耐着。

如果女儿或是我试着将他抱起来，他就会快速逃走，径直跑到我丈夫那里——最不欢迎他的地方。查理还是一个杂技演员，当查理轻轻地趴在躺椅的后背，然后从我的丈夫的头上跳过，落在他的腿上时，有好几次，我的丈夫差点被吓得心力衰竭。而查理每次这样做的时候，我的丈夫都没有准备好应该如何对付头顶上的袭击。

而只有一项游戏是查理愿意跟我和女儿一起玩的，而这还要哄着他才能玩呢。我们站在查理的面前，来回摆动我们的睡衣。查理的尾巴也会跟着来回摇摆。然后他就会摆出一副准备攻击的姿势前后摆动着。最后，我们尖叫着在房间里穿来穿去，而查理则在我们后面疯狂地紧追不舍。

我认为查理特别不喜欢女性。我雇了一个女清洁工，一个星期来打扫一次卫生。查理很明确地表现出对她的憎恶。一天早上，在我还没有换好工作服的时候她就来了。她走到楼上去拿床单。查理躲在一间卧室的门后等着她。这场偷袭来得非常迅速，而结果是传来一阵令人毛骨悚然的尖叫声。从那天起，在清洁工来之前我一定会事先确保查理没有在房间里。即便如此，查理也没有放过她。他知道清洁工一定会到外面倒垃圾。查理很耐心地等着，然后再一次偷袭了她。现在，那个清洁工都不愿意去外面倒垃圾了。

查理以他自己喜欢的方式生活。如果他想过得浪漫些，就会到附近寻找异性同伴。我的姐姐有一只母狗，她想要查理和她家的狗狗交配。当时机成熟的时候，我抓着查理，将他放在车里带到姐姐家。到了之后，我们将库房的门锁上，然后站在后面观看那浪漫的一幕。我从未听到过这样的咆哮声！他们在车底走来走去、上窜下跳，听起来好像在彼此厮杀。我想，这次是肯定成功不了的。查理竟然拒绝她的狗，这让姐姐很愤怒，她说道："很显然，你的狗是个同性恋。"

"不，不是那样的，"我回应道，"查理只是有些挑剔而已。我们只是需要将一个纸袋子套在你家狗的头上，那样就好了。"

我和查理回到了家，彼此都有些生气。到此为止吧，我再也不会让查理处于如此可笑的境地了。几个星期之后，姐姐给我打来电话，说她家的狗生了一只小狗，而且看起来真的很像查理！

查理渐渐衰老了，动作也相对缓慢了很多。当他看到一只小鸟栖息在附近，就只是满意地摇着尾巴，并不冲上去捕猎。他也不再与我和女儿做游戏了。我可以从他的眼里看出有些事情不对劲了。在兽医所里给他做了全身检查,医生告诉我查理患了肾功能衰竭。他建议让查理从痛苦中解脱出来,因为现在他已经无药可救了。

将这个消息告诉我的女儿并不是一件容易的事情。她还是一个十几岁的孩子,让查理安乐死对于她来说是一件不可思议的事。她每天都会带着查理去医院输液。这样过了将近一个月,查理没有什么好转。我在储藏室给查理做了一张小床,他原来的那个稍高一点的床也不再用了,因为查理太虚弱了,下不了床。他只有在去医院的时候才下床。

我和丈夫都知道,我们应该结束查理的痛苦,但是女儿会哭,这使得我们一再放弃这个念头。可是我再也不能让一只动物长时间地遭受这样的痛苦了。查理需要离开,我们必须让他离开了。

甚至是我的那位声称不喜欢查理的丈夫也下定决心要好好地安葬查理,并开始给查理做棺材了。后来查理走出了储藏室,这是两个多星期以来他第一次出来。他慢慢地走向我,我将他抱起来,放在我的腿上,这是他第一次让我抚摸他而没有试图逃走。我们就这样坐着,好像过了很长时间。然后查理决定离开了。他慢慢地走向门后,当我让他出去的时候,他走到平台停顿了一会儿,看着我的丈夫给他做的棺材。他走下台阶,又转过身,再看了我一眼,然后就走了。

查理知道离开的时候到了,他向我们道别,然后做了上帝创造出来的所有生灵都会做的事,他走到他的安睡之地,安息了。他的棺材成了一个花坛,多年来一直是那些漂亮的天竺葵的家园,不过这样做的真正目的是希望我们能够想起查理。

175 <<<<*The Soul of the Dogs*

Charlie

Anonymous

I didn't want to write Charlie's story because I knew I would cry. He's been gone for a long time, but he's still close to my heart. After reading some very good stories about other dogs, I decided that Charlie needed to be remembered too.

How do I begin to tell about Charlie? He was all dogs, Charlie, from the tip of his little pug nose to the end of his ever-swinging tail. Beautiful, is how I'd describe him. Though just a stray, he had the carriage of royalty. His long gray silvery coat spotted a white star just under his neck. I could almost imagine that one of his forefathers belonged to a Persian Princess.

Charlie loved us as much as a real dog can love humans, but mostly he tolerated us. My daughter and I wanted to hold him and snuggle. Charlie would tolerate it just so long then he was gone. On the other hand, my husband Charles, clearly had no interest in Charlie, and often made the comment that dogs weren't good for anything. I often thought that his resentment towards Charlie had something to do with the fact that Charlie was named after him without his consent.

I once heard that dogs will chose only one person in a family with which to bond, and to everyone's dismay, Charlie choose Charles. Each night Charlie would finish his meal, and then preen himself for nearly an hour before he jumped into my husband's lap for a long nap. Neither touched the other, they simply tolerated one another.

If my daughter or I tried to pick Charlie up and hold him, he would quickly scamper away and head straight back to where he was least wanted. Charlie was an acrobat too. Many times my husband was almost brought to the point of heart failure when Charlie would silently creep up behind the recliner and Jump over my husband's head and into his lap. As many times as Charlie did this, my husband was never prepared for the overhead assault.

There was one game that Charlie would play with my daughter and me, but it took a lot of coaxing. We would stand in front of Charlie and wave our nightgowns back and forth. Charlie's tail would begin to sway. Then he would position himself for the launch by rocking back and forth. Eventually it ended with us screaming and running through the house and Charlie in hot pursuit.

Charlie had a particular dislike for all females, I think. I had a lady that came once a week to clean for me and Charlie clearly hated her. One morning she arrived before I had finished dressing for work, and had gone upstairs to get the bed linens. Charlie was waiting for her just inside one of the bedroom doorways. The attack was swift and the result was a blood curdling scream that would wake the dead. From that day on, I had to make sure that Charlie was out of the house before the cleaning lady would come inside. Even so, Charlie was not through with her. He knew that she would come outside to put the trash in the garbage can. Charlie was patient. He wait-ed, and he nailed her again. Now she refused to take the trash out.

Charlie lived his life pretty much like be wanted to. If he felt romantic, he would scour the neighborhood in search of female companionship. My sister had a female dog and wanted Charlie to mate with her dog. When the time was right, I grabbed Charlie, put him in the car and off we went to my sister's. Once there, We closed the garage door and stood back to watch the romantic scene unfold. Never have I heard such growling and howling! Back and forth they went under the cars, darting here and there, it sounded like they were killing each other. This is not working I thought. Indignant that Charlie would spurn her dog, my sister said, "Your dog is obviously gay."

"No, not at all," I replied, "Charlie is just a little choosy. We just need to put a small paper sack over your dog's head, that's all."

Charlie and I went home, both a little huffy. So much for that. Never again would I put Charlie up for such ridicule. Then, weeks later, my sister called. Her dog had one lone pup, and he looked exactly like Charlie!

As Charlie got older he slowed down considerably. He was more content to just swish his tail when he saw a bird perched nearby, rather than go for the hunt. He didn't play the game with my daughter and me anymore. I could look into his eyes and tell, something was just not right. After a thorough examination from the vet, I was informed that Charlie had kidney failure. His advice was to put Charlie out of his misery. There is no cure he said.

Breaking the news to may daughter was not easy. She was a teenager and to put Charlie to sleep was unthinkable. Everyday she would take Charlie to the vet and he would be hydrated. This went on for almost a month, but Charlie didn't get better. I made a bed for Charlie in the utility room, his litter box sat unused. Charlie was too weak to get out of his bed. The only time he was out of it was when he went to the vet.

My husband and I knew that we should put Charlie out of his misery, but my daughter cried and put up such a fuss that we always backed off. Never again will I let an animal suffer that long. Charlie needed to go. We needed to let go.

Even my husband who professed not to like Charlie was determined to properly bury him. He had begun to build a coffin for Charlie. Then out of the blue Charlie came out of the utility room. It was the first time he had walked in over two weeks. He slowly came up to me and I picked him up and held him in my lap. For the first time he let me stroke his head without trying to get away. We sat like this for what seemed like a very long time, and then Charlie decided it was time to leave. Slowly he walked to the back door and as I let him out, he paused on the deck as he watched my husband building the coffin. He descended the steps, then turned and looked back at me one more time, and then he was gone.

Charlie knew that his hour had come, he said his good-byes, and then did what all of God's creatures do. He went to his resting place. His little coffin was turned in-to a planter and over the years has been the home for many bright geraniums, but its true purpose is to remind us of Charlie.

一只名字叫 B 的狗

苏珊娜·斯特罗

狗的寿命太短,这真的是它们唯一的缺点。

——艾格尼斯

　　当我还是个 15 岁的小女孩时,有人给我介绍了一只小狗,这一品种在这个国家是非常少见的。他和我之间有着一种非比寻常的关系。他有着极强的个性,与之相配的是一个响亮的名字,开头字母是 B 的单音节词。每天放学后,我都会去看 B。在我离开这只狗上了大学之后,我非常思念他。10 年过去了,我联系了一个饲养员,向他咨询有没有像 B 一样的小狗。他告诉我,在纽约,单亲家庭是不可以饲养这种名贵的小狗的,他们是不会卖给我的。

　　我在动物保护协会进行了登记,第二天,我就去另一个国家出差了。在那里,一个朋友把我带到他母亲在乡下的房子里过周末。她在很久之前就想见我了。用餐的时候,我们总会给这位女士留个空位,然而她一直没有出现。星期日,我们开车沿着林荫小道回城时,碰到一位高个子的女士,她表情严肃,身旁各有一只我看到过的最高大、最安静的拾猎。她就是朋友的母亲,于是朋友把我介绍给了她,我并没有从车里走出来,她只和我说了几句话。我看着她说话,她对明显的缺席情况并未做出任何解释,而她说话时的那种感觉却震撼着我,那是自从和 B 在一起的学校生涯之后就不曾拥有的。这个女人和她身旁站着的两只狗之间仿佛有一种相似的难以言表的亲缘关系。我们作了简短的告别之后,就开车走了。

　　回到纽约大概两个星期之后的一个早上,我接到一个电话,是动物保护协会打来的。他们说有一只大品种的小狗可以领养,其实他们对此已经放弃了,因为在出国的这段时间里,他们打来的所有电话都无人接听。我给单位打电话请了病假,坐上出租车直接去了东河边 92 大街上的动物保护协会。有人带着我进了一个小房间，里面有一只小笼子。这个房间仿佛就是一个由三层狗舍组成的巨大迷宫。笼子的最底层躺着一只无精打采的小黑狗。他有点瘦弱，除了这一点，他看起来像极了 B。我打开门，蹲了下去，想尽可能让他到我的面前来。严厉而又冷漠的管理员断言我不会收养这只小狗，因为这只狗太有个性了。我站了起来，转过身打算离开。正在这时，不知道什么原因"本"这个字眼出现在我的脑海里。我高声地叫出这个名字，停下脚步原地不动。就在我转身的时候，小狗从笼子里跳了出来，向上一跃，将他的爪子搭在我的脖子上，舔着我的脸，还把我的前胸尿湿了。尽管管理员坚决反对，我还是领养了这只名叫本的小狗。

　　那天夜里，我们很晚才回到公寓，我感觉精疲力竭。我把门打开，看到有一个蓝色的航空信封放在门槛上，看起来像是一封投错了的信件。小狗停住脚步，一直盯着那封信，直到我将它拣起来，他才进屋。他就坐在那里，看着我读信。这封信是朋友的母亲写的，就是那个住在国外的女人。她为唐突地写这封信而向我致歉，因为我们几乎不认识。她从她的儿子那里知道了我的住址。她这样写道，因为某些原因，她感到必须要告诉我，她的本——就是我在林荫道上看到的那只狗——突然死去了。她只想让我知道这件事。结尾处，她询问我是否已经找到了我一直在寻找的小狗。

The Dog Was Named B

Suzanne Stroh

As a girl of fifteen, I was introduced to a dog whose breed was quite rare in this country. There was a **remarkable**[1] chemistry between us. He had a strong personality and a strong name to go with it, a single syllable beginning with the letter B. I visited B every day after school. When I went off to college and left the dog behind, I missed him terribly. Ten years later, I contacted a **breeder**[2] and inquired about a puppy like B. I was told that a single-parent household in New York City was no place for such a noble puppy. They refused to sell me one.

I registered with the SPCA and left the next day on a business trip to another country. There a friend took me to spend a weekend at his mother's country house. She had wanted to meet me. A place was always set for her at mealtime, but the woman never showed up. On Sunday, driving down a wooded lane on our way back to the city, we came upon a very tall, austere woman flanked by two of the biggest, quietest retrievers I had ever seen. She was my friend's mother. My friend introduced me to his mother. I didn't get out of the car, and she only said a word or two to me. As I watched her speaking, giving no excuse for her **conspicuous**[3] absence, I was struck by a feeling I had not felt since my school days with B. There seemed to be the same inexplicable kinship between the woman and the two dogs standing beside her. We said a brief good-bye and drove on.

Back in New York one morning about two weeks later, I got a call from the SPCA. There was a large-breed puppy for adoption. They had given up on me because I had not answered any of their previous calls during the time I was out of the country. I called in sick at work, got a taxi, and went straight to the SPCA on Ninety-second Street by the East River. I was taken to a small cage in a small room in a vast maze of kennels three levels high. Lying there listlessly on ground level was a black puppy.

Except for the fact that he was emaciated, he looked exactly like B. I opened the door, crouched low, and tried everything I could to get the puppy to come to me. The stern, emotionless orderly assured me I did not want this puppy. He was obviously too willful. I stood up and turned to leave. But then for some reason the word "Ben" came to mind. I said the name aloud and stopped in my tracks. When I turned around, the puppy bounded out of the cage, jumped up, put his paws around my neck, licked my face, and peed all down my front. Against the protestations of the orderly, I adopted the retriever puppy called Ben.

Both of us were exhausted when we arrived at my apartment late that night. When I opened the door, a blue air-mail envelope, apparently mis-delivered, was lying on the threshold. The puppy froze, fixed on the envelope, and would not enter my apartment until I had picked it up. He sat and looked at me as I read the letter. It was from my friend's mother, the one who lived abroad. She apologized for writing, since we hardly knew each other. She had gotten my address from her son. For some reason, she wrote, she felt that it was important to tell me that her dog, Ben, the one I had met on the wooded lane, had died suddenly. She just wanted me to know. She asked, in closing, if I had found the puppy I had been looking for.

熱詞空間

1. remarkable [riˈmaːkəbl] *adj.* 不平常的；平凡的
2. breeder [ˈbriːdə] *n.* （动物）饲养者；种畜
3. conspicuous [kənˈspikjuəs] *adj.* 显著的

礼物

> 对于我来说,那是我们一家共同的新生活的完美开始,就像我一直梦寐以求的那样——
> 我和丈夫,还有我的狗。
>
> ——狗迷

对于丈夫的逝世,斯特拉早有心理准备。自从医生发出癌症晚期的通知起,他们便不得不正视那必然的结局,只好努力争取共度更多的生命余光。善于理财的戴夫病逝后,斯特拉并未增添新的经济负担,只有可怕的孤独……她的生活失去了方向。

他们选择不要孩子,但他们的生活充实而富足。他们对繁忙的工作心满意足,彼此和谐地相处着。他们曾经有过许多朋友,而现在,"曾经有过"已经成为一个常用词了。失去你倾心相爱的人已经够痛苦的了。但在过去的几年中,她和戴夫经历了朋友和亲戚的相继辞世。他们都到了人体机能开始衰竭的年龄。是该正视现实,面对死亡了,人都有那个年龄——年老体衰的时候!

戴夫过世后的第一个圣诞节就要到了,斯特拉深知今年的圣诞节她不得不一个人过。

她用颤抖的手指把收音机的音量调低,圣诞音乐渐弱成柔和的背景音乐。斯特拉惊讶地发现有邮件到了。她皱着眉头强忍着关节炎的巨痛,弯身去拾地上的那些白色信封,然后坐在钢琴凳上拆开来看。里面装的大多是圣诞节贺卡。她用那忧郁的眼神,微笑地看着贺卡上那些熟悉的传统圣诞节景象和爱意绵绵的寄语。她把刚收到的圣诞卡与以前的全部放到钢琴顶上,它们是整栋房子里唯一的节日装饰品。离圣诞节不到一个星期了,可她根本没有心思去装饰不再有任何意义的圣诞树,甚至不愿将戴夫亲手做的马厩模型摆出来。

突然间，一种极度难耐的孤单感吞噬着斯特拉，她用手捂着脸，任凭泪水不停地流。她该怎样熬过圣诞节和此后的漫漫寒冬呢？

门铃突然响了，斯特拉克制住小声的惊叫。谁会来探望她呢？她把木门打开，怀着惊恐的心情透过玻璃风门往外看。一个陌生的年轻人站在前廊，双手捧着一个大盒子，几乎把他的整个脸都挡住了。她看了看那人身后的车道，可是他的小汽车也丝毫没有表明来者的身份。年迈的斯特拉鼓起勇气，把门稍稍开了一点缝，那人侧了侧身，站到了一边，并隔着门缝说道："您是桑霍普太太吧？"

她点了点头。他接着说，"这儿有您的一盒东西。"

好奇心驱散了戒备心。她把门打开，那人走了进来，他微笑着把盒子小心翼翼地放到地上，然后直起身从口袋里掏出一个半露在外边的信封。那人递给她信封时，从盒子里传出一个声音。她吓了一跳。那人笑着连连道歉，他俯下身来，打开纸箱上的盖，让她看。

是一只狗！确切地说，那是一只金黄色的拉布拉多小猎犬。年轻人抱起那只小狗，解释说："这是给您的，夫人。"那个小家伙从拘禁中获释，高兴地不停地扭动着身体，欣喜若狂地舔着年轻人的脸。"我们本应在圣诞夜把他送来的，"因为要设法让下巴躲开小狗的湿舌头，他说话有些困难，"可养狗场的人明天就开始放假了，希望您不要介意我把这份礼物提前送到。"

斯特拉惊讶极了，以至于不能保持清醒的头脑来思考问题，就连话都说不利索了，她结结巴巴地问："可是……我不……我的意思是……谁……？"

年轻人把小狗放在他和斯特拉之间的门垫上，并用一个手指碰了碰她手里的那个信封。

"这儿有封信，信上差不多解释了一切。买这只狗时，他还在妈妈的肚子里呢。他是特意为圣诞节准备的礼物。"

那陌生人转身要走，斯特拉急忙问道："可是……是谁买的啊？"

他停在门口，答道："是您的丈夫，夫人。"说完就走了。

一切都写在信里。那熟悉的字体一映入眼帘，斯特拉就把小狗忘到了九霄云外，梦游似的挪到窗前的椅子旁边。她努力将热泪盈眶的双眼睁开，仔细读着丈夫写给她的这封信。他在去世的前三周就写好了这封信,并把他留给了养狗场主,要他连同狗一起作为他的最后一个圣诞礼物送给她。整封信洋溢着爱与希望,他要她坚强,给了她鼓励与忠告。他发誓要等着她,直到来到他的身边。他送来这只小狗,就是想让他陪着她,直到两人再次相聚。

读到这里,斯特拉才忽然想起那只小狗,她吃惊地发现他正静静地望着她,气喘吁吁的小嘴像是在滑稽地笑着。斯特拉把信搁在一边,伸手去够那金黄色的毛毛团。他比她想象的要轻,大小和重量就跟沙发垫差不多,软软的、暖暖的。她把他搂在怀里,他舔着她的颚骨,然后舒舒服服地蜷入她脖颈的凹陷处。温情的交流又使她禁不住潸然泪下,小狗乖乖地一动不动,任由她哭泣。

最后,斯特拉把小狗放在膝盖上,一本正经地看着他。她匆匆地拭去面颊上的泪水,勉强露出笑脸。

"小家伙,我想以后的日子该咱俩一起过了。"小狗吐出粉红的舌头,喘着气似乎在表示同意。斯特拉开心地笑了,目光移向旁边的窗子,夜色已经降临。透过漫天飞雪,她看到邻居们的屋顶边缘上挂着明亮的圣诞彩灯。《普天同庆》的旋律也从厨房传入她的耳朵。

刹那间,斯特拉觉得自己完全沉浸在一片幸福祥和的美妙感情中,像是被爱意盈盈的怀抱包围着。她的心吃力地跳动着,不是因为悲伤和孤独,而是因为欣喜和惊异。以后她再也不会感到孤独寂寞了。

斯特拉又把注意力转到小狗身上,对他说:"小家伙,知道吗,地下室有个盒子,我想你会喜欢的。里面有一棵圣诞树,还有一些装饰物和彩灯,你一定会特别特别喜欢的! 我想那个旧马厩模型我也是可以找到的。怎么样,咱俩下去找找吧? "

那只小狗似乎听明白了她的话,高兴地叫着表示同意。斯特拉起身把小狗放在地上,然后他们两个一起向地下室走去,为共同的圣诞节而做准备。

Present

Anonymous

Stella had been prepared for her husband's death. Since the doctor's pronounce-
ment of **terminal**[1] cancer, they had both faced the inevitable, striving to make the
most of their remaining time together. Dave's financial affairs had always been in order. There were no new burdens in her widowed state. It was just the awful alone-
ness... the lack of purpose to her days.

They had been a childless couple by choice. Their lives had been so full and
rich. They had been content with busy careers and with each other. They had many
friends. Had. That was the operative word these days. It was bad enough losing the
one person you loved with all your heart. But over the past few years, she and Dave
repeatedly coped with the deaths of their friends and relations. They were all of an
age—an age when human bodies began giving up. Dying. Face it—they were old!

And now, approaching the first Christmas without Dave, Stella was all too aware
she was on her own.

With shaky fingers, she lowered the volume of her radio so that the Christmas
music faded to a muted background. To her surprise, she saw that the mail had arrived. With the **inevitable**[2] wince of pain from her arthritis, she bent to retrieve the
white envelopes from the floor. She opened them while sitting on the piano bench.
They were mostly Christmas cards, and her sad eyes smiled at the familiarity of the
traditional scenes and at the loving messages inside. She arranged them among the
others on the piano top. In her entire house, they were the only seasonal decoration.
The holiday was less than a week away, but she just did not have the heart to put up
a silly tree, or even set up the stable that Dave had built with his own hands.

Suddenly engulfed by the loneliness of it all, Stella buried her face in her hands and let the tears come. How would she possibly get through Christmas and the winter beyond it!

The ring of the doorbell was so unexpected that Stella had to stifle a small scream of surprise. Now who could possibly be calling on her? She opened the wooden door and stared through the window of the storm door with consternation. On her front porch stood a strange young man, whose head was barely visible above the large carton in his arms. She peered beyond him to the driveway, but there was nothing about the small car to give a clue as to his identity. Summoning courage, the elderly lady opened the door slightly, and he stepped sideways to speak into the space. "Mrs. Thornhope?"

She nodded. He continued, "I have a package for you."

Curiosity drove caution from her mind. She pushed the door open, and he entered. Smiling, he placed his burden carefully on the floor and stood to retrieve an envelope that protruded from his pocket. As he handed it to her, a sound came from the box. Stella jumped. The man laughed in apology and bent to **straighten up**[3] the cardboard flaps, holding them open in an invitation for her to peek inside.

It was a dog! To be more exact, a golden Labrador retriever puppy. As the young gentleman lifted its squirming body up into his arms, he explained, "This is for you, ma'am." The young pup wiggled in happiness at being released from captivity and thrust ecstatic, wet kisses in the direction of the young man's face. "We were supposed to deliver him on Christmas Eve," he continued with some difficulty, as he strove to rescue his chin from the wet little tongue, "but the staff at the kennels start their holidays tomorrow. Hope you don't mind an early present."

Shock has stolen Stella's ability to think clearly. Unable to form coherent sentences, she stammered, "But... I don't... I mean... who...?"

The young fellow set the animal down on the doormat between them and then reached out a finger to tap the envelope she was still holding.

"There's a letter in there that explains everything, pretty much. The dog was bought while his mother was still pregnant. It was meant to be a Christmas gift."

The stranger turned to go. Desperation forced the words from her lips. "But who... who bought it?"

Pausing in the open doorway, he replied, "Your husband, ma'am." And then he was gone.

It was all in the letter. Forgetting the puppy entirely at the sight of the familiar handwriting, Stella walked like a sleepwalker to her chair by the window. She forced her tear-filled eyes to read her husband's words. He had written the letter three weeks before his death and had left it with the kennel owners, to be delivered along with the puppy as his last Christmas gift to her. It was full of love and encouragement and admonishments to be strong. He vowed that he was waiting for the day when she would join him. And he had sent her this young animal to keep her company until then.

Remembering the little creature for the first time, she was surprised to find him quietly looking up at her, his small panting mouth **resembling**[4] a comic smile. Stella put the pages aside and reached for the bundle of golden fur. She thought that he would be heavier, but he was only the size and weight of a sofa pillow. And so soft and warm. She cradled him in her arms and he licked her **jawbone**[5], then cuddled into the hollow of her neck. The tears began anew at this exchange of affection and the dog endured her crying without moving.

Finally, Stella lowered him to her lap, where she regarded him solemnly. She wiped vaguely at her wet cheeks, then somehow mustered a smile.

"Well, little guy, I guess it's you and me." His pink tongue panted in agreement. Stella's smile strengthened, and her gaze shifted sideways to the window. Dusk had fallen. Through fluffy flakes that were now drifting down, she saw the cheery Christmas lights edging the roof lines of her neighbors' homes. The strains of Joy to the world floated in from the kitchen.

Suddenly Stella felt the most amazing sensation of peace and benediction wash over her. It was like being enfolded in a loving embrace. Her heart beat painfully, but it was with joy and wonder, not grief or loneliness. She need never feel alone again.

Returning her attention to the dog, she spoke to him. "You know, fella, I have a box in the basement that I think you'd like. There's a tree in it and some decorations and lights that will impress you like crazy! And I think I can find that old stable down there, too. What d'ya say we go hunt it up?"

The puppy barked happily in agreement, as if he understood every word. Stella got up, placed the puppy on the floor and together they went down to the basement, ready to make a Christmas together.

1. terminal ['tə:minl] *adj.* 末期的
2. inevitable [in'evitəbl] *adj.* 不可避免的；必须的
3. straighten up *v.* 好转；直起来；改正；清理
4. resemble [ri'zembl] *v.* 像；类似
5. jawbone [dʒɔ:bəun] *n.* 颚骨；下颚骨
6. decoration [ˌdekə'reiʃən] *n.* 装饰；装饰品

和狗的对话

佚名

在这个世界上，一个人唯一不自私的朋友，唯一不抛弃自己的朋友，唯一不忘恩负义的朋友，就是他的狗。

——狗迷

那天，我走进火车站的一个酒吧，要了一杯啤酒，独自坐了下来，开始思索，我想人类的孤独感是一种必然，也是一种悲惨。刚开始我想到自然界存在着某种必然，并因此感到欣慰，但是我继而想到不能这样想，人类的灵魂需要其他的东西。我用了好长时间思索其他的词汇，这时，命运之神或是某个福星把一只长毛茶色且油光闪亮的狗送到我的面前。

如果说每个国家都有属于自己的狗，那么英国人的狗是最好的，因为她们最快活、最友善。但是，我遇到的这只狗，就算是与英国狗相比，也是格外聪明和友善——尤其是友善。她轻轻一跳，跳到了我的腿上，安稳地卧在那里，用她那可爱的右前爪小心翼翼地触摸着我的胳膊，算是自我介绍，她的目光可爱而无暇，看了我一眼，接着偷偷地微笑了一下，算是接受我了。

受到这样亲近的问候，没有人会不做出反应的。所以我伸出手去抚摩阿玛西亚(我正因为这个名字才有了这番幻想)，尽管我的动作是出于尊重和对陌生人的礼貌，但很快我们之间产生了亲密感，我为能在西南部 99 路的地铁终点站，找到这样的好朋友而高兴。然后，我从抚摸到说话(当然是以恰当的方式)，我说，"阿玛西亚，最漂亮的狗，你想得到爱抚，为什么偏偏选中我呢? 你认为我是所有生灵的朋友吗? 还是你自己特别孤单(尽管我知道你的可爱的家离此不远)? 还是因为动物和人类一样拥有同情心? 那么你为什么要这样做呢? 会不会因为我太傻了，问这样的问题，却不愿意接受上帝赐予的美好事物呢？"

阿玛西亚回应了我提出的问题，她咕噜咕噜地叫着，闭着眼睛，对我们的相遇表示非常惊喜。

"阿玛西亚，你永远都不会离开我的。"我说，"你睡吧，我要陪在你身边，我永远坐在这里，我把你抱在怀里，任你做最美丽的梦，没有任何东西能够将我们分离，我的阿玛西亚。我是你的人，你是我的狗，从现在一直到最完美的安宁。"

接着，阿玛西亚再次站了起来，轻盈、小心地跳到地板上，那动作可爱得犹如波浪。她就这样慢慢离开了，头也不回。她另有打算，当她端庄地走到她要找的门时，一个身材矮小的人弯下身去抚摸她的头后部，她说着："汪！汪。"她甚至没有看他一眼，只是蹭蹭他的腿，以表达她单纯而深沉的爱，并以此来表达友谊的圣洁与不朽。

A Conversation with a Dog

Anonymous

The other day I went into the bar of a railway station and, taking a glass of beer, I sat down at a little table by myself to meditate upon the necessary but tragic isolation of the human soul. I began my meditations by consoling myself with the truth that something in common runs through all nature, but I went on to consider that this cut no ice, and that the heart needed something more. I might by long research have discovered some third term a little les **hackneyed**[1] than these two, when fate, or some other fostering star, sent me a tawny silky, long–haired dog.

If it be true that nations have the dogs they deserve, then the English people deserve well in dogs, for there are none so prosperous or so friendly in the world. But even for an English dog this dog was exceptionally friendly and fine—especially friendly. It leapt at one graceful bound into my lap, **nestled**[2] there, put out an engaging right front paw to touch my arm with a pretty timidity by way of introduction, rolled up at me an eye of bright but innocent affection, and then smiled a secret smile of approval.

No man could be so timid after such an approach as not to make some manner of response. So did I. I even took the liberty of **stroking**[3] Amathea (for by that name did I receive this vision), and though I began this gesture in a respectful fashion, after the best models of polite deportment with strangers, I was soon lending it some warmth, for I was touched to find that I had a friend; yes, even here, at the ends of the tubes in Southwest 99. I proceeded (as is right) from caress to speech, and said, "Amathea, most beautiful of dogs, why have you deigned to single me out for so much favour? Did you recognize in me a friend to all that breathes, or were you your-self suffering from loneliness (though I take it you are near your own dear home), or is there pity in the hearts of animals as there is in the hearts of some humans? What, then, was your motive? Or am I, indeed, foolish to ask, and not rather to take whatev-er good comes to me in whatever way from the gods?"

To these questions Amathea answered with a loud purring noise, expressing with closed eyes of ecstasy her delight in the encounter.

"You will never leave me, Amathea," I said. "I will respect your sleep and we will sit here together through all uncounted time, I holding you in my arms and you dreaming of the fields of Paradise. Nor shall anything part us, Amathea; you are my dog and I am your human. Now and onwards into the fullness of peace."

Then it was that Amathea lifted herself once more, and with delicate, discreet, unweighted movement of perfect limbs leapt lightly to the floor as lovely as a wave. She walked slowly away from me without so much as looking back over her shoulder; she had another purpose in her mind; and as she so gracefully and so majestically neared the door which she was seeking, a short man standing at the bar said, "Bark! Bark!" and stooped to scratch her gently behind the ear. With what a wealth of sin-gular affection, pure and profound, did she not gaze up at him, and then rub herself a-gainst his leg in token and external expression of a sacramental friendship that should never die.

1. hackneyed ['hæknid] *adj.* 不新奇的；陈腐的；常见的
2. nestle ['nesl] *v.* 舒适地坐定；偎依
3. strok [strəuk] *v.* 抚摸

我的一位朋友

J. B. 卡林顿

我第一次看见他，就被他朦胧的眼神吸引住了。那是一双忧郁的眼睛，会使你想到古老的哀痛、古老的梦境以及古老的生命秘密。毫无疑问，那就是他灵魂的窗口。我们很快成了熟客，我注意到，他对亲和的语言反应迅速，而且对任何小事都抱有热切的兴趣。

我们很快就从熟客发展成了好朋友，经常一起散步。不管什么时候，他都沉默寡言，仅仅能从他的行为举止可以确定他正在享受乡村小道的美景，我习惯欣赏他的快乐、他的友谊、他那成为一位朋友的感觉。很明显，他的心里没有诡计，有他的陪伴，我多年来的压抑感都会消失。我也可以放缓步伐，感受奔跑和跳跃的刺激，让一切苦闷随风飘散。当哀伤的眼睛闪烁着光芒时，当每一个步伐都出卖了喜悦时，我无法平静，我听到了歌声，我感受到年老的皱纹体会着新的跃动。至少这是在我和我的朋友一起散步的时候。

有时我看到他安静地、忧虑地坐在那里，好像是在眺望远处蓝色山岗以外的东西，我希望我能够读懂他的想法，希望能从他忧郁的棕色眼睛中探究他的心思。那信赖而又无助的眼神一直很吸引人。他依赖人类的仁慈，我不认为有谁会粗鲁地对待他，或是在进餐时，有他在旁边，而不愿与他共享。他感激的态度从不夸大，或是你觉得他仅仅是因为有好处才表示友善，其实许多人在他们寻找好处时都会很和善。他们对待亲和言语的感激程度超过了得到任何其他礼物。他因相信人类是友好的而感到幸福。你们一定遇到过这样的人。我并不是特指那些哀诉者和乞求者，但是他的付出、友谊和爱的真诚、仁慈之心只要求有一个善意的回报。

我的朋友曾经是一个流浪者，我认为他的历程主要是寻找富有同情心和友好的伙伴。他很快就可以注意到他的接近得到了理解，于是他的整个状态从哀伤转到喜悦和朝气。我坦白对他的友谊的依赖，这让我很满意。我很高兴我跟他同属一个类型，我们能够相遇和互致祝福，一起散步，不用他的支言片语，我们都可以意识到我们满意于彼此的世界。

对于我们来说，过去的日子充斥着哀伤的回忆。真正的朋友很少，在这个现代化生活的重压下，正直、率真的灵魂很容易被遗忘。当然，麦克只是一只狗，但是我不得不相信狗是有灵魂的，通过我们对他们那种真诚的爱和信任所做出的回应，我们自己也会变得越来越好。

A Friend of Mine

J. B. Garrington

The first time I met him I was impressed by the far–away look in his eyes. They were such sad eyes, eyes that made you think of old sorrows, old dreams, old **mysteries**[1] of life. They were certainly the windows of his soul. We were soon on familiar terms and I noticed a quick response to a kindly spoken word, a manner that expressed keen interest in any small attention.

Our mere **acquaintance**[2] developed early into a warm friendship and we had numerous walks together. He was ever a silent friendship and only by his manner were you sure he was enjoying the beauty of the country roads. I used to enjoy watching his enjoyment, his feeling of companionship, his sense of being in friendly company. There was no guile in his heart, evidently, and with him I often forgot the pressing cares of the years. I, too, could walk with a lighter step, feel the impulse to run and jump and let cold care go hang. When sad eyes sparkles and every step betrays enjoyment it's hard to be a clam and not hear singing voices, feel new thrills in old veins. At least this is the way it always seemed to me when I walked with my friend.

I've seen him sitting quietly, **pensively**[3], as if trying to look beyond the distant blue hills, and I wished I could read his thoughts, and fathom the soul in those sad brown eyes. They were always appealing, the eyes of a trusting helpless one, one dependent on human kindness, and I couldn't think of anyone wanting to be rude to him, or being unwilling to share a friendly meal if he happened to be around when the dinner bell rang. He was so appreciative of attention, he never overdid it, or made you feel that he was only nice for what there was in it. So many can be nice when they are looking for some profit. This fellow was more thankful for a kind word than for any other gift. He simply couldn't be happy without believing the human world was a friendly one. You have met this kind. I don't mean the whiners, the fellows that beg, but the genuinely kind soul that gives himself and his friendship and love and only asks a return in kind.

My friend was ever a wanderer and I thought his wanderings were chiefly in search of sympathetic and friendly companionship. He was quick to see when his advances were understood and then his whole manner changed from one of sadness to one of joy and animation. I confess I liked his friendship. It flattered me. I was glad I was one of his sort, and that we could meet and exchange greetings, walk the roads together, and without a word on his part, be conscious we were enjoying each other's society.

The older years are so full of sad memories for all of us. True friends are few and the honest simple souls are easily forgotten in the stress of life these modern days. Of course Mike is only a dog, but somehow I can't help believing that dogs have souls and that our own are made better by our response to their honest love and faith.

1. mystery ['mistəri] *n.* 神秘的事物；神秘
2. acquaintance [ə'kweintəns] *n.* 相识；熟人
3. pensively ['pensivli] *adv.* 沉思地；焦虑地

颂狗

乔治·格雷厄姆·维斯特

　　在这个世界上，一个人最好的朋友可能会背叛他，并成为他的敌人。他悉心关爱的儿女可能会忘恩负义。那些我们最亲、最爱的人，那些我们用我们的幸福和良好的名誉来信任的人，都可能会背叛你。

　　一个富人可能会变得一贫如洗，或许在他最需要安慰的时候，朋友们会离他而去。一个人的名誉，可能会断送在考虑欠周的一瞬间。那些在我们成功的时候和我们在一起时对我们尊敬有加的人，或许就是当失败的阴云降临在我们头顶上时首先进攻我们的人。在一个私欲横流的世界中，或许有一个唯一的、慷慨的朋友是绝对不会抛弃你的，那个绝对不会忘恩负义或是背信弃义的朋友就是狗。

　　狗始终会陪在主人的身边，无论主人富有与否，健康与否。每当寒风凛冽、大雪纷飞时，他会睡在冰冷的地板上，只要能陪在主人的身边。他会亲吻没有食物可以给他的主人的手。他会舔舐在严酷的世界中所遭遇到的创伤和痛处。他会在贫穷的主人睡觉时守护着主人，就像守护着王子一样。

　　当所有的朋友抛弃主人时，他依旧陪在他的身边。不管主人飞黄腾达还是名誉扫地，他始终像太阳按着轨道运行一样地对主人付出他的爱。如果主人运气不好、遭到社会抛弃、无亲无故、无家可归时，忠实的狗只会要求与他一起面对、共御强敌。当最后一幕来临时，主人走了，尸体被安放在冰冷的土地里，虽然其他所有的朋友都已经离他远去，但是有一只狗总会陪在他的墓旁，他的头趴在两只爪子之间，眼神忧郁，却时刻保持警觉——即使主人走了，可是狗的忠实与真诚依然长存。

A Tribute to the Dog

George Grham Vest

The best friend a man has in this world may turn against him and become his enemy. His son or daughter whom he has reared with loving care may prove ungrateful. Those who are nearest and dearest to us, those whom we trust with our happiness and our good name, may become traitors to their faith.

The money that a man has may lose. It flies away from him, perhaps when he needs it most. A man's reputation may be sacrificed in a moment of ill–considered action. The people who are prone to all on their knees to do us honor when success is with us may be the first to throw the stone of malice when failure settles its cloud upon our heads. This one absolute, unselfish friend a man may have in this selfish world, the one that never deserts him, the one that never proves ungrateful or treacherous, is his dog.

A man's dog stands beside him in prosperity and in poverty, in health and in sickness. He will sleep on the cold ground when the wintry winds blow and the snow drives fiercely, if only he can be near his master's side. He will kiss the hand that has no food to offer. He will lick the sores and wounds that come in the encounter with the roughness of the world. He guards the sleep of his pauper master as if he were a prince.

When all other friends desert, he remains. When riches take wings and reputation falls to pieces, he is as constant in his love as the sun in its journey through the heavens. If fortune drives the master forth, an outcast in the world, friendless and homeless, the faithful dog asks no higher privilege than that of accompanying him to guard him against danger, to fight against his enemies. And when the last scene of all comes and death takes the master in its embrace and the body is laid away in the cold ground, no matter if all other friends pursue their way, there by his graveside will the noble dog be found, his head between his paws, his eyes sad but open in alert watchfulness—faithful and true even in death.

喜爱飞翔的狗

利·安妮·雅舍维–布赖恩特

很显然,库伯渴望飞翔的愿望是从小就有的。为了在工作时防止他来找我麻烦,我在他的床边围了栅栏,可是从那一天起,他就证明了这并不能阻止他飞出地球的英勇尝试,这里没有什么可以让他停止。

就是库伯的那种想要高飞的精神使他成为我的第一只狗。而其他剩下的小狗,也只是一些可爱的传统小狗。然而,库伯并没有用鼻子碰触我或是拥抱我。他只是将自己放到沙发顶上,在人们阻止他之前,从上面跳下来。他"噗"的一声下来了,像是从肚子里吐出一口气。7个星期大的狗腿并不能支撑在他的高空降落。我知道这一点,可是他不知道。

我在他娇小的耳朵旁边低声说:"我喜欢你,小飞狗。你难道不想和我一起回家吗?"他专心地看着我,好像在说:"好的,但是不要指望我能够遵从牛顿的万有引力定律!"

当我们一回到家,库伯的飞行训练就开始了。他视察了地形,确定最高点,在他以后的日子里只要是能到的地方,他就会跑到最高点,然后从那里飞下来。几个月中,房间的地板上到处都是枕头、毯子、毛巾,只要我能找到的任何柔软的东西,都是他着陆的垫子。

当他5个月大的时候,有一天,我回到家里发现库伯站在餐厅的中央,他脸上的表情好像在说:"系好你的椅带,我要乘它飞下来了!"我飞快地朝他跑过去,想抓住他,但是我还没有喊出"不要在餐厅里飞"时,他已经着陆了。

从那天起,每天早晨在我上班之前,都会将餐厅的椅子放在桌子下面。当朋友和邻居问我为什么要这样做时,我只是耸耸肩,说这是德国的一个旧习俗。

我希望库伯能够喜欢去做一些正常的德国猎犬的活动——嗅着地毯、散发出一些古怪的味道、朝着松鼠狂叫以及学习服从两种语言,但是这一切在他的身上都没有体现出来。"我该拿你怎么办啊,小飞狗?"每天晚上我下班回家都会这样问他。

我给他找来一条形状类似飞机的狗绳,并祈祷他能够足够坚强,在他飞行的时候不要伤害到自己。

在他5岁时的一天,库伯蹦到躺椅的后背,然后飞走。当他着陆的时候,他伤到了背部。我匆忙地带着他去看兽医,医生说他伤到了椎骨间的软骨,需要进行手术。我的心都要碎了。我想,如果我是一个好的狗妈妈,就应该找到一种方法,让他停止飞翔。

库伯从手术中恢复过来,摇着尾巴,眼睛里也闪耀着叛逆的光芒。因为他在手术之后做了一个溜冰的倒立动作,使他轻松了许多。我听到医生最后说:"不要再让他从高处跳跃了!"

我试着去做,也确实做了。3个星期,只要我不在他的身边,我就会将库伯锁在一个板条箱里。他看着我,仿佛在说:"你怎么能剥夺我的自由、我的灵魂、我赖以生存的条件呢?"他是对的,我圈起来的不仅仅是他的肉体,还有他的灵魂。所以,当他更强壮一些的时候,我开始让他走出箱子。我给他一套严厉的警告,规范他的行为,不过我和他都知道,他是不会遵守的。

时光流逝,库伯发现很难放弃这个习惯。当他老得不能够轻易地攀上沙发时,我给他做了一个斜坡。当然,首先他用这个斜坡作为他起跳的跳板。而且,就像以前那样为自己感到自豪。

在他13岁的时候,库伯背部的尾端瘫痪了,他再也不能跳跃了。库伯飞翔的日子结束了,我不知道他和我谁更伤心。

兽医也查不出任何毛病,于是我给库伯买了一辆K-9手推车——一种专门为狗狗准备的轮椅。"现在,库伯,"我说,"我去寻找带有翅膀的手推车,但是他们没有。所以我想从现在起你不得不待在地上,做一只普通的狗。"

几分钟之后,当我在厨房做饭的时候,起居室里传来一个奇怪的声音。我跑过去,看到库伯站在斜坡上。在任何人阻止他之前,他转过来,全速滑了下来,他的耳朵飞了起来。

库伯仍然可以飞翔。这些我应该更能理解,不应该去怀疑他翱翔的精神。而他一旦着陆在他的新"飞行器"上,他就会滑到斜坡上,再次起飞,就像莱特兄弟那样,对自己的这项功绩他感到很高兴。

库伯利用他身后的纺纱用的轮子在斜坡上飞上飞下,又度过了最后的三年时光,直到他从这片土地上永远离开。

The Dog Who Loved to Fly

Leigh Anne Jasheway–Bryant

Copper's yearning to fly was apparent from puppy–hood, but From the day he cleared the rail of the **playpen**[1] that was supposed to keep him out of trouble while I was at work, to his last valiant effort at leaving the Earth, there was no stopping him.

It was Copper's soaring spirit that made me choose him as my first dog. The rest of the litter was cute in the traditional puppy way. Copper, however, would have nothing to do with touching noses or **cuddling up**[2] next to me. He managed to drag himself up on top of the sofa, and before anyone could stop him, off he jumped. He landed with a "poof!" as the air escaped from his tiny belly. Seven–week dog legs aren't meant to support skydiving. I knew that, but he didn't.

I whispered in his little ear, "I like you, flying dog. Do you want to come home with me?" He stared at me intently as if to say, Okay, but don't expect me to obey Newton's Law of Gravity!

Copper's pilot training began the moment we arrived home. He surveyed the landscape, identified the highest elevations and spent his days scampering up and flying down from everything he could. For months, every floor in the house was covered with pillows, blankets, towels and anything soft I could find to **cushion**[3] his landings.

One day when he was about five months old, I came home to find Copper standing in the middle of the dining– room table with that look on his face that said, Fasten your seat belts and hang on for the ride! I ran as fast as I could toward him to catch him, but he hit the ground before I could yell, "No flying in the dining room!"

From that day on, I put the dining–room chairs upside down on the table every morning before I went to work. When friends and neighbors asked why, I'd just shrug and say it was an old German custom.

I wished Copper could be happy doing regular dachshund stuff—sniffing the carpet, rolling in strange smells, barking at **squirrels**[4] and learning to be disobedient in two languages, but it just wasn't in him. "What am I going to do with you, flying dog?" I'd ask him every night when I got home from work. I got him a dog tag shaped like an airplane and prayed that he was strong enough not to get hurt in his airborne escapades.

One day when he was five, Copper jumped up on the back of the couch and flew off. When he landed, he hurt his back. I rushed him to the vet, who said he'd blown a disc and would need surgery. My heart was broken. If I had been a good dog-parent, I thought, I'd have found a way to stop him from flying.

Copper pulled through the surgery with a wagging tail and that same rebellious spark in his eyes. And now that he had a reverse Mohawk from the surgery, he looked even more independent. The last words I heard at the vet were, "Don't let him jump off things!"

I tried, really I did. For three weeks, whenever I wasn't with him, I kept Copper in a crate. He gave me a look that said, How can you take away my freedom, my spirit, my reason for living? And he was right, I had grounded not only his body, but his spirit as well. So as he got stronger, I started letting him out of the crate. I gave him a stern warning to behave himself, but he and I both knew he wouldn't.

As the years went by, Copper found it harder to get around. When he got too old to easily clamber onto the sofa with me, I built him a ramp. Of course, the first thing he did was to use it as a springboard to fly from. And he was just as proud of himself as he ever was.

Then at age thirteen, Copper's entire back end became paralyzed; he couldn't jump at all. I don't know who was sadder that Copper's flying days were over, him or me.

The vet couldn't find anything wrong, so I got Copper a K-9 cart, a little wheelchair for dogs. "Now, Copper," I said, "I looked for a little cart with wings, but they just didn't have one. So I guess you'll just have to stay on the floor like a real dog from now on."

A few minutes later, while I was in the kitchen cooking dinner, I heard a noise in the living room. I ran in and saw Copper at the top of the ramp, with that look in his eye. Before anyone could stop him, he turned and wheeled down the ramp at full speed, his ears flying behind him.

Copper could still fly. I should have known better than to doubt his soaring spirit. And once he landed his new "aircraft," he wheeled back up the ramp and took off again, as **elated**[5] by his accomplishment as the Wright Brothers must have been.

Copper flew up and down that ramp with his wheels spinning behind him for almost three more years before he escaped the bonds of Earth once and for all.

1. playpen ['pleipən] *n.* 婴儿用围栏
2. cuddle up *v.* 蜷缩着睡
3. cushion ['kuʃən] *v.* 加衬垫
4. squirrel ['skwirəl] *n.* 松鼠
5. elated [i'leitid] *adj.* 兴高采烈的；得意洋洋的

萨米的笑脸

盖尔·戴尔哈根

　　在我很小的时候，朱丽姨妈有一只名叫萨米的小狗，他是一只黑色的混血吉娃娃，舌头几乎和身体一样长。萨米会跑到你的身旁舔你的脸，然后在你明白发生了什么之前又跑到你的另一边。这只可爱的小黑狗总是用"狗狗的笑脸"来欢迎你。家里的每一个人都知道萨米和朱丽阿姨很亲密。

　　一天中午，我去拜访姨妈。我们穿戴整齐，准备出发。我忘了要去哪里，但是我清楚地记得当时我们都急匆匆的。长久以来，我们家有个习惯，就是如果你不能提前15分钟进入一个场合，那就算迟到了！就像平常一样，时间是最重要的。然而，萨米却无所事事，唯一能让他感到有趣的就是得到一些注意力。

　　"不，萨米，我们不能玩了。"我的姨妈责备道，"现在我们必须走了！"

　　而问题是我们不能"走"，因为朱丽姨妈的假牙忘记放在哪里了。我们寻找她的牙齿时间越长，到的就越晚，朱丽姨妈变得更生气了，而萨米看起来就越想得到更多的注意力。我们忽略了萨米的叫声，因为我们都在疯狂地寻找着丢失的假牙。

　　最后，朱丽姨妈到达了她忍耐的极点，放弃了。她"砰"的一声坐到楼梯的台阶上，哭了起来。我坐在她的旁边，用一种超过8岁智龄的方式安慰她："没关系，朱丽姨妈，不要哭。我们还能去的，只是笑不出来了。"而这使她哭得更伤心。

　　就在那时，萨米发出了几声尖叫，而这次是从楼梯的顶上传来的，然后就安静了。当我们转过身去看她想要什么的时候，我们都大笑了起来。萨米露出了一张大大的"笑脸"，衔着朱丽姨妈的假牙站在那里，尾巴摇得有每小时100英里那么快。她那闪闪发光的眼睛很明显在告诉我们：半个小时前我就告诉你们了——我知道你的牙齿在哪里！那一幕，在30年之后，还会让我开怀大笑。

Sammy's Smile

Gayle Delhagen

When I was a child my Aunt Julie had a dog named Sammy, a little black Chihuahua mix with a tongue as long as her body. Sammy could run up one side of your body, lick your face clean and run down the other side before you knew what happened. This adorable black dog always greeted you with a "doggy smile." Sammy owned my Aunt Julie, and everyone in our family knew it.

One afternoon I was visiting my aunt. We were all dressed up and going out. I don't remember the occasion, but I do remember that we were in an awful rush. My family comes from a long line of people who feel that if you're not fifteen minutes early for an event, you are late! As usual, time was of the essence. Sammy, however, wasn't in any rush. The only thing Sammy was interested in was getting some attention.

"No, Sammy, we cannot play," my aunt scolded, "We have to go! Now! "

The problem was that we couldn't "go," because Aunt Julie had misplaced her false teeth. The longer we searched for her teeth, the later we got for the event and the angrier Aunt Julie became—and the more attention Sammy seemed to demand. We ignored Sammy's barking, as we looked frantically for the missing dentures.

Finally, Aunt Julie reached her breaking point and gave up. She plunked herself down at the bottom of the stairs and cried. I sat next to her, counseling her with that special brand of wisdom eight-year-olds possess. "It's okay, Aunt Julie, don't cry. We can still go, just don't smile," I said, which made her cry even harder.

At that moment, Sammy gave a few shrill barks, this time from the top of the stairs, and then was quiet. As we tuned around to see what she wanted, we both exploded into laughter. There stood a "smiling" Sammy—with Aunt Julie's false teeth in her mouth—her tail wagging a hundred miles an hour. The message in her sparkling eyes was obvious: I've been trying to tell you for a half hour—I know where your teeth are! A vision that, thirty years later, still makes me laugh out loud.

狗狗在法庭上的一天

玛丽·K.希蒙斯

> 不养狗的人才养孩子。狗儿引领我们进入一个更慈爱，更温柔的世界。
>
> ——哈妮

在我长大之后，距我居住的地方约0.25英里的地方有一个火车道交叉口。我们的狗——兰尼，有一个非常恼人的坏习惯：当火车通过并鸣响警笛时，兰尼就会狂叫不已，这可能是因为他的听觉非常灵敏吧，不管他是在屋外还是在屋内。他一直狂吠着，直到火车驶过。有些时候，当火车在远处顺风驶过时，他也会狂吠不已。我们已经学会忍受他骚动的犬吠声了，因为我们非常爱我们的宠物。

一天早晨，我们正在吃早餐，在一声骇人的撞击声后，我们听到了火车紧急刹闸的尖锐的鸣叫声。哥哥冲出屋，跑向小路的尽头，发现在巨大的火车头排障器的旁边，挤满了骚乱的人。一辆车的零件掉得到处都是。很不幸，汽车司机当场死亡。

回到屋里，我们猜测撞车之后有人给当地的救援队打了电话。但我们马上又说："兰尼没有叫！警笛肯定没有响起！"

在这种情形下，哥哥忽然意识到，他伙伴的父亲还在车上，现在这个悲伤的消息应该已经传到了他的家人耳中。当救援队的领导人赶到的时候，哥哥对他说："火车经过的时候，司机并没有鸣响火车的警笛，因为我家的狗没有叫！而在一般情况下，他都会叫的！"

当每一个人都在分担着这位妻子和家庭的不幸时,兰尼的嚎叫故事也很快传遍小镇。人们激烈讨论着司机是否开启了火车的警笛。有些人甚至目击"嚎叫的狗"的现象,确信警笛根本没有响起!

没有了收入,这个九口之家陷入了可怕的境地。当地最负盛名、胜诉经验最多的律师决定帮他们起诉现在已经臭名昭著的苏兰公司(当然了,律师是很少这样做的)。这名律师雇了一个调查人,对技术员的证词做了记录。几天来,这两个人频繁来到我家的院子和家里,每当火车来临,他们就会认真地记录下兰尼的嚎叫声。按照兰尼的性格,他是从来不会放弃嚎叫的,当他走近悲剧发生的十字路口时就会发出刺耳尖锐的嚎叫声。他们甚至记录下了火车在顺风时,经过的方向相同的两个领近的交叉口警笛鸣响时兰尼的嚎叫声。律师深信不疑了。

这盒磁带证据在法庭被出示的时候,伴随着我的家人的证词,从而说服了法官和陪审团。最后的判决是保障不幸家庭的安全和未来。县法庭表示将证据的成功归功于"狗狗在法庭上的一天"。

A Dog's Day in Court

Mary K. Himens

When I was growing up, we lived about a quarter mile from a train crossing. Our dog, Lenny, had a very annoying habit: he howled whenever a train whistled for the crossing. It probably **stemmed**[1] from his very sensitive hearing. It did not matter if he was outside or in the house. He howled and howled until the train went by. On some days, when the wind was right, he would even howl for the crossings farther down the track. We learned to put up with the noisy ruckus, mainly because we loved our pet so much.

Early one morning while we were eating breakfast, we heard the squeal of a train's braking efforts followed by a terrible crash. My brother dashed out of the house, ran to the end of our lane and discovered a mangled mass jammed on the cowcatcher of the massive **locomotive**[2]. Parts of a car were strewn everywhere. Unfortunately, the driver of the car had died instantly.

Back in the house, we guessed there had been a crash and called the local rescue squad. But we all immediately said to each other, "Lenny didn't howl. The whistle must not have blown! "

At the scene, my brother recognized what was left of the car as that of his buddy's father and knew immediately the sad, sad news that would now have to be conveyed to the family. When the chief of the rescue squad arrived, my brother told him, "The engineer could not have blown the whistle for the crossing, because our dog did not howl. And he always does! "

The story of Lenny's howling circulated rapidly around our small town as everyone shared in the grief of the wife and family. Speculation ran high as to whether the whistle had truly been blown as the engineer claimed. Some folks even came to witness the "howling dog" phenomenon and left convinced the whistle must not have sounded!

Left without the breadwinner, the family of nine was in dire straits. One of the county's best-known and most successful lawyers decided to pursue a claim against the, by now, infamous Soo Line on behalf of the widow and children. (On contingency, of course!) The lawyer hired an investigator and recording technician. For days, at all hours, the two men frequented our yard and our home listening for oncoming trains and faithfully recording Lenny's howl. Lenny never failed to echo with his characteristic, piercing howl the sharp wail of an approaching freight as it neared the crossing at which the tragedy had occurred. They even recorded his howling as a whistle was blown at the neighboring crossings in both directions when the wind was right. The lawyer was convinced.

The taped evidence, presented in court, along with the **testimony**[3] of my family members, convinced the judge and jury. The settlement awarded to the family secured their home and future. County court records give evidence of the success of a "dog's day in court! "

1. stem [stem] *v.* 滋生；阻止
2. locomotive [ˌləukə'məutiv] *n.* 机车；火车头
3. testimony ['testiməni] *n.* 证词；宣言；陈述

不管我睡得多沉，依旧能听到你们的呼唤，所有的死神都无力阻止我兴奋快乐地对你们摇尾巴的心意。

狗是我们与天堂的联结。它们不懂何为邪恶、嫉妒、不满。在美丽的黄昏,和狗儿并肩坐在河边,有如重回伊甸园。即使什么事也不做也不觉得无聊——只有幸福平和。

在这个世界上,一个人的好友可能背叛他;倾注全部心血培养的儿女也可能变得不忠不孝;那些亲近的人,也可能会远离他……在这个世界上,一个人唯一不自私的朋友,唯一不抛弃他的朋友,唯一不忘恩负义的朋友,就是他的狗。